Advance Praise for *Tartarus*

"Myth rolls forth from the ocean of story and breaks in waves against the changing times in new patterns. Eric Andrews-Katz grafts the crazy force of classical Greece upon the everyday domestic life of a gay American. It's a nervy conceit and an exciting one."—Gregory Maguire, *New York Times* Best-Selling Author of *Wicked: The Life and Times of the Wicked Witch of the West* and *After Alice*

"From Gay comedy to gruesome horror to Greek mythology to hot sex and back—this rollicking ride takes its smart-assed gay hero—and his hot lesbian sister!—all the way from Seattle's Puget Sound to the River Styx! One minute they're dishing over cocktails at an art gallery, the next doing supernatural battle with monsters out of *Army of Darkness*. I'm hoping the three surprise 'superheroes' introduced here become a series. Chill the champagne—Release the Kraken!"—Alison A, Best-Selling Author of *Confessi*

"Blending myth, romance, and a ___ ___ling rivalry, Andrews-Katz's fantasy keeps you ___ked from bitchy brunches in gay Seattle to harrowing adventures in the Greek underworld itself."—Christian Baines, author of *Puppet Boy* and *The Orchard of Flesh*

Praise for Eric Andrews-Katz

The Jesus Injection

"Fast-paced and readable, Eric Andrew-Katz's *The Jesus Injection* is a character-driven mystery with familiar political scenery and a well put together paranoic's nightmare of a credible story line."—Felice Picano, author of *Like People In History* and *The Lure*

"A hilariously irreverent satire."—John Rechy, author of *City of Night*

"Meet the hero for the new century…Agent Buck 98."—*New York Times* Best-Selling Author Alison Arngrim

"And there is lots of action. Andrews-Katz certainly knows his way around a fight scene, and the climax is nicely terse and well done."—*Out in Print*

"Andrews-Katz displays a keen ear for dialogue and a good sense of style and humor. I look forward to more from him." —*Seattle Gay News*

Balls & Chain

"This is a fun read—one that gives you a good reading experience. The writing is smooth and polished, the plot is cute, and there are many interesting personalities."—*Reviews by Amos Lassen*

"It was a very enjoyable, and to me, lighthearted read, with a bit of mystery, unforeseen catastrophes, creative use of a straw and nails, and some unexpected reveals."—*Rainbow Gold Reviews*

"Andrews-Katz keeps the action speeding merrily along… all in the best tradition of James Bond (albeit a queer James Bond). Andrews-Katz is actually more the literary descendant of Mabel Maney than Ian Fleming."—*Chelsea Station*

"The story is an enjoyable detective thriller as Buck tries to infiltrate the group that has kidnapped the governor's son… the story is fast-paced and ties up everything in a car chase." —*GLBT Reviews*

By the Author

The Agent Buck 98 series

The Jesus Injection

Balls & Chain

Tartarus

TARTARUS

by

Eric Andrews-Katz

A Division of Bold Strokes Books

2016

TARTARUS

ISBN 13: 978-1-62639-746-0

THIS TRADE PAPERBACK ORIGINAL IS PUBLISHED BY
BOLD STROKES BOOKS, INC.
P.O. BOX 249
VALLEY FALLS, NY 12185

FIRST EDITION: DECEMBER 2016

CREDITS
EDITOR: GREG HERREN
PRODUCTION DESIGN: STACIA SEAMAN
COVER DESIGN BY JEANINE HENNING

Acknowledgments

There are many things to be grateful for, and the people in my life are only some of the reasons to celebrate.

I'd like to start by thanking the team at Bold Strokes Books, in particular Radclyffe, Sandy, Ruth, Stacia, and my ever-patient editor, Greg Herren. Without your help and belief in my work, none of this would be possible.

By the same right, and for different reasons, my business clients and friends. I appreciate all of your feedback, ideas, and/or you going to sleep so that I may mentally think through another chapter. In particular Kathryn, Lynn, and Sally for their helpful insights and suggestions. Jay, Shaun, James, and Brad for their patience and friendships beyond.

My indomitable proofreaders. Susan—I'm amazed that despite an incredibly full schedule you still manage to find time to help with all I ask of you and never show any faltering. Robert—to say I appreciate your editorial eye is to undermine your skills; to say how much I appreciate your friendship would hardly be sufficient. I am very grateful for both—in very different ways.

Many thanks for the feedback and commentary from Alison, Christian, and Gregory.

For Chris and Dave, I appreciate your friendship and discussions on music from jazz to classical and back again.

For Michelle—thank you for all of your advice and help.

For Felice: I appreciate all the insight, suggestions, help, and advice you so easily and generously provide. Most of all I am grateful for your conversations and friendship.

Many thanks to Bryan (and his team) for providing a secluded writing retreat. It is much appreciated.

Most of all I thank Alan for his unending support, limitless patience, unquestionable love, and for giving me Sundays to myself.

Jama:
Like the Moon you are radiant and magical

Alan:
I'd do it again—I'd be a fool not to

PROLOGUE

Far beneath the Earth's surface she lay entombed. Below rotting corpses and stifled mantles were miles of compacted mountains leading down to the darkest reaches. Beyond deep layers of fire and lava lay the remnants of the Kingdom of the Dead. Four rivers flowed at its dark center: Phlegethon, the River of Fire, marked the extreme limits forming the barrier of her confinement; the Acheron's calm waters of rebirth dissected the Underworld and provided passage from one end to the other. Those drinking from the waters of the Cocytus ended their sorrowful wailing, as the dark waters stole their voices and provided a comforting numbness. At the farthest edge, closest to the upper realms, the Great River Styx swiftly flowed, carrying away the damned and forsaken and forming a natural boundary between the living and the dead.

Echidna's eyes snapped open, no longer detecting the difference between sight and the surrounding darkness. The hollow eyes were sunk deeply in their sockets, and the leathery skin hung gauntly to her skull. Her amber pupils were vertical and shifted with precision to scan for movement in the eternal dark; she had learned to rely more on instinct than sight during her vast imprisonment. The forked tongue flickered, tracing her cracked, gristly lips, trying to detect something other than the cold staleness around her or the subtle breathing of the Earth.

Echidna stretched her arms with a heavy yawn. Her human torso was naked, but she had become accustomed to the prison's chill long ago. Leaning forward, she slithered from her nest, constructed of found debris, excrement, and the discarded flesh and bones of creatures that somehow came her way. Her movements were slow due to the subterranean temperatures. Since the prison's cavern door was sealed with powerful magic, the temperature never changed. A collar weighed heavily around her neck, causing calluses and chafing the skin. A chain forged by the Smith God himself connected the collar to a deeply embedded hook anchored to the wall. Her futile screams had ceased centuries ago, as only a mocking silence answered, and she had not bothered with using her voice because of it. She was left here, imprisoned and forgotten.

She pulled the plastered strings of knotted hair from her face. Her tongue flickered out to sense any water droplets trickling down the cavern sides. She detected something else in the darkness, and her body went still. The leather tongue waved slowly, searching for the slightest motion. The Mother of Monsters was immortal, but food was strength, and every morsel helped.

The slightest movement again registered. Some worm inched through a crack on the wall. Her eyes narrowed in the dark. Her dragon's body recoiled and the serpent tail vibrated, readying to strike, her human arms subtly reaching outward. The forked tongue nodded, using heightened precision to detect the maggot's wriggling. Her tail snapped, pounding on the wall and causing the larva to fall into her waiting clawed hand.

The worm twisted between her coarse fingertips. It was not much, but it was fresh, alive, and that's where the power lay. It was more than the residual nourishment left to her. She threw the larva into her mouth, feeling it turn on her tongue before swallowing it whole. Her mind tormented her with fading memories, back to a time when she feasted on blood…human blood.

Long before the Olympians ruled, Echidna and her brother-mate Typhaeon held immense power. They were the first children of Mother Gaia and ruled all of Heaven, Earth, and beyond. When the more godlike Titans were born, Echidna and Typhaeon divided the Universe among them, and inadvertently created Chaos.

Olive and pomegranate trees once veiled the entrance to Echidna's island lair. Fresh water cascading from the hilltops easily seduced passing ships, luring them into the inlet's calm waters. Mighty vessels would anchor in her domain, not aware of the jagged angled rocks hidden below the water's deceptive surface. Neither ship nor human ever left her island after their arrival.

Echidna birthed a litter of monsters in her paradise. One by one she ripped them from her body; hydra, sphinx, python, and the others she proudly bred. Her firm breasts were plump and full of powerful venom, and her offspring suckled it from her. One by one she sent them off into the world. One by one they were hunted until only the three-headed puppy, Cerberus, remained.

Through deceit and trickery Chaos secretly allowed the Usurper to be born. He was hidden until an army was raised, and once summoned, they rose in revolt. Battles lit the skies, shaking the very core of the Earth. On the verge of destruction, the great mother Gaia succumbed and yielded by betraying the Titans' stronghold. The new Olympians hurled their predecessors from their thrones, punishing the Titans with great cruelty.

Typhaeon was imprisoned in a cave, his tantrums shaking the mountains above him. Over time his rage faded and lapsed, and eventually he succumbed to a perpetual dormancy. The Usurper hurled thunder at the Earth, causing it to crack open. He took Echidna by the tail and cast her downward into Tartarus, the prison of the gods, from which there was no escape, and she fell deep into the bowels of the Earth until even Time held no meaning. She landed, broken, where waiting wraiths quickly collared and chained her to the prison wall. Her tomb was sealed, and she was left to rot for eternity.

Echidna stopped and sniffed the air. It was oppressive, cold and still. She sensed something rumbling from far away. It was approaching fast, shaking the walls and causing the cave to become unstable. Stalactite rocks were shaken loose, releasing a hailstorm of stone. The earth rolled beneath her body, throwing her to the ground. She curled into a ball, covering her head with her arms. Rocks rained down, burying her where she fell.

After a long time the rumbling slowed and dulled until it gave way to silence. Dust and debris floated in the air, making the darkness thicker and heavier than before. She pushed the stones off until the pile started to tumble away. Pain rippled through her body with each movement. Her hands clawed their way out and she pulled herself free from the cairn of stones.

It was in the dark stillness that Echidna noticed a subtle difference in the air. A new smell emerged among the floating dust and debris. It was a crisp chill from the outside world, and she inhaled it deeply, feeling it scratching the inside of her nostrils. She greedily took another breath.

There was something else. A whispering sound slushed through her prison. It was the unmistakable fatal gasp and hiss of expiration. Mother Gaia, the last of the great gods and her infinite jailor, exhaled her last breath with a low death rattle, and was no more.

With a newfound boldness, Echidna reached up and took firm hold of the collar at her neck. She summoned her strength and pulled at the metal. The resistance ripped at her skin until she felt the collar's lock give way. She doubled her efforts, feeling the collar break apart in her hands, falling from her shoulders.

Echidna let the idea wash over her; she was free for the first time in over three thousand years. The thought made her cracked lips spread over jagged teeth into something resembling a smile. Gaia, the Mother of the Gods, was dead! And she—Echidna, Mother of all Monsters—was alive, and free to seek revenge.

CHAPTER ONE

*A*drian felt himself being lifted higher into the sky. Neither the wind burning against his face nor the eagle's talons tightly gripping his outstretched arms bothered him. The loincloth offered little protection from the elements. His body felt only a gentle breeze and the rays of the sun warming his skin. Looking downward, he saw clouds passing like discarded strips of gauze, and a hazy view of the blue sky beneath. The snowy caps of mountains pierced the clouds. Adrian could not remember ever feeling more alive.

There had been no surprise when he spotted the great eagle circling above him. He felt no fear as the winged creature swooped down and took him from the field. Adrian had spread his arms, and the bird took hold. He felt safe in the bird's clutches. The back of his hand stroked the eagle's strong leg, feeling leathery skin giving way to tufts of feathers.

An electric charge burnt beneath his skin. It flowed from the bird's legs down into his arms and chest, causing his heartbeat to race with exhilaration. The bolt moved lower into his groin. Adrian's flaccid penis crept into motion, growing and pressing against the flimsy cloth around his waist. The material loosened until the wind tore it from his hips and it floated away. The air caressing his chest caused his nipples to become erect.

The underside of the great bird rustled with each beating of the powerful wings. Orange talons wrapped around each of Adrian's biceps, holding tight without ripping the tender flesh. Brown breast feathers gave way to a black neck with a pure white hood. Adrian could see the sharp curve of the creature's beak. He felt no fear, knowing the *majestic eagle wouldn't hurt him, and relaxed within its hold. The eagle lowered its head to stare into his eyes.*

A screech sounded through the air. The eagle lifted its head into the wind and opened its mouth to let out another majestic cry. Instead, the sounds of string instruments cut through the air along with a roll of drums. The eagle opened its mouth again and the familiar musical refrain sounded a second time. The rushing winds went silent and the racing of string instruments filled the air. Adrian listened...

The first thing Adrian noticed when his eyes fluttered open was the hardness of his erection. The second thing he noticed was his phone ringing. He took a deep breath, debating which required his attention more urgently. The phone prevailed.

"You have the absolute worst timing in the world," Adrian grumbled upon answering.

"I usually do."

"I'm going to have to assign you a ringtone. And learn to ignore it," Adrian mumbled. His erection was already dissipating.

Talking to your sister would do that.

"It wouldn't help," Annelise said. "We'll always know it's the other one no matter what ringtone. The joys of being twins."

It was true. More often than not, each knew when it was the other calling...or sometimes when the other was feeling an extreme emotion such as pain or happiness. If it was above average on the emotional scale, the other twin would feel it. There were times Adrian resented his sister's multiorgasmic capabilities. He swung his legs off the bed.

"Did you have a reason for waking me?"

"Yeah," Annelise answered. "I need your truck to clear out my showcase for the next exhibit."

"That's not a good enough reason for waking me."

Adrian braced the phone between his right ear and shoulder. He pulled a pair of black gym shorts over his muscular legs and stood to lift them to his waist. He padded his way out to the kitchen.

"I'm sorry," Annelise purred. Her voice was laced with saccharine. "I meant to say, 'Can you help me move a few things from my showroom? There's dinner in it for you.' Is that better?"

"Much better." Adrian tapped his fingers on the counter waiting for the coffee to brew. "And for dinner, something other than seafood."

"Done. What time can you be here?"

Adrian looked for the digital clock tucked in the counter's corner. It blinked 10:27 a.m. He'd slept later than expected.

"Let me hit the shower, and I'll head out. You're lucky I don't have any work at either of the apartments today. I want to be home early to work on a new project, but I will take you up on dinner."

"A new piece?" Her tone was surprised and skeptical. "What kind of new work?"

"Some sketching I'm doing." Adrian winced at the lie, hoping she didn't pick up on it.

"It's going well, is it?" Her sarcasm was evident. "What's it about?"

Adrian thought about the easel and blank canvas in the other room. "I'd rather not discuss it until it's a little more on its way. Superstitious and all."

"Superstitious," Annelise repeated. "That must be it."

"Do you want my truck or not?"

"Definitely." She backpedaled. "Sorry."

"What exactly am I getting myself into here?" Adrian asked.

"I need you to help return a few delicate pieces to the artist. Don't worry, he lives on the peninsula, and it won't take too long."

"Aren't you supposed to be the butch one?"

"I'm lipstick only, dear brother. I defy stereotypes."

"Can't you call a handyman for this?" Adrian mumbled.

"Funny thing, I thought I did," she bantered. "Look, the gallery's truck is in the shop, and I need to make room for a new exhibit. Besides, it's an excuse to see you. It has been a while."

"Ten days."

"Okay then," Annelise conceded. "Do I have your help or do I have to rent a truck?"

"Fine."

"Thanks. I owe you one."

"You owe me a lot more than that." He hung up the phone.

Adrian poured himself a cup of coffee and sat on the couch in the center room of his home. The place was spacious—considering the Capitol Hill location, adjacent to downtown Seattle. He'd bought the place when rates were low and the economy lower, and with his handyman talents, spent the next year reconstructing the lower half of the house and converting it into two separate one-bedroom apartments. Adrian continued the renovations until he had a comfortable, independent second-story two-bedroom home. A back stairwell provided a private entrance.

Adrian tossed his phone onto the table. He leaned back into the sofa cushions and finished his coffee. Closing his eyes, he tried to conjure the dream from his memory. A smile crawled across his lips. His free hand crept across his leg so that his fingertips could slide up his inner thigh and into the leg opening of his shorts. He took a deep breath as his hand squeezed his hard-on. He went into the bathroom and started the shower.

When he finished drying off, Adrian stood in front of the full-length mirror hanging behind the bedroom door. He pulled on square-cut black underwear and a pair of jeans torn at the knee, and slipped a russet-colored T-shirt over his head. He pushed a hand through the drying waves of his black hair, then ran it over the olive skin of his face, debating shaving. He could go a week without touching a razor and only the hints of dark stubble in random patches would appear. Adrian Petrakis felt good as he grabbed his keys from the table.

He opened the hall closet and reached for his worn leather jacket. His eyes fell on an old cloth messenger bag tucked into the corner. He smiled, reaching for the bag. Inside were an 11x14 sketchpad and an assortment of drawing pencils, sharpeners, and pens.

"What the hell," he muttered, throwing the bag's strap across his shoulder. "Maybe it'll actually inspire me."

The Bainbridge Island ferry was far from crowded on a Tuesday in early April. The boat was barely half full of cars. Adrian went up to the sundeck as soon as the sailing signal sounded. It was warm for Seattle. Only a few passengers got out of their cars, most preferring to doze for the short thirty-five-minute crossing. Adrian found a seat at the stern to enjoy the view of the Olympic mountain range.

A loudspeaker's tinny voice sounded. "A small pod of whales has surfaced along the port side of the ferry."

The few passengers on the deck lined up against the railing. The mammals resurfaced, blowing water from their spouts. Adrian watched the two whales swimming not far from the boat. The sleek polished color of their arched backs glistened, and they smacked the water with their great tails before submerging.

Adrian sat gazing out over the water. The sun felt good. The ferry engine's steady humming lulled thoughts away until his mind was blank. He removed the messenger bag from across his shoulders, took out his pad, and started to draw.

The ferry motor's vibrations faded away until it was just white noise. His hand flitted across the paper, drawing of its own accord. He smeared lines and shapes, smudging edges and allowing shadow to create the illusion of depth.

The shrill alarm signaling the boat's approach to dock made Adrian jump. He looked at the sketching pad in his lap. He had drawn his dream. A majestic eagle flew through the air holding on to a handsome young man. The outstretched wings spread across the page. Sharp talons held on to the man's rib cage. The figure was naked except for a simple cloth.

The man's face was blissful. The dark curls of hair cascaded around a classically handsome face. The figure's left hand reached upward, lovingly curling around the eagle's neck. The right hand hung at his waist, holding a single lightning bolt.

Adrian smiled, contented. He threw his tools back into the messenger bag and ran for the stairwell. He managed to return to his truck just before the cars in front began to drive off the boat.

When Adrian arrived, he parked his red Nissan pickup in the reserved space by the loading platform behind the gallery. The truck's tarp was rolled up and a blanket lined the open bed. Giving the horn a double honk from habit, Adrian got out and went around to the gallery's entrance. He paused with a smile to read *Petrakis Gallery* across the thick-glassed window set in the heavy oaken frame. The gallery's hours were printed below in smaller print.

The front door opened to a small foyer with a large desk. On either side of the desk an entrance led into to the next room. An attractive Asian woman dressed in a light blue blouse and a gray jacket matching her skirt sat behind the desk. She looked around the large computer screen and greeted him with a smile.

"Hi, Adrian," she said casually. "Annelise is expecting you."

"Thanks, Lily. Are those new glasses?"

"Yes." She perked. "Do you like them?"

"They add a softness to your face," Adrian said, "with your hair pulled back in a ponytail like that. Very attractive."

"Why can't straight men be like you?" Lily sighed.

Adrian entered the main gallery. The large space was empty except for five crates. An open folding ladder leaned against the far wall next to a dolly cart. Four pedestals were lined up along several dividing partitions. A few panels in the ceilings were shifted out of place to allow track lighting to be dismantled and moved. At the far end, another open door led out to the loading zone.

"There you are," Annelise said. She was holding a closed ledger book and a business-sized envelope. "I was beginning to wonder if you were still coming."

"I texted when I got onto the ferry," Adrian said. "Not my fault you don't check your phone."

Annelise Petrakis was the same height as her brother, if she wasn't wearing heels. Her legs were shapely. Her black skirt ended just above the knee and was cinched at the waist. She wore a white blouse open at the collar with a smart, short black jacket. Her hair was pulled back from her face in a ponytail. The high cheekbones and olive-toned skin set off her brown eyes.

"You'll have to excuse me if I've been busy," she replied, giving her brother a hug and an affectionate peck on the cheek.

"All this needs to be moved?" Adrian asked.

"No," Annelise replied. She gestured to the first few crates. "These five are from the artist that didn't sell. He'll be coming to pick those up later. There are two crates in the back for Zack. We sold four pieces of Zack's work. He's very good."

"Zack," Adrian muttered to himself. "And why can't Zack pick up his own leftovers?"

"Because I thought I'd have the truck today," Annelise answered, too quickly. "And I told him I'd do it. I don't go back on my word, do you?"

"Fine." He said with a sigh. "You win."

Annelise handed him an envelope with an address.

Zack Wilson
Eagle's Nest Farm
5871 Kingston Way

"Don't lose that. It's his check," she said. "Stop with that look; the crates aren't heavy."

"What are they?" Adrian asked, putting the envelope into his back pocket.

He gave the first crate a gentle push.

"The packaging is probably heavier than the actual statue," Annelise answered. "Zack's a carpenter turned wood-carver. People love his work. These were only a few samples to fill in the exhibit. He said he had several more pieces. I'm hoping to build an entire exhibit around his work."

"More tree-stump troll carvings for the tourists, I assume," Adrian said.

"Yeah," Annelise teased. "There aren't enough places selling those horrible statues around the peninsula."

Adrian smiled and walked out the back door. He took a deep breath, leaning on the dolly. "Don't suppose you're going to give me a hand loading these up?"

"I'm front of the house," Annelise purred. "You're the help."

"Thanks, you butch thing!"

"Lipstick only," she sang over her shoulder. She paused at the doorway with a light smile. "You're bitter because I have a life."

Adrian snapped, "I have a life."

"Really." She raised her eyebrow. "When was the last time you had a boyfriend or even got laid? Hmm, that's what I thought."

"You don't know me."

Annelise smiled. "I'm comfortable being alone, but at least I socialize. There's got to be half a dozen apps for you to meet available guys. Do you have any of them downloaded? You're the only single gay man I know that doesn't."

"And what's the app on your phone called?"

"Lickety Split," Annelise immediately answered. "It's an app for lesbians who want to meet in real time."

Adrian incredulously stared at her for a silent minute. "You're kidding, right?"

Annelise burst out laughing.

"Anyway," she continued, "Zack lives by Jefferson Point. Swing by my place after and I'll cook dinner. You can catch a later ferry back to Seattle."

Adrian shook his head and slid the dolly's lip under the first crate. He easily moved the crate down the ramp to the lowered tailgate of his truck. Carefully, he secured it in the truck's bed and went back for the second one.

Adrian took his seat behind the driver's wheel and honked twice to let Annelise know he was leaving. He programmed the envelope's address into his phone's GPS, plugged the phone into the charger, and turned on the engine.

"Zack Wilson." Adrian read the name off the envelope and put it into his bag on the passenger's seat. "Why do I get the feeling you are some five-toothed yokel wood-carver with only seven fingers left?"

He lowered the front windows. The crisp air circulated through the truck's cab. He clicked on the local NPR station to find himself midway through Bizet's *Carmen*. Smiling, he reached over and opened the armrest compartment, taking out a metallic cylinder roughly the size of a tire gauge.

Adrian clicked the vaporizer switch, waiting for it to warm up. After a moment he put the plastic mouthpiece to his lips, inhaling the marijuana mist into his lungs.

"In one-quarter mile turn left onto unpaved road," the GPS said. "Then destination in three-quarter miles."

Adrian came to a long curve and slowed down, looking for the turnoff. He saw the sign declaring *Eagle's Nest Farm* and made the turn. The dirt road was rough and Adrian slowed. The single lane curled through a forest to a beautiful home. The path became part of a crescent driveway. Adrian parked at its crest.

The house was built on a ten-foot-high platform to allow parking and a workspace underneath. A set of stairs led up from either side. The underside was divided into three parts, lit with fluorescent bulbs. A large black truck occupied the first spot, while the middle section was clear except for a grill and a table. The far side was a workshop with another table and a large tree stump in the process of being shaved and sanded. Three ceiling-to-floor pillars separated each space, and a wall of hanging tools stretched across the back.

Adrian walked past the first two stalls. The tree stump was about a yard high and two feet across. Sawdust and shavings blanketed the area at its base. The sides were sanded smooth. The top was being broken up by chisel cuts.

An electric handsaw lay next to the table. Nine carving chisels, sorted by size, were displayed across the tabletop.

"Careful," a voice warned casually from behind him. "They're sharp."

CHAPTER TWO

*L*ong before the Titans existed, the Veiled Lady Hecate appeared in the Underworld. No one remembered when she first emerged from the shadowy lands, where she previously came from, or when she claimed the Land of the Dead as her kingdom. It was always so, and therefore never challenged. The Night Pack, a den of large hounds constantly at her side, ensured her rule of the Underworld. Hecate kept her face hidden by several veils, and she came to be worshipped as a revealer of secret portals and doorways.

Hecate built the Black Palace among the numerous lakes of the Underworld. The walls were constructed of solid onyx. The grand palatial doors were forged from iron and always kept open without fear.

The Night Pack was set to digging a moat to divide the Lands of the Living from the Kingdom of the Dead. The Veiled Lady straddled the empty riverbed and cut her inner wrist. Her blood spilled into the trench, slowly filling the moat. The great River Styx created an impenetrable boundary for Hecate's kingdom.

Standing on the banks, the Dark Goddess removed one of her veils and set it afloat in the water. The translucent material shimmered, solidified, and expanded, becoming a crescent-shaped boat. Benches lined the deck for thirty passengers. Hecate removed another veil and threw it into the air. It caught hold on the boat and transformed into a black sail, embroidered with a silver weeping willow.

Hecate reached between her thighs and opened herself to the darkness. She allowed Chaos inside her and became pregnant. When the time came, she ripped the shadowy child from her womb and watched as it grew to a towering height, taking the form of an ogre.

Kharian stood ominously silent. Dark fires burned within deeply set eyes, and a thick braid of coal black hair hung down his back. The squared head sat on a thick neck and a set of broad shoulders. Powerful arms hung at his side, and a leather harness divided the muscled pectorals. A kilt made of leather straps hung around his waist, over thick thighs.

Hecate reached her hands up to write the secret of life on Kharian's forehead. She caressed his face and gave him his charge.

"Only those with the obols may be ferried from those shores to my kingdom. I bless you with indifference to all else."

Kharian bowed silently to his mother. She kissed his brow. He strode past her to take his place at the rear of the boat. He wrapped his fingers around the tiller and waited.

Hecate picked up a small handful of black stones from the beach and threw them into the river. As they sank beneath the surface, they changed shape, becoming massive creatures swimming in the waters.

"Leviathan. Kraken," the goddess called. "I give you the names of fear to patrol the waters of the world."

The Veiled Lady walked the plank and gracefully climbed into the body of the ship. She called two of the Night Pack to her side; the rest remained waiting on the shore. She gently took each of the dog's heads in her hands.

"I call you Orthos, the Vigilant."

Hecate nudged the two dogs closer together until they meshed, becoming one animal with two heads. She lifted the dog into the air, transforming the living creature into the mast's figurehead. A red lantern hung tightly clenched in each set of snarling teeth.

Kharian pushed the vessel from the dock, steering from the rear with a pole. The barge sped forward, disappearing into a mist hanging in the air. At the river's center, the ferryman brought the vessel to a stop.

Hecate stood at the bow and removed another veil. She let it loose, and it was quickly swallowed by the mist. The air shimmered before them, coming alive with sparkling lights. A set of gates formed, stretching across the vast river. Each gate only opened one way. A gentle rain fell over the gate entering the kingdom.

"I name you Lethe," the goddess proclaimed. "All those passing through shall forget the previous lives they've known."

Hecate moved to the side of the barge, looking at the waters in each direction. She threw another stone, letting it skim across the Styx. A new spout of water erupted. With a deep exhale of breath, Hecate changed the stream and forced its flow away from the River Styx. She saw the new river flowing to the edge of her kingdom, until it bubbled up into a huge lake. Across the lake, a path could be seen leading into a thick void.

The rest was beyond her domain and of little interest to her.

"I name you Acheron," the goddess stated to the river. "Your water shall divide my kingdom."

The goddess returned to the bow and signaled for the return to her shores. The Night Pack took their place at her side when she docked. A pathway spread before her, leading from Kharian's boat to the Dark Palace. Hecate stopped halfway, removing another veil from her face.

"Go with peace," Hecate commanded. She raised her arm, pointing between the castle and the ferry dock. A new path paved its way into the distance. "I name you Elysium, and you shall be known as Paradise."

Once her boundaries were established, the Veiled Lady reached into the rich ground and withdrew titanium. She created a magnificent throne and placed it in the main hall of the palace. Next, she created a crown, embedding it with jewels and powerful magic. Hecate placed the crown on her head and retired to her castle to rule. She was content, knowing that all livings things would eventually come to her.

Hecate watched the courtship between earth Gaia and Uranus, the Sky Lord. She saw the birth of their children and had no interest when the Titan Cronus overthrew his father Uranus, taking control of the heavens and earth. She watched with apathy when the cycle repeated, with Zeus rebelling against his father Cronus.

Hades, the Brooding One, entered her kingdom with humility and charm, bringing an offering for its sovereign, with a deceivingly handsome face masking his chicanery. The eldest brother of the new Sky Lord, Hades, knelt before the Dark Queen, presenting her with his offering, a pitch-black puppy. The tiny creature sat in his large palm, barely strong enough to lift its three heads. Only one set of eyes had opened and quickly found Hecate. The creature squeaked out its bark, setting off the other two heads, much to the Veiled Lady's delight. She named the dog Cerberus and accepted both god and beast into her home.

Hades was clever and seduced the Dark Queen. He used the darker spells of Love to cast a haze over the Veiled Lady's eyes, and she became lost in his charisma. He kenneled the Night Pack and prepared a banquet. He toasted his queen with poisoned wine, and after Hecate drank, she fell into an enchanted sleep.

When the Veiled Lady awoke, she found herself magically bound and her kingdom raped. Her crown was lost. The Night Pack was slain and condemned to roam as soulless wraiths, and Hades declared himself Lord of the Dead.

The overthrown queen was brought to the docks. It was then that Hecate saw how her borders were breached. The Olympian, Poseidon, was sitting in a saddle on the back of the Kraken. In his hand he tightly held a powerful weapon.

The ferry arrived and Hecate was placed aboard, the ghostly Night Pack at her side. Kharian did not protest, being bound by her own spells to ferry her across. The boat cast off and Poseidon rode the Kraken under the water. Once at the Shores of the Living, the Veiled Lady was put on land and left to wander with the soulless wraiths and the poor souls unfortunate enough not to be buried with the ferryman's payment. With the last of her magic, Hecate carved out a secret temple deep within the rocks and resigned herself to oblivion.

The Black Palace loomed in front of Echidna at last.

The quake's rumblings had shifted the earth so much it changed the course of the River Phlegethon. The lava rose slowly, fallen boulders causing the flow to splinter off in various minor tributaries.

Echidna picked her way across the lava flow by climbing from one dislodged rock to another. With great patience Echidna crossed over the river of fire. She could see the paved road in the near distance, and her strength renewed. The various lakes lining the way had become brackish and silted and were now festering marshes. The closer she got to the palace, the stronger the foul smells grew.

Echidna stopped as she approached the center of a crossroad. The Dark Palace towered in the distance to her right. The gate had been left open. She took a step forward and stopped by instinct. Her body coiled onto itself and she brought her human arm to her mouth. She opened her jaw and bit into her wrist. Her fanged incisors tore the loose skin until beads of her black blood appeared.

"Blood returned for blood stolen," she whispered. "Veiled Lady of the Crossroad, I honor you."

Echidna held her wrist over the pavement. Her tongue flickered as she squeezed three drops from her veins. She continued across the intersection until she found herself standing on the edge of the dock. The waters slapped against the six posts. The river held power, and Echidna listened to its chatter: *I am all that is. I am all that was. I am all that will ever be.*

She slithered to the dock's edge, standing under the burning torch on the last post. Below the sconce, a thick cord trailed out of the bottom of a box. Echidna pulled the cord, feeling it resist at first. Her amber eyes scanned the horizon.

From the thick mist, a dark cloud appeared in the distance. It grew thicker and took the form of a ship. It rapidly approached and silently docked in front of her. A ramp plank was extended from the ship's side as the sails snapped in the windless breeze.

Kharian stepped down onto the loading platform. Neither surprise nor recognition registered in his burning eyes. He stepped aside, letting Echidna pass and board the vessel. He returned to his position in the stern and cast off without a word.

The shore disappeared. The Gates of Lethe appeared from the mist and Echidna marveled at their magic. The boat carefully turned, avoiding the raining-down Shower of Forgetting. Echidna looked away, holding on to her bitter memories.

The shoreline appeared from the darkness. Echidna noticed shadows flooding onto the planks' edge. The shadows became throngs of individual specters, wraiths of lost souls crowding forward, desperate for passage.

The boat moored at the dock. Kharian lowered the platform and waited for Echidna to disembark. At first sight of the Mother of Monsters, the wraiths pushed forward, drawn to her life force. But as she took her first steps onto the dock, the throngs parted and backed away from her with fear.

Echidna watched Kharian. He was already choosing his passengers, collecting coins and jewels for payment. She turned away and slithered from the dock. She crossed the black sand and found the broken path leading up the rocky cliffs. This was the path that led to the World of the Living, and she instinctively knew it was not the way she needed to follow. Echidna reached into her memory for the ancient spells she would need and spoke aloud the spells of revealing.

A green flame appeared before her. It hovered in the air before moving along the path until it came to the side of the mountain. The glowing light disappeared into the rock, leaving an outlined door behind.

Taking a deep breath, Echidna began her long journey up from the Underworld to find the last Temple of Hecate.

CHAPTER THREE

Adrian spun around. The man was older, dressed in a worn, faded pair of overalls covering a rust and gray plaid flannel shirt. His arms were folded across his broad chest and his sleeves were rolled up. His gray hair was brushed roughly up and away from his handsome face.

"Sorry," Adrian said. He stuck out his hand. "I'm Adrian Petrakis, Annelise's brother. She sent me to bring your work back."

"Oh yeah," the man said. The smile flickered wider. "I see the resemblance now. Zack Wilson."

The man stepped forward. Adrian reached out to shake hands and noticed the details of a tattoo disappearing under the sleeve. It looked like a bushy treetop with gold branches rooting through the crown. When their hands touched, tiny pinpoints of light flashed around Zack's head. Adrian was surprised by how strong the grip was and the short bursts of electricity that pulsed up his arm.

He smiled and looked away.

"You all right?" Zack asked.

"Yeah," Adrian said. "Your statues are back here. Tell me where you want 'em. Give me a hand, and it should only take a few minutes."

Adrian lowered the tailgate. Zack leapt up onto the bed.

"I'll push these two to the front," Zack said. "We can get them to the ground and then move them to the workshop."

"Try not to scratch the bed, please."

"Don't worry, pretty boy. I won't." Zack squatted down and pulled the crate from the back. He winked at Adrian.

"So, Annelise runs an art gallery. What do you do?"

"I manage two apartment buildings," Adrian reluctantly answered. "And I do some drawing and painting."

"Really? What kind of drawing?"

"Sketching mostly."

"People or inanimate objects?"

"Whatever I feel like doing," Adrian answered.

"Okay." Zack patted the side of the crate. "I'll need a hand getting them back to the storeroom. You ready?" He squatted down to take hold of the bottom end. "I take it you're more of a city mouse to your sister being a country one?"

"You could say that," Adrian said. He took hold of the crate's bottom.

"Why do you prefer the urban opposed to the rural?"

They lifted the box and moved it off the truck and into the middle workspace.

"I like the convenience, I guess," Adrian answered. "I could live out here like her, but I'd miss the conveniences of going out and doing stuff."

"Are you a party boy? One of the circuit crowd?"

"Hardly." Adrian chuckled. "I'm more of a recluse. I want to feel like I can go out if the mood hits. Out here, it would be a lot easier to talk myself out of going anywhere before I even got ready to go."

"If it's not worth the effort"—they put the first crate down, and Zack stood back up with a grin—"then it should no longer be an issue."

"Annelise likes it out here," Adrian said. They headed back for the second crate. "When our parents died, she jumped at the chance of opening a gallery out here. I bought a house and converted the bottom half into two one-bedroom apartments. It pays my bills, and I can still live in the city. Both have their pros and cons, I guess. I think we appreciate the other's lifestyle while preferring our own."

"Do you hand-pick the tenants?" Zack asked.

"Hardly. It's not always a good thing to rent an apartment to a friend," Adrian said. "My tenants are nice enough, but I wouldn't call them friends. We don't hang out much."

"Wouldn't you like living out here?" Zack spread his arms outward with a smile. "All this fresh air and quiet?"

"No offense, but honestly, all this quiet would drive me batshit cray-cray. And I know Annelise feels the same way about city noise."

Zack laughed. "No doubt. Your sister is definitely a country girl."

"How well do you know her?" Adrian wondered if Zack knew his sister was a lesbian.

Adrian felt Zack take him by the shoulders and spin him around as if he were a rag doll. He lost his breath when both of Zack's strong arms wrapped around his lower back. Firm hands slid down over the jeans, feeling the curve of Adrian's ass. Zack's hands began kneading the rounded muscles.

"You're tight," Zack whispered.

Adrian felt the strong hands pulling him close. He could feel Zack's breath against his neck. Their breathing became one, coming heavier and faster. Zack leaned in and Adrian closed his eyes as their lips were about to touch.

"Your sister?" Zack asked once again.

Adrian blinked, realizing he'd slipped into fantasy. He looked down where Zack was squatting next to the crate, waiting for his help. His blue eyes climbed up Adrian's body.

"I've known your sister for about a year," Zack continued "Maybe two. We met through mutual friends, you know how island life is, and they told her about my artwork. Ready on three?"

Zack nudged the crate between them. Together they lifted the box.

"You all right?" Zack asked.

"Yeah," Adrian answered. He quickly reached down, readjusting the bulge in his pants.

They put the crate down a few feet from the first. Zack stood up.

"You sure you're okay?" He reached out for Adrian's shoulder.

"Yeah," Adrian said. He stepped out of reach. "Just an odd dream I had this morning."

"What was it about?"

"Nothing," Adrian said. He began walking back to the truck. "Never mind."

"Oh." The knowing acknowledgment. "One of *those* dreams. It's cool. I get ya."

"Get your mind out of the gutter. It would take too long to explain, that's all."

"No problem," Zack said. "Any desire to see what you've been haulin' across the island?"

"Sure."

Zack popped off the top of the first crate. He reached inside and lifted out a statue, placing it gently on the ground. The statue was stained a dark color and carved from a single piece of wood. A horse, galloping hard against the wind. The animal's tail whipped out behind muscled flanks. The animal's neck extended, the windblown mane trailing.

As Adrian studied the details of the animal's face, he noticed the human figure curled along the neck. The tiny human legs were wrapped in front of the animal's chest. The figure leaned in so that his pixielike head peered out from the tangled mane. One hand held firmly on to the horse's neck. Grasped tightly in the rider's other hand was a clutch of lightning bolts.

"I call it *The Centaur*," Zack said.

"That's really cool," Adrian replied. "Much better than the troll-stumps I thought I'd be seeing."

Zack laughed, clapping Adrian on the shoulder.

Adrian's body tensed. The electric pulses started racing through his body again.

"Can I use your bathroom?" he managed to squeak out.

"Sure," Zack answered, still laughing. "Inside the front door to the left, and two doors down. Easy to find."

"Thanks," Adrian said. He started up toward the house.

"Did Annelise happen to give you an envelope for me?"

"Yeah," Adrian said. He looked over the stairs' railing. Zack was standing next to his truck, his hands on his hips. "It should be right inside my bag. Passenger seat, the door's open."

The house's front door opened to a large room with a glass sliding door on the opposite wall. A cloth couch faced the extended outside deck. There was a kitchen to the left, and to the right was an open door leading into the master bedroom. A hallway on the left led down to the guest bathroom and bedroom.

Adrian started down the hallway, looking at the framed photos decorating the wall. Some were scenic from locations around the world, while others had people posing in front of famous sites.

"I guess he only knows pretty people."

Adrian flipped on the bathroom light. Above the switch was a framed black-and-white photo taken on a beach verandah with the ocean behind. Two men sat at a table in the picture's center. They were both slim-built, bare chested, well tanned. Their palms were locked, arm wrestling. The man on the left was mostly smooth-chested, only a central darker patch of chest hair. The man on the right had tight curls of dark hair rolling down his chest. Both men were grinning directly at the camera.

Adrian noticed the tattoo on the right man's inner arm. It was a younger version of Zack. His hair was dark and curly, a bushy mustache covering his lip. Adrian's eyes studied the tattoo closer. It wasn't a tree, but a storm cloud with lightning rippling through it.

"Handsome man." Adrian smiled, closing the bathroom door. "For a seventies Castro clone."

❖

Adrian started down the outside wooden stairs and stopped halfway down. "What are you doing?" he yelled over the railing.

Zack looked up from the passenger seat of the truck and waved. His legs sprawled over the seat as he went over the drawings in the sketchpad held in his lap.

"These are pretty good," Zack called back cheerfully. "Are they yours?"

"Hey! I said you could get your check, not go through my stuff." Adrian stomped down the remaining stairs. "Do you mind?"

Zack continued flipping through the pages. "Some of these early ones are okay at best, but not bad. You can see definite progress with the latter ones. This one here." He stopped. "The details on the eagle feathers are incredible for a pencil drawing. Not to mention the guy. I like your homage to the Renaissance Braghettone by painting a loincloth over the crotch. Leaves a little something to the imagination, that's hot."

Zack looked up into Adrian's face. "Oh my God! It's you, isn't it?"

"I said they were personal!" Adrian snatched the pad from Zack's hands, the top page ripping off the first metal ring. "I don't like people seeing my work until *I'm* ready to show them."

"I'm saying they're really good. You don't have to get all pissy, pretty boy."

"Would you mind getting the hell out of my truck?" Adrian stepped aside.

"All right." Zack chuckled awkwardly. "Learn to take a compliment."

Adrian slammed the passenger car door. "Oh, fuck you!"

He stomped around the truck and got into the driver's seat. He tossed the pad onto the bag lying on the seat.

"Did you get your check?"

Zack nodded.

"Good. It was nice meeting you," Adrian started the engine. "Buh-bye."

The truck sped off, kicking up a cloud of dust as it drove away. Adrian looked into the rearview to see Zack still standing in the driveway.

The truck pulled out onto the two-lane road, and Adrian reached behind to open the truck's sliding rear window. With the Eagle's Nest Farm growing distant behind him, Adrian released a heavy sigh and reached into the armrest to withdraw his vaporizer. He clicked the button, inhaling deeply and feeling the THC-laced mist in his lungs.

"Arrogant bastard." Adrian huffed aloud, blowing out the smoke. "Some fucking nerve going through my shit without asking."

He reached out and turned on the CD player. He turned the music up, taking another toke off the vaporizer. By the time he drove into Annelise's driveway, he'd banished Zack Wilson from his thoughts and was already in a much calmer state of mind. He parked behind Annelise's metallic blue Subaru Crosstrek.

"I'm in the kitchen," Annelise called out, hearing the front door open.

Annelise was at the counter chopping red and green peppers. She had changed from her work clothes to a pair of gray sweatpants and a casual T-shirt advertising the Seattle Art Museum.

"What's wrong with you?" Annelise asked.

"Nothing. I don't want to talk about it."

"Get the statues delivered?" she asked after a long moment's silence.

"Yes," Adrian snapped.

"Give Zack his check?"

"Of course I did. What a son of a bitch!"

"Really?" Annelise asked. "He's always nice to me."

"He's nice to you because you make him money!"

"That's because he's talented," Annelise said calmly. "Did you see any of his work? You have to admit, it is original and well done."

"Yeah." Adrian shrugged. "He showed me his *Centaur*."

"That sounds naughty."

Adrian corrected her. "I don't go for old men. How old is he anyway?"

Annelise pushed the peppers from her cutting board into a small bowl and moved on to the chicken breast.

"I think he said he turned sixty a few months ago," Annelise answered. "He's only twelve years older than us. That's not that old."

"Old enough," Adrian muttered. He popped a piece of cut pepper into his mouth.

"*The Centaur* is a great piece," Annelise gushed. "I had two offers for that one, but Zack didn't want to sell it. It's beautiful and a little homoerotic. Didn't you think so?"

"Yeah. Maybe a little." Adrian paused. "You know I hate it when you do that."

"Do what?" She checked the temperature of the wok's oil.

"Disarm me when I'm pissed off," Adrian said.

Annelise put the chicken pieces into the oil and began to stir. "So what did Zack do that pissed you off?"

"He," Adrian paused for a breath, "he went into my bag without asking."

"That doesn't sound like him at all," Annelise said. "He's usually very respectful of boundaries."

"When I went to the bathroom I told him he could get his check from my bag," Adrian said. "I didn't say he could browse through my sketchpad."

"Not to change subjects or anything," Annelise said. "But when did you start carrying a sketchpad with you?"

"Not the point," he protested. "I told you I was working on a project."

Annelise snorted. "So you got all pissy because he went into your bag, after giving your permission."

"To get the check, not to go through my drawings."

"He showed you his," Annelise teased. "Isn't that how these boy things work?"

"You're really not funny, you know."

"And you're being childish," she snapped back. "He saw a couple of drawings, waaaaah."

"He actually said he liked them."

"Now there's a reason to get pissed off."

"Actually," Adrian said, "he said I should show them to you."

"Then maybe you should."

"They're nothing special." Adrian shook his head. "Except for the one I did today. It's really good."

"Today?" Annelise said with a cocked eyebrow. "Then what are you working on back at home?"

Adrian grinned sheepishly.

"That's what I thought," she concluded. "So if your easel is still buried in your hoarding room, what made you decide to start drawing today?"

"Don't know," Adrian admitted with a shrug. "I woke up from a dream this morning. It's been haunting me all day. Maybe that's what did it."

"Really?" Annelise added the food to the brown rice already on each plate. "That's funny. I had a really interesting dream last night, too."

She offered one of the plates to her brother.

"And it was hot."

CHAPTER FOUR

*A*nnelise walked along the beach with a chocolate Labrador. The dog leapt in the water a few yards behind her, barking playfully. The crescent moon hung in the dark night sky, stars spreading out around it. The waves softly rolled in with a gentle motion, rushing over and cooling Annelise's feet.

Her dark hair was pulled back and pinned in a small round bun. A white gown with strap ties hung loosely over her chest. Her breasts swayed underneath the garment with every movement. A silver braided rope belted the dress, skirting out just above her knees. Her leather sandals had cords bound up the lower part of her calves. A quiver of arrows hung over her back, and a wooden bow was slung over her shoulder.

The dog rushed ahead of her, barking several times. Annelise leaned forward, clapping her palms to her thighs. The Labrador responded by quickly running back in her direction.

She slid the bow from her shoulder. In a flash she notched an arrow. Annelise arched her body, aiming at the sky. The dog barked from her side and galloped across the wet sand, chasing after the launched arrow.

The dog came bounding over the sand with the silver arrow clutched in its mouth. She dropped the bow as the dog leapt up, knocking her down to the water and wet sand.

"Selina!" Annelise called.

The Labrador stood over her. It barked twice. Without warning, the dog bounded away down the beach.

Annelise sat up, leaning back on her hands. She looked out at the ocean and the black sky stretching before her. The moon's silver crescent slowly turned upside down, frowning. Red dripped down from the points like running paint, changing its color to a burning blinking in the sky.

Annelise blinked her eyes to clear the daydream from her mind. The last vision of the pulsing moon faded. Her cell phone screen lit up. The phone vibrated again.

"Hello?"

Annelise wiped her eyelids with her thumb and index finger.

"No, I was just lost in a daydream," she went on. "I gave Lily the day off, so I'm here by myself. Not much, paperwork, some filing and stuff like that. No, I haven't seen the exhibit yet…I could do that. There's not much more to do here."

Annelise cradled the cell phone between her ear and shoulder.

"No, I don't mind," she said. She turned the computer off. "Perfect. When you're done, meet me at Juno's and we can go to the exhibit after lunch…yes, that's the one. Thanks, I appreciate it."

Annelise stood at her desk and stretched with a yawn. She popped an Altoid in her mouth and left the office.

Annelise looked up over the menu as her brother approached the table.

"What brings you into the big city?" Adrian asked after greeting her with a peck on the cheek.

"Glad to see you, too." Annelise smiled.

"Not that I wasn't happy to hear from you." Adrian draped his wet jacket across the back of the empty chair to his left and sat down opposite his sister. "You're just not usually one for last-minute visits to the mainland."

"Mainland? Give me a break." Annelise laughed. "There's not much to do between shows, so I thought I'd check out the Calder exhibit at the Seattle Art Museum. Want to join me?"

"No, thanks." Adrian looked over the menu. "Mobiles aren't really my thing, you know?"

A squat man in a black waiter's apron approached the table, pencil and pad poised and ready in his hands. Once they ordered, he reached for the remaining place settings.

"Please leave one," Annelise said. "We're waiting on a third."

"Should I wait to put in the order?" the waiter asked.

"No," she said. "I'm not sure if he'll be eating or just joining us."

"I'll put your order in and be right back with your drinks."

"And who is the third?" Adrian asked once the waiter was gone.

"Zack," Annelise said. "It was his idea to go to the exhibit, and since I've been meaning to go for a while it worked out."

"Now I'm really glad I'm not going," Adrian mumbled.

"Get over yourself." Annelise sat back in her chair with an exasperated expression. "Zack's a nice guy. Don't take this the wrong way, but you *can* be an asshole. I'm sure he didn't mean to insult you."

"So where is he?" Adrian turned, looking over his shoulder. "Didn't you take the ferry together?"

"He had a few errands to run and dropped me off. He said he would meet me here afterward."

"Adios."

"Hold on," Annelise said. "Sit back down and enjoy lunch. I thought you'd appreciate me coming to you for a change, and he may not be here for a while. He might arrive in five minutes, or it might be an hour. You can keep me company until he gets here, at least. Just try to be cordial."

The waiter returned with their drinks.

"Is it too late to get a beer?" Adrian asked. "Redhook, or whatever you have on tap. The largest you got."

"Very good." The waiter disappeared.

"I have another reason for wanting to see you," Annelise said. She leaned closer. "Is everything okay with you? In your personal life?"

Adrian straightened the place setting. "Nothing out of the ordinary. Why do you ask?"

"Curious."

"You're never just curious. You always have a reason. What's up?"

Annelise rested her arms on the table. "You don't have a secret boyfriend or something like that that I should know about, do you?"

"First of all," Adrian answered, "I don't have any boyfriend, secret or otherwise. What in the world would make you think that?"

"I keep having these intense dreams and figured they must be related to you somehow."

"Why me?"

"Because there's nothing abnormal in *my* life."

"What kind of dreams are you having?" Adrian asked.

"Odd ones," Annelise said. She wrinkled her nose and whispered, "More like erotic ones."

"Really?" Adrian replied. "And who is in these dreams with you?"

"No one."

"Then what do you think is causing these dreams? Are you looking for a girlfriend?"

"No." Annelise took another sip from her glass, giving her a moment's thought. "Not really. If one came along I wouldn't mind it, but I'm pretty content by myself. Maybe all I need is a dog. I was thinking about a chocolate Labrador."

"A dog?"

The waiter approached with their meals. "Can I get you anything else?" he asked before leaving.

"My life is mostly routine," Annelise said. "There's the gallery, and that's pretty much it. That's why I figured the dreams must have something to do with you. So what's up?"

"Nothing," Adrian insisted. "Really. There's absolutely nothing going on in my life. No issues whatsoever. And I'm not anxious to start looking for trouble."

He took another bite and chewed.

"I was referring more to your social life," Annelise said. "Are my dreams mirroring you somehow?"

Adrian stopped and swallowed. "No," he finally replied after a sip of beer. "Actually, I've been having dreams, too. I don't usually remember my dreams, but I sure as hell do with these."

"What kind of dreams?"

"Odd dreams," Adrian continued. "Also with an erotic bent to them."

"That's uncanny." Her eyes sparkled. "I do love being a twin, don't you? It's odd that we're both having these types of dreams. What do you think is the cause?"

"I don't know. Strange things happen with twins all the time." Adrian took another bite of his burger. "Are your dreams explicit?

Vivid? I mean, when I wake—even if it's a daydream—my heart is racing, and I feel like I returned from a different world."

"Exactly!" Annelise slapped the table. "When the phone buzzing brought me out of it, I was still hearing the dog barking in my head."

"What's with the freakin' dog?" Adrian wiped his mouth after finishing the last bite.

"I honestly have no idea." Annelise looked over Adrian's shoulder. "Zack's coming. Remember," she whispered to him, "you promised to be nice."

"I hope I'm not interrupting," Zack Wilson said as he approached the table.

"Actually," Adrian said, "we're almost finished." He removed his jacket from the back of the empty chair and put it over his own.

"Hope you don't mind if I catch up." Zack sat next to him. He raised his arm and signaled for the waiter.

"Yes, sir." The waiter returned. "Would you like a menu?"

"Don't bother." Zack quickly glanced at the remnants on the table. "Can I get a blue-cheese burger and…what is that, a beer? I'll have one of those, as well. Whatever he had is fine."

"Very good, sir." The waiter left.

"Good to see you again, Adrian. How are you?" Zack grinned.

"Fine," came the stiff reply.

"Get everything you needed?" Annelise asked.

"Yes," Zack answered, shiftng in his seat. "I have to special-order a lot of my tools. They let me know when they come in, and I get them."

"Why don't you have them delivered to your house?" Adrian asked.

"Eh." Zack waved off the suggestion. "It's not a big deal. Plus it gives me an excuse to come to the mainland."

"Oh shit," Annelise mumbled.

"Ha." Adrian pounced. He snapped forward, leaning over the table at Annelise. "'Mainland.' See?"

"What?" Zack asked. "Did I say something wrong?" His amusement mixed with his slight confusion.

"Nothing." Adrian dismissed it.

"Adrian's being a bitch," Annelise explained. "I mocked him when he said 'mainland' earlier."

"What do you have to bitch about, pretty boy," Zack asked.

"We can start with I don't like people calling me pretty boy."

"If that's the worst thing you get called," Zack gave a jovial laugh, "then you really got no bitch at all."

The waiter returned with the burger and beer.

Adrian shot his sister a look. "I'm gonna get going."

"Come on," Annelise said in a hushed tone. "Wait until he's done and don't be rude. Please."

"Fine." Adrian slumped in his chair.

"Adrian," Zack said. "Did you hear about the earthquake?"

"Adrian gets his all of his worldly information from Facebook only," Annelise said. "He's not one to watch the news."

"No," Adrian said to Zack. "I evidently missed that Facebook feed."

"They're calling it 'the quake that murdered Mother Earth,'" Zack said.

"Really?" Annelise sat up. "I didn't realize it was that bad."

"They didn't think it was that bad at first, but it seems it has gone beyond what they expected."

"What happened?" Adrian asked sitting up in his chair.

"There was a major earthquake in the middle of the Pacific Ocean," Zack explained. "They were doing some deep oceanic drilling and hit some pivotal point beneath the surface. It caused an underwater volcano to erupt, starting this massive shift in the earth's core. Lava has been erupting since about two in the morning."

"Are you serious?" Adrian asked.

"There's been so much lava flow they're predicting it'll cause a change in the ecosystem."

"I heard that tsunamis have been hitting Hawaii," Annelise added. "And as far as Guam. The coasts of Australia and Japan have been hit pretty hard, too."

"Holy shit!" Adrian said. "How could I have missed this?"

"Those Facebook feeds can go by pretty fast," Annelise teased.

"It's supposed to be really serious," Zack continued. "All sorts of sea life has been killed, and the lava flow doesn't seem to be stopping any time soon."

"I read that one scientist is calling the tsunami 'Triton's Revenge,'" Annelise said. "They say the effects could wipe out some of the smaller Pacific island chains."

"Holy shit!" Adrian faced Zack fully, and their knees brushed against one another.

"Thousands have been killed," Zack went on. "The coastlines are being torn up. In some cases, the smaller islands are being completely overrun with waves. Some of them aren't expected to resurface. There's all sorts of international rescue and relief programs being undertaken to help, but with it all still raging on in full force, it's difficult."

"I guess that explains the weather," Adrian muttered.

"You think?" Annelise said. "You didn't notice the rain and wonder why it's coming down so hard?"

"It's Seattle in late April; who can tell?"

"You really notice nothing," Annelise said, shaking her head.

"Hey," Zack said. "It happened at two in the morning. Not everyone got the memo."

"See?" Adrian defended himself. "I was asleep."

"Pretty boys need their beauty rest."

"Do you mind?" Adrian snapped. "I asked you not to call me that."

"Sorry." Zack held up his hands, surrendering with a smile to try and defuse the tension. "It just slipped out. I'll do my best not to let it happen again. Can you put the attitude on hold for a bit?"

Adrian's eyes grew wide and his body went rigid.

"Oh no," Annelise mumbled. "Calm down, Adrian, he didn't mean anything by it. What is your problem?"

"Really," Zack said. "I didn't mean anything by it. Calm down, we'll forget it. Let me buy you another beer."

"Don't tell me what to do." Adrian scooted the chair back from the table. "And you can shove your beer up your ass."

"Hey," Zack said sternly.

"Look," Adrian said. "You just rub me the wrong way. Can I make it any more succinct?"

"Nope," Zack answered. "Got it, loud and clear."

"I am so outta here," Adrian said, exasperated. "Enjoy the exhibit."

Adrian grabbed his jacket. He slammed his arms into the sleeves and reached for his wallet, dropping twenty dollars on the table.

"I'll talk to you later," he said to his sister before storming out of the restaurant.

"Well," Annelise said quietly. "That went well."

"Yeah," Zack added. "I think he's starting to like me."

CHAPTER FIVE

Echidna made her way deeper into the earth. Eventually the pathway ended at the solid rock base of a mountain. She paused, looking for any hidden passages or doorways.

She stared at the wall, debating retracing her steps, when she noticed subtle differences in the stone. Blending perfectly with the shadows was a doorway, carved from slightly darker rock than that around it. Echidna leaned closer, letting her eyes adjust until she saw a design etched into the stone. It was a weeping willow tree, with a lantern carved in the center.

Echidna placed both palms flat against the rock's surface on either side of the tree trunk. She closed her eyes, took a deep breath, and leaned her weight against the stone.

"Mighty Hecate," Echidna whispered in the ancient tongue. "With howls in the night, I call to you. Blood at the crossroads, I have left for you. Triple-faced goddess, she who sees through darkness, let me be your vengeance or strike me down. Veiled One, I seek out your help."

The branches of the willow tree slowly became animated. The long whips glided across the stone, brushing against the back of Echidna's hands. Two branches wrapped themselves around her wrists, binding her arms against the stone. She tried to pull free but the ties were too tight. The slivered edges drilled into her wrists, pumping blood from her veins. Her black blood flowed into the branches, emptying into the tree's center. The markings on the lantern slowly started to rise.

When the lantern was full of blood it started to glow dark ivy green. The willow branches detached themselves from Echidna's palms, slowly unbinding from her wrists. They once again became branches etched in stone. The lamp's handle jutted out of the rock. Echidna's hand trembled as she reached for it and gave the latch a firm twist.

The door slid away to reveal a large triangular room. Mounted on the wall to the right were three torches. Dominating the space from the center pedestal was a large statue of the three-headed goddess Hecate. Each face blankly stared into a different corner.

The wall to the left held an intricately woven tapestry hanging from two pillars. The left column was carved from the darkest onyx and polished smooth, while the other was pure ivory. A carved pomegranate sat on top of each one with a large snake curling its way down. The tapestry was woven in pastel hues of green, blue, and purple. At the front left side was the back of a woman dressed in a peplos. It was exactly like the one on the statue except amethyst purple instead of ivy green. Black hair cascaded down her back. Her hands hung relaxed at her sides.

At the center of the tapestry was a huge wheel. Signs of the zodiac were woven on the outer lip, each symbol resting above a mounted chair. Five chairs were in use at various places on the wheel.

Echidna looked at the wall beyond the statue. She slithered across the floor until she could see the words clearly. The words were written in an ancient language and she had to stretch her memory to remember.

Two burn as one when the three align
Then stone lips shall speak—three at one time

She committed them to memory before turning away. She made her way around the triangular perimeter, studying the room as she went. In each of the corners she noticed burn marks rubbed onto the stone. The scorches were low on the walls with long black streaks burned onto the stone. She noticed a small hole in the tiled floor. It took only a quick glance at the mounted torches to understand the chamber's secret.

Echidna slithered over to the three mounted sconces burning with the same black flame as the torches on the shores of the Styx. Their handles could be removed from the wall. Taking one staff in each hand, Echidna slid over to the nearest corner. After a moment's consideration, she put the shorter shaft into the hole in the floor tile.

The pole sank deep until the flame burned only a short distance off the floor. The black fire danced several inches higher than the burn marks. Echidna watched. Several long moments passed, and when nothing occurred, she removed the first torch and replaced it with the other. The pole sank into the tile until the fire aligned with the scorching on the wall. The flame grew several shades lighter, turning from black to the rich color of wine.

Echidna smiled and returned to take the third torch from the wall. Scurrying to the other corners, she placed the shafts into the holes matching the fire to the wall markings. When the last flame changed to the color of burning amethyst, the statue of the goddess came to life.

Echidna looked up into the faces of the triple goddess. The empty eyes became the color of opal moonlight, and the three faces became flesh once more.

"Mother of Monsters, welcome to my Temple." The black veils billowed out with each breath. "What is it you seek?"

Echidna pressed herself against the stone floor, prostrating her body before the goddess. Her human arms extended outward as far as they could go.

"Black Mother," Echidna croaked into the ground, her voice wavering. "You share my suffering by the Olympians. I beg for your help."

"Rise, Dark Sister," Hecate commanded. "It is true. You are the last. I've waited for you."

Echidna lifted her head. She rose until she stood on her clawed dragon's feet and extended to her full eight-foot height. She looked up at the faces of the veiled goddess and waited.

"Many years the world has turned," Hecate said. "Many gods the world has spurned. When there is no one left to keep their faith, even the mightiest becomes a wraith."

"Why me?" Echidna asked. "Why am I the last?"

"The reason you have kept so well—Olympian magic created your cell."

"The reign of the Olympian is over?" Echidna anxiously asked.

"Their reign has faded and their power gone," Hecate said. "But a line of lesser demigods was spawned. If they realize their heritage true, it can mean the end of you."

"Dark Mother," Echidna beseeched. She tried to understand the goddess's oracle. "I ask that I may return to seek revenge. Let me find the Olympians' offspring. I will destroy their children like they murdered mine. Let me avenge you."

"If you kill them as you say," Hecate said, "I shall bless you on that day."

"Dark Mother," Echidna vowed, "I shall not fail you."

"Your powers will not be as they were, and mighty foes you shall incur."

"You honor me, Dark Lady." Echidna bowed her head. "I fear them not."

"Before you are bound by magic gird, make sure you hear my every word."

The two torches in Hecate's hands burst into flame, their light filling the upper half of the chamber. As sparks flew free they disappeared into the ceiling's impenetrable darkness. The three heads stared directly forward, seeing far beyond the Temple's walls. Hecate's ominous voice thundered throughout the chamber.

"When the ground starts to shake, then the earth shall split and volcanoes give up their fire; for revenge is found when prisoners are freed and their captors feel their ire. Beware the meshing of sun and moon when thunder shakes the skies, for if Heaven shall journey into the World of Night, the mightiest can die."

The torches on either side of the tapestry suddenly grew. The flames launched two feet in the air. The woven picture swayed. The standing priestess arched her back and raised her arms above her head in offering. The Harlequin sitting at the wheel's center leaned forward and turned the crank. The wheel slowly started to spin. The zodiac signs on the wheel's edge began to blend together, becoming a solid blurred line of color.

When the Wheel of Fortune spun so fast it appeared to change direction, the priestess lowered her arms. She reached from inside the picture and pulled aside the tapestry, granting Echidna access.

"The wheel shall turn and you begin again," Hecate's triple voice declared. "Enter the portal to the world of men."

The three faces of the goddess blinked in unison. When they opened their eyes, the pupils were empty. The black veils slowly drifted to stillness over cold stone lips, and the color drained from the three faces. The torches in either hand of the goddess burst into large fires.

The flames in the corners of the room exploded in size, casting the room into blinding light and searing heat. Suddenly all flames were extinguished; only an ethereal light radiated around the tapestry and the ghostly turning Wheel of Fortune.

Echidna found that she had already entered the tapestry. Hecate's Temple was seen through opaque glass, and the turning wheel was perfectly clear. Her amber eyes locked onto those of the Harlequin, sitting in the wheel's center and turning the crank. As she watched the wheel spin, Echidna felt the pit of her stomach being clawed from the inside. She felt as if a grappling hook ripped into her belly before feeling the sensation of being pulled into the vortex of the spinning wheel.

The Mother of Monsters found herself rolling on the floor of a small, dank cave. Bats took flight out into the darkening sky. Light filtered in along with rain from the downpour outside. Echidna pressed her body against the cold floor, fearing she was back in her Tartarus cell. The spinning subsided and she glanced around her new surroundings.

At the back of the cave she found a crude coal drawing on the wall. It was a large circle with an "X" crossing in the center. A tight spiral was drawn inside the circle, giving the illusion of a hypnotist's wheel. To the right stood a crudely drawn stick figure.

Echidna slithered to the cave's mouth, a short ledge extending the lip outside. Some body of water stretched far before her and disappeared into the horizon. It did not look familiar, and she recognized no scents the howling wind offered. Stepping outside, she ignored the pelting rain. The cave was a short distance from the top of the cliff. There was the opportunity that creatures would fall, or climb, down into her lair on their own accord.

The idea of devouring living food made her ravenous. Reaching up, she took hold of the first secure rock and pulled herself up.

There was a new world, with new tastes to be offered.

❖

Camille Beaumont woke on the grass of Myrtle Edwards Park not knowing where she had passed out. She lay on her stomach with her left cheek pressed into the cold, wet grass. She tried to spit out the dirt coating her lips. Camille roughly pushed herself up from her current facedown position. Her hair matted to her cheek and was caked with mud.

The rain came down hard. She crawled a few inches. She felt solid ground through the mud and realized she was protected under a tree a short distance from a cliff's edge. Camille pulled herself farther under the tree, collapsing and catching her breath.

She closed her clouded hazel eyes. Malaysia had been almost a year ago, and she'd managed to survive that. The rain brought back memories of the unexpected flooding sweeping over the country, drowning those on the Lower Peninsula. She could still feel the warm tidal waters rising all around. The panic still rose in her chest.

She looked down at her left arm, feeling soreness in her inner elbow, relaxing immediately when she saw the dirty ribbon still loosely wrapped around her bicep. She leaned back against the tree trunk with a smack to her skull.

She was with…Breydon. Breydon. Breydon knew where to get a fix. He always did and was happy to share with her; she was his favorite. Breydon was always broke, but getting money was not difficult for Camille. Breydon had taken her from the shelter and showed her how to earn money. He'd rescued her from that Red Cross hell, and she would do anything to make him happy.

"That guy keeps texting me," Breydon had told her. "That old fuck likes your accent. He wants you to visit."

"No," Camille said hesitantly. "He's mean to me and calls me disgusting names."

"He pays good, don't he?"

Camille considered it for a moment.

"All you have to do is speak some French bullshit to him, play with his Tootsie Roll dick, and we can have ourselves a partay."

She started picking at her unkempt brittle gray hair.

"Come on, baby." Breydon pouted. "Don't ya want to party with me?"

Camille nodded.

"That's my baby girl." Breydon's face lit up. "I'll text him and bring you over."

An hour later she was coming out of the client's building with a fat lip and cash. That was the last thing she remembered before waking up in Myrtle Edwards Park.

Camille tried to calculate how long she had been passed out. It could have been an hour; it could have been a day.

"Bastard," Camille hissed. Breydon had left her with no cash and no fix.

She sank back against the tree trunk. This was not the first time she'd been abandoned; she would survive. Camille was tired of surviving. She'd survived a tsunami, only to be rescued from a Red Cross camp by a pimp, to become a prostitute and an addict. What was the point? Breydon would move on to others. He didn't love her. She could run the twenty yards, leap from the edge, and be done with it. No one would miss her.

Camille sat up. She froze and rubbed her eyes, not sure if what she was seeing was real or the drugs. Two arms extended over the edge. Slowly, a woman's head and naked torso emerged.

The creature struggled to get its reptilian body atop the cliff. It finally stretched on the edge, prone on its belly. The long tail thumped the ground before curling beside its body, the spike end dragging in the mud. The human body lazily turned its head, resting its chin on her folded arms.

"It's a mermaid," Camille whispered.

The creature's head lifted and propped the upper half up with its human hands. It opened its human mouth and a tongue flickered out. The head turned and locked eyes with Camille. The creature lowered her head, keeping her eyes fixed on her prey.

The mermaid dug its fists into the ground. The tail wriggled behind her like a giant rudder propelling her over the land. It was rearing up before Camille could move. The creature towered over her. Camille tried to push back, only to be pinned against the tree trunk.

The tail swung around and collided with Camille's skull. Her head hit the tree and she blacked out.

Camille opened her eyes a short while later. Familiar scents flooded her nostrils; warm smells from long ago. The smells of her childhood back in the French countryside. She tried to focus on the blurred figure of a woman.

"Mama," Camille softly cooed in French. "Is that you?"

The woman didn't answer. She reached out and hugged Camille closer. Camille felt secure, the embrace tight around her arms and body.

"Mama," Camille playfully cried in French. "Please, you will crush me."

Camille looked into her mother's amber eyes. The vertical pupils seemed to vibrate. Her mother held her closer and she felt the rough lips brush her neck. Camille winced at the brief pinch under her ear and floated away in the warm waters of oblivion.

CHAPTER SIX

Unofficially dubbed "Gay Bucks," the coffee house was an open room with ample seating. Adrian sat at the back of the room, sipping his double-shot cappuccino. His hand lightly sketched the details of a serpent's face. The snake's body was roughly outlined at the page bottom, and a nude male figure was not far away.

"Hey, buddy." Teddy stripped off his jacket, draping it over the back of his chair.

Adrian closed his sketchpad and put the pencil down. He was supposed to meet up with Marcus; Adrian should have assumed Teddy would come along.

"Not having anything?" Adrian asked.

"Marcus is getting it," came the reply. "How are you?"

"All right," Adrian answered.

Teddy Bolloun flopped into one of the empty chairs at the table. His face was full, his hair cut down to dirty blond stubble. He wore Lennon-style glasses over his green eyes. His body's frame was stout without being heavy. His phone was perpetually in his hands.

"What's that?" Teddy gestured to the pad on the table.

"Oh," Adrian said. "My sketchpad."

"I never knew you draw."

"When the mood strikes," Adrian explained. "Lately I've been in the—"

Two short buzzing sounds interrupted him.

"Hold on." Teddy picked up his phone and tapped the screen to open the app. "I'm trying to make plans for tonight."

"I got you a Market Blend plain drip with milk." Marcus Acivo sat down at the table. He rolled his eyes and looked at Adrian.

"I'm assuming he's already lost in Scruff-land?"

"The moment he sat down," Adrian answered. "How are you?"

"Doing well," Marcus answered. "Or at least well enough."

"I'm a little sick of this rain," said Adrian.

"You heard about the earthquake and tsunami, right?"

"Of course," Adrian answered. "It's all anyone's talking about. I know it's all related, but four days of this torrential downpour is enough. I'm ready to build an ark."

"You're in the right place." Marcus gazed around the room. "There's at least two of everything on Capitol Hill."

Marcus's smile was contagious. His body was lean, with well-developed round shoulders. His olive green shirt stretched over his broad chest and flat stomach. The long face was clean-shaven. His black hair was buzzed on the side with the long tufts on top brushed over.

"You're going to get whiplash turning your head that fast," Adrian commented.

"Never you mind," Marcus answered. "Mens are everywhere today."

"The two of you are incorrigible," Adrian replied.

"That's why we're the best of friends," Teddy answered.

"What's that?" Marcus asked.

"It's a sketchpad," Teddy answered. His eyes never left his phone's screen.

"You draw?" Marcus asked. "Can I see?"

"Sure," Adrian said.

He reached over and handed the pad to his best friend. Marcus opened the book to the picture of the eagle carrying the nude male.

"This is good," Marcus said.

"Thanks."

Adrian watched Marcus flip through pretending to be interested in everything but the naked figures. He knew Marcus pretty well. They'd dated for the first year, followed by another two years of avoiding each other. After the next chance meeting, they started what would become a very close friendship.

Teddy came along with the deal like a "gift with purchase." The two friends were strictly platonic, but one rarely went anywhere without the other.

"What's going on here?" Marcus pointed to the undetailed serpent's body.

Teddy glanced up.

"It looks like a giant penis," Teddy said.

"It's a snake," Adrian said. "And the figure in the back is going to be a hunter, or Saint Patrick or something. I haven't decided yet."

"What brought this on?" Marcus asked.

Teddy's phone buzzed and he reached for it.

"I've been having a few dreams lately," Adrian said to Marcus. "I thought I'd draw what I remember of them. See what comes of it, if anything."

"Dreaming of pythons, eh?" Teddy said. "That's an easy one, Dr. Freud. You need to get laid."

"Thanks," Adrian said. "No matter the ailment, sex is your answer."

Teddy declared, "If you're happy, then sex is a great way to celebrate. If you're sad, sex is a great way of cheering yourself up."

"Trust me," Marcus said in a stage whisper. "There's no reasoning with him."

"How can there be?" Adrian asked. "He's consistently reliving puberty."

Marcus turned to Teddy. "How old is this one?"

"Twenty-six," came the answer.

Adrian and Marcus both rolled their eyes.

"He's twenty-six," Teddy protested. "That does not make me a pedophile."

"You're twenty years older than him. What do you have in common?" Adrian teased back. "I have shoes older than him. You could be his father."

"Hell." Marcus choked on his coffee. "Half the guys hit him up with ''S up, Dad.'"

"Are you kidding me?"

"What can I say?" Teddy beamed proudly. "I still got it."

"But what you have," Marcus answered, "nobody wants."

"Evidently, they do. And often," Teddy replied. "You know how often I see Marcus's sad little face enviously looking at me when I leave the house? Don't give me that look, Adrian."

"Sorry," Adrian said with a shake of his head. "Rule number one: No one calls me 'Daddy' if it could be a biological possibility."

"Who are you kidding?" Teddy answered. "Nobody calls you Daddy."

Another set of short buzzes sounded. Teddy snatched up the phone and grinned at the screen.

"Look at him." Teddy turned the phone around so they could see the naked photo of the young man. "He's hot!"

Adrian took the phone.

"He's shaved every inch of his body including his pubic hair," Adrian argued. He handed the phone to Marcus.

"There is nothing wrong with a summer/winter romance," Teddy said. "It happens all the time."

"What if you're the summer?" Adrian asked.

"Please," Marcus said. "At our age we're more into fall."

"Okay," Adrian said. "What do you call someone who is our age dating someone who is, maybe, early sixties?"

"That's not a summer/winter romance," Teddy sneered. "That's a summer/Labor Day romance."

"Is there someone on your radar?" Marcus asked.

"No," Adrian said. "I was only curious."

"Come clean, Adrian."

"Really, no one in particular." Adrian paused for a moment. "I do I think I am ready to get back in the dating game."

"About time," Marcus said. "It's been a while since you've dated anyone."

"That we know of." Teddy gave Adrian a sly glance. "Something tells me he has his dance card punched when he wants it to be."

"Something tells me not," Marcus said. He took a sip of his coffee. "If you are ready, then good for you. When was your last relationship? I can't even remember."

"The last time I had a relationship…" Adrian thought a moment. "Was probably you."

"Really?"

"I told you," Adrian defended himself. "I'm particular about who I get involved with when it comes to relationships."

"And the last time you hooked up with someone?" Teddy leered.

"You mean you don't remember?" Adrian pouted. "Now I'm hurt. It meant so much more to me."

"Seriously," Marcus pursued. "When was it?"

"Not your business," Adrian protested.

"You need to get out more," Marcus said. "Socialize and meet people."

"I'm open to dating if I meet someone that I connect with. If not, oh well."

"Famous last words." Marcus sneered.

"Time's running out," Teddy said. "Tick tock. You're not looking any younger, you know."

"There's always someone that's going to look better than you, and someone that looks worse." Marcus smiled. "The trick is, when it comes to the lineup, always stand next to the person that looks worse."

The three men saluted each other with their coffee cups.

CHAPTER SEVEN

Echidna felt power spreading through her body, warming her blood. Her senses were sharpening. Camille's life was not much, but the essence was better than the maggots and larvae in her prison.

Camille's dehydrated body was ripped apart like strips from a rag. Her bones were broken and crushed. Echidna mixed the bone powder with water and used it to bind together her nest. She felt the magic growing inside her like a child. And like a child, she needed to nurture it and let it grow.

Echidna's body tingled, alerting her to another presence in her lair, and she cautiously slithered to the back of her cave. Her eye slits focused on the crude coal drawing on the back wall.

The stick figure became animated and moved across the stone. It reached over and took hold of the crank at the wheel's center. The figure turned the crank and the wheel began to spin. It gained speed until the spokes became a whirling blur.

Echidna's eyes locked on the hypnotic pinwheel. World images flashed and burned into her mind, as if awakening memories. Wars destroyed the world she knew, while voyagers discovered new lands to conquer. Gods rose and fell over the centuries, exchanged for science and technology. Empires expanded only to be conquered in turn, becoming lost in the dusts of time. She watched as three thousand years became part of her consciousness, blending with Camille's personal memories.

A full day passed before the wheel ceased flooding Echidna with images and knowledge. The wheel slowed until it stopped. The stick figure returned to its corner, and the animation returned to a crude coal drawing.

Echidna turned from the wall. She slithered to the cave's mouth, understanding just how far she'd come from her home in ancient Arcadia.

She looked up into the rain, ready to explore her new homeland. She reached for the rocky edge and pulled herself up to ground level. Raising her arms to the pouring sky, Echidna closed her eyes and deeply inhaled the sharp smells of the salt water. From the recesses of Camille's mind, Echidna plucked a visual, playing it over and over until she could see every detail.

"Conceal," she whispered into the storm.

Her arms fell to her sides, letting warmth wash over her body. She felt her body shift under the illusion and become the figure from Camille's memory. She inhaled deeply, the scents of a new world awakening her appetite. Mortal flesh lay in wait, unaware of the fierce predator in their midst.

"Camille!" The sound was distant and far.

Echidna watched a ship cruising the water below her.

"God damn it, Camille! Answer me!"

She heard the shouting several more times before recognizing the name as hers.

"Don't you hear me, Camille? I've been looking for your French ass for days. Don't just stand there, bitch!" Breydon said as he approached.

It took a moment before Echidna could pluck Breydon from Camille's memories. The pimp walked toward her. The UW baseball cap worn backward made his brown eyes seem larger than they were. A scowl tightened his ebony face. His denim pants were soaked from the rain and hung below his waist.

"God damn it, girl," Breydon said. "I've been yelling at you from across the field. Didn't you hear me? I should beat your ass."

Breydon slowed as he approached. "What did you do to yourself? You look diff'rent."

Echidna stood still, studying Breydon. Her attention focused on the sparkling phantom lights hovering around his shoulders. There was no pattern, flashing like a sprinkling of red fireflies.

This pathetic creature yelling before her was of an ancient lineage. The hovering wyre-lights were evidence of magical ancestry. Centuries of mortal blood had diluted the purity, but it was of Arcadia, and that meant power.

"When did you color your hair? Look at you," Breydon said. "You looking fine."

Echidna smiled.

The moment his fingers touched her skin, Echidna knew the illusion was shattered. Breydon's brown eyes widened with fear. His mouth opened, silently trembling, his body shaking where he stood.

"What the fuck?"

Echidna's hand snapped up and yanked Breydon's arm away from her face. The force pulled the bone from the socket. The strong tail wrapped around his legs and yanked him from a standing position. Slowly, she lifted him until he hung upside down. His working arm swung desperately, falling short of range.

"I'll...I'll fucking kill you." Breydon spat out blood.

Echidna held him dangling in the air. Her tongue flickered out. The twin edges of her forked tongue brushed against his skin, and she relished the delicious salty tastes of sweat, fear, and adrenaline.

"Kill me?" Echidna whispered. "I think not."

Breydon whimpered.

Echidna sank her fangs into Breydon's neck. Her powerful teeth tore a gap in the flesh until his blood gushed freely in her mouth. She pressed her lips to his neck, gulping as much as she could. She drank until she felt the dehydrated skin clinging to his bones.

The power surged through her body. She heard the rumbling in her ears and turned her head to look over the waters of Puget Sound. White tips formed on angry waves.

Poseidon's phantom horses crashed on the ledge, deluging Echidna in enchanted waters. She felt her body ingesting the magical strength and power Breydon never knew he possessed. She ransacked his pockets, finding $123 in loose bills in his wallet, a heroin packet, and a single unmarked key. The money she kept, knowing its value. With a single motion of her tail, she knocked his body over the cliff's edge.

CHAPTER EIGHT

*T*he larger-than-average-sized stallion galloped hard across the sky. The triangular ears jutted out from a mane of pure white. The horse's muscled shoulders and strong legs hurtled both animal and rider at an incredible speed with natural grace. Pegasus followed the clouds as easily as any road marks on the ground below them. The horse snorted and galloped onward.

Adrian was aware that this body was not his own, yet he controlled all movements with the same sharp dexterity as if it were. His body slowly rocked to and fro with the motion of the horse's gallop. Both hands held loosely to the mane. The wind brushed the black wavy hair from his face, and he felt the sun warming his naked skin. A quiver of arrows was strapped across his back, the bow strung across his chest. A large spear rested in a holder off the saddle.

The saddle made his nakedness more comfortable, and the blazing sun heated the soft leather. Adrian leaned forward, pressing his body against the horse's chest, and ran a comforting hand down its side.

The horse's large wings beat a steady rhythm like the gentle rolling of summer thunder. The ground below was becoming less green, more broken rocks and stone. They were climbing up toward the mountains. He did not recognize the terrain, but the horse knew the way, and Adrian trusted the animal's instincts.

They slowed as they entered the mountain range's center. Snow covered the peaks, but he still felt the warm sun on his skin. The horse flew in tight circles, drawing closer to the ledge with each passing. Adrian could see the bones of animals strewn about the lip's surface. Steam rolled out, with the strong stench of decay.

A frightful roar thundered from inside the cave. Small rocks rolled down either side. The steam grew thicker as another roar sounded.

A great lion emerged from the cave. The creature raised its head with a deafening cry. The gigantic lion crept farther out onto the ledge. From behind the great beast a sharp tail snapped; at its end the hood of a cobra opened, venom dripping from exposed fangs. The chimera released a final warning roar. It crouched down, the cobra tail hovering behind, as a goat's head reared up on a neck from the center of the creature's back and shot out a stream of fire.

The winged horse reared back, kicking its powerful front legs. Adrian reached over his shoulder and loosely notched an arrow to the string of the bow.

Adrian pulled at the bow and fired a storm of arrows in quick succession. The first arrow missed, disappearing into the cave. The second arrow was notched and released, only to be batted aside by the lion's paw. The third shot barely missed the lion's leg. Adrian notched the next arrow and shot.

The arrow pierced the cobra's hood. The chimera howled with anger and crouched low, readying to pounce. It leapt, the lion's paw deeply scratching the lower part of Adrian's leg.

Adrian's heart pounded in his chest as the winged horse reared back and out of range. Blood ran down his calf. He could feel adrenaline racing through his body. His hand crept to the quill strapped to his back.

Adrian notched the arrow and took a breath. Slowly, he drew the bow back and took careful aim at the creature on the cliff's ledge.

The chimera leapt to the side, managing to avoid the full force of the arrow flying toward it. The attack grazed both animal heads and fully hit the center of the tail. The snake's head was cut from the monster's body. The remaining heads let out a howl of pain and rage. It crouched low, two sets of black beady eyes studying the hovering enemy.

Adrian shifted the bow to his shoulder. He took hold of the spear and took a deep breath.

The lion's mouth opened and the chimera leapt into the air, clawing at the exposed flesh of his legs. Adrian leaned back against the horse's flanks, raising the spear and tightening his grip.

Adrian hurled his weapon.

Adrian woke with his heart pounding in his chest. Both hands gripped the bedsheets. He lay still, trying to catch his breath. The clock on the counter read 6:43 a.m.

Adrian closed his eyes and tried to drift back to sleep. Images of his dream returned. He got out of bed, retrieving the discarded cotton shorts and T-shirt from the floor. Visions of the horse and rider still flitted through his mind as he made coffee. He poured a cup and went to the back bedroom.

The floor of the guest room was a mess. Boxes, some open and others still taped shut, lay strewn about the room. Books were stacked along three walls, and garbage bags of clothes were torn open, their contents pulled out and sifted through on the floor. Abandoned in the back corner lay a folded easel pressed against the closet door. Propped next to it was an empty rectangular canvas.

Adrian tucked the empty canvas under his arm and took hold of the easel. He carried them back into the main room and set them in front of the sofa, pushing the table out of the way. His sketchpad was propped against the couch and his messenger bag lay open on the table's surface.

Adrian reached inside the cloth bag and removed an assortment of colored pencils and his ear buds. He brushed a dry dish towel over the canvas to clear any traces of dust and listened to Mussorgsky's *Night on Bald Mountain*.

It only took a moment before Adrian found the music's soul. The basic drawing began with wide curves and grand sweeps as his hand moved to the music. Between sips of coffee, an outline emerged. He sketched a horse in midair outside a mountain cave. The ambiguous form of a rider was penciled onto the horse's back, and he added wings to the horse's sides. A monstrous creature with three heads lay crouching on the mountain's edge, waiting to leap at horse and rider.

Adrian didn't notice at first when Beethoven's Fifth Symphony interrupted his classical music playlist. It played twice before he made the connection and reached for the phone. The photo of Marcus with the time stamp 10:06 a.m. flashed on the screen.

"Good morning." Adrian stifled a yawn.

"Answering the phone at ten a.m.?" Marcus replied. "I was expecting your voice mail."

"I can hang up and you can call back." Adrian made a few

adjustments to the drawing. "Not all of us get up at five a.m. to hit the gym."

"Some of us really need to," Marcus mumbled.

"Did you want something?"

"Actually, I have a favor to ask. A big favor."

"Okay. What is it?" Adrian scanned his sketch of the Greek hero Bellerophon fighting Chimera with a sense of pride. The sketched outlines were clear and the figures were definitely recognizable.

"I was hoping I could borrow your truck this weekend?"

"This weekend?" Adrian asked. "As in tomorrow?"

"Yeah." There was a pause. "My mom gave my sister that large dresser and dining room set. The one she had in her old house; the one that has been in storage for the last two years. You remember that beautiful oak antique set?"

"I remember."

"Well," Marcus continued, "my sister was going to use our brother's truck, but the clutch went out."

"Why can't they move it when the clutch is fixed?" Adrian gently smudged a line under Chimera's feet, extending the creature's shadow.

"Mom didn't tell me she closed her storage unit down," Marcus said. "She has to have everything out of the unit by this weekend. If not, she'll have to pay for the month of June. You know how cheap my mother is."

"Promise me you won't drive me crazy, and I'll consider it."

"I promise."

"And your mother owes me a pot of chicken adobo."

"Deal."

"When do you want it?" Adrian asked.

"Can I pick it up this afternoon?" Marcus asked. "I'll come by after work. This way I don't have to bother you tomorrow. I'll drive up to Bellingham in the morning and have the truck back by Sunday evening."

"You're pushing it."

"At least I'm not asking you to help move it."

"Roped Teddy into it?" Adrian asked.

"It was easy," Marcus immediately confirmed. "Can I come by your place around six thirty? I'll take you out for a drink first."

"Yeah," Adrian said. "I don't think you having a drink before taking my truck is a good idea. I've seen how you drive sober."

"Anyway," Marcus muttered, "thanks. My mother says thank you, and so does my sister. I'll text you before leaving my last client."

"Do me a favor," Adrian teased. "Please shower before coming over."

"In this rain? What's the point? Thanks, Adrian. I really appreciate it."

"You owe me," Adrian replied. "And so does your mother."

It was over an hour later that a second interruption broke through his music. Taking the phone from his waistband, Adrian glanced at the message from his sister.

Coming over today, the text read. *Will you be home @ 2 pm?*

Sure, Adrian answered. *What's up?*

Last minute stuff for opening this weekend. Need 2 kill time. Have favor to ask.

Seems to be the day4it. See you then.

When Adrian stepped back from the picture later, an extremely pleased smile crossed his lips. He added color to different parts of the drawing while leaving others purposely in black and white. He brought the vaporizer to his lips and took another inhale from the mouthpiece. After a toke, he sharpened another colored pencil with renewed inspiration.

CHAPTER NINE

Annelise climbed the outside steps to the house's second level. At the top she could hear the classical music playing from inside. Annelise smiled, knowing her twin's intuition was right; Adrian was in a good mood, and she hoped it would work in her favor. She knocked loudly to be heard over the music.

"Come in!"

Adrian was sitting on the couch, his legs propped onto the coffee table. In his right hand he held an open bottle of beer, paused midair between sips. His left arm lay across the cushions.

"Beer at this hour," Annelise teased, with a glance at her watch. It was half past three.

"There's more in the fridge," Adrian replied. "Help yourself. There's also a bottle of white wine in there."

"I don't mind if I do."

Annelise put her purse down by the door and took off her jacket.

"Beer's not your usual flavor." Annelise poured herself a glass of wine. "What's going on?"

Annelise took a seat next to her brother on the couch, putting her cell phone on the tabletop.

"It's my day off," Adrian confessed. "I've been pretty busy, and beer sounded good."

"You remind me of Dad right now." She nodded at the green bottle in his hand. "The tone in your voice, and the way you're sitting there. He always enjoyed a cold bottle of Mythos."

"Believe me, it's not easy to find with all of Seattle's microbreweries." He took a sip from the bottle. "I couldn't tell you the last time I saw Mythos in a store around here, and picked it up on whim the other day. I figured it wouldn't go to waste. Teddy and Marcus both like it."

"So what's the occasion?" Annelise asked.

Adrian smiled. He put the bottle on the table and nodded toward the easel.

Annelise walked over to the easel. She tucked her left hand behind her back, a position she took when studying any artist's work.

"How long have you been working on this?"

"Since early this morning." Adrian replied.

"No. Really?" she said, impressed. "What brought this on?"

"A dream I had last night."

"You're telling me this is all from today?"

"From about nine thirty this morning."

"This shows great promise," Annelise said. "You have good detail on the chest muscles. The spear cutting across the body with the shaft covering the rider's dick is quite a bold metaphor, if not very subtly erotic."

"Thank you."

"Even this chimera emits a certain masculinity." Annelise looked up at her brother, impressed. "This is good. This is very good."

Adrian smiled. "I was inspired."

"Whatever did it," Annelise turned back to study the painting and took another sip, "I hope it lasts."

"I wasn't sure if I should color it in or not," Adrian said. "That's why it's not all the way done."

"Good," Annelise replied. "I like it the way it is, not fully colored. I love how the sun isn't in the picture except captured in the helmet's reflection. Wait, it's not a sunburst, it's a design?"

"I thought I'd give him sort of a sigil. It seemed appropriate."

Annelise looked again at the front of the helmet. "A sigil for what?"

"I don't know," Adrian confessed. "It felt right."

"I'd say the beer is well-earned," Annelise said.

Annelise sat back against the couch's cushions and kicked off her shoes. Stretching her arm across the sofa's top, she swung her stocking feet onto the table and crossed her ankles.

"Dad once told Mom Uncle Nico drew a lot as a kid," Annelise said. "Nico supposedly had potential, but after they escaped to the US, Nico had to work and couldn't pursue his art."

"Dad encouraged his younger brother to draw?" Adrian said. "That doesn't sound like him."

"Don't start," Annelise said.

"Even you have to admit Dad never was into the arts."

"When did he have time? When he first came to the United States, his family needed him to work. Then he had his own family. When did Dad have time?"

"Mom found time," Adrian said.

"Exactly. Mom found time. Dad worked constantly so that Mom could stay home and raise us. Besides," Annelise said, "where do you think you get your love of classical music? Didn't you know that Dad loved listening to the symphony?"

Annelise smiled. "Mom used to tell me that he would come home from work, go to the bedroom and take off his shirt. While she took care of us, he'd wash off with a cloth. They'd listen to the radio or the stereo without talking. It was how Dad unwound from work."

"How come I never knew any of this? Why didn't Mom ever tell me?" Adrian said.

"You and Dad had issues," Annelise said. "You probably blocked it out. You remember the music during dinner?"

"I almost forgot about that."

"You were always closer to Mom," Annelise said.

"I'm getting another beer. Want a refill?"

"Sure."

Annelise leaned over to her side and snatched up the sketchpad leaning on the table's leg.

"What are you doing?" Adrian said.

"You have been busy," Annelise said.

She glanced up from the fourth page of the sketchpad, flipping the cover over. She put the closed book back against the table.

"If you really want to know the truth, you have real talent. And that's a gallery owner speaking, not your favorite sibling."

"Only sibling," Adrian muttered.

"You know," she went on, "there could be a show in this."

"I don't think so," Adrian said.

"A few more like that chimera over there…we could do an amateur's exhibit showing the process from these earlier sketches, and going up to that one, and whatever else you come up with for me. I need an exhibit for the first part of fall through Christmas. If you can get me, say, two or three more in the next four months, I can work with that."

"I don't know if I'm ready to show these yet," Adrian said.

"We have four months. If you're still uncertain in three months, no big deal. We don't have to do it."

"You're being serious," Adrian said. "You really think I have talent?"

"Why would I say it if I didn't?"

"So what's the new exhibit?" Adrian changed the subject.

"It's a collection of local artists," Annelise said. "One makes flowers, baskets, and other creations from wire and beads. One creates small ceramics—animals, small-lidded containers, and such. Another paints local scenes in watercolors and oils. The exhibit should be perfect for this time of year, and the local factor plays well with tourists."

"Sounds good," Adrian said.

"That brings me to my favor." Annelise smiled.

"I was wondering when we'd get to that," Adrian said. "What is it?"

"I need a couple of waiters for the grand opening?" Annelise squinted her eyes with anxious anticipation. She held her breath and waited.

"When?" Adrian asked.

"This weekend," she answered.

"Nothing like a little notice."

"I'm in a real bind," Annelise said. "I had two waiters lined up and they both canceled this morning…within an hour of each other."

"Fine. What do you need me to do and when?"

"Thank you!" Annelise said. She leaned over and gave her brother a hug. "It's only simple stuff. Meandering among the guests, serving champagne, stuff like that. Nothing too difficult and nothing you haven't done several times before now. It's only for a few hours on Saturday evening. Come over before three that afternoon and all is good. I'll pay your ferry. You can spend the night if you want, and I'll pay you fifty bucks."

The sounds of a slide whistle briefly echoed and Annelise's phone screen lit up. She picked it up and read the text message.

"Hey," she said. "I need to cut this short. My client changed her mind and wants me to leave brochures at her shop."

"You had brochures made up?"

"And there's my next favor. I need you to give me a lift downtown to Louise's gallery."

"What happened to your car?" Adrian asked. "I know the gallery's truck is in the shop, how come you're without your car?"

"I wasn't planning on being here that long." Annelise settled farther into the couch with a heavy sigh. "I thought the brochures were being delivered. Lily forgot to mention they needed picking up. And once I realized I was going to be here until after five," Annelise continued, "well, you know how it is to try and drive onto the ferry on a Friday night. Never mind the rain."

"I don't mind Seattle's rain, but this was exceptional."

"It's all about the tsunamis, remember?" Annelise answered.

"Sure." Adrian picked up his phone from the table. "Marcus is coming by in two hours. That's more than enough time. Even in this weather."

"At least the rain is slowing," Annelise said. She put on her shoes as Adrian texted his change in plans.

Adrian stood up facing his sister. "It's almost three o'clock now. What time will you be done with your client?"

"After this client, I'm meeting Yvonne at six up in Shoreline."

"Yvonne, your ex?"

"Yeah," Annelise said. "But don't worry. I'm not asking you to meet me."

"Okay." Adrian sat back. "Say hi for me. Hey, how are you getting home from the ferry?"

"Lily knows to pick me up by the donut shop," Annelise confirmed. "So what time are you going to meet Marcus?"

"When he gets off work," Adrian answered. "You excited about the opening?"

Annelise grinned. "Excited. Nervous. Scared. The usual."

"You'll be fine," Adrian assured her. "You go through this with every opening. You get nervous, and then everything always turns out perfect."

"Yeah, I know," Annelise said. "I have an odd feeling about this."

"You say *that* every time, too."

"Not the same thing," Annelise said.

"Okay," Adrian said. "Let's get going."

Chapter Ten

Echidna moved along the streets of downtown Seattle still under the concealment spell. She was becoming more familiar with the Pike Market. She hunted with caution, resigning herself to the few junkies and homeless she could find.

The power in Breydon's blood revived her lust for human flesh. His untapped energy brought her new life. Poor soul. Poor fool.

Echidna approached a woman with a baby stroller waiting to cross the street. Carefully balancing an umbrella between her neck and shoulder, the woman bent down to struggle with the plastic bonnet covering her child in the stroller.

Echidna watched the child with care, noticing the red wyre-lights brightly flashing through the stroller's covering. These lights did not flutter weakly, but pulsed with the rhythm of a strong heartbeat. The infant's innocence radiated with power, pure and untainted.

"No," the child said.

The little boy looked around and focused directly on Camille. The baby blue eyes stared up at her, filling with tears. The bottom lip trembled and the child started to cry. It kicked its feet wildly, flailing its hands outside the stroller.

"No!" the child yelled.

The light changed and the woman pushed the stroller across First Avenue. A small clump of people darted across the street. Echidna meandered behind, keeping the mother and child in sight. She saw them browse through windows, eventually going into a store with *The Garden—A Boutique Gallery* written on the window.

The child could see through my concealment. And couldn't tell a soul. What delicious irony.

Echidna stood three storefronts away from the gallery and could still smell the infant's power. Her hunger grew at the thought of the hunt, and she could feel her mouth watering. A red truck pulled curbside in front of the boutique. Echidna halted in her tracks, stepping back to watch.

Yellow lights blinked on either side of the license plate, A545QRT. A slim-figured woman dressed in black pants and jacket jumped out of the passenger's side. A man leapt from the driver's side and raced around the front of the truck. He carried a rectangular brown box under his arm. He darted over and gave the package to the waiting woman.

Echidna noticed the red wyre-lights around both of them. These lights didn't pulse or flutter; they glowed. A steady strong river of red flowed around both of their heads and shoulders. As they stood in front of one another, Echidna noticed their physical similarities.

The wyre-lights were strong in both of them, and that meant power. Bile cramped her stomach. Echidna knew they were danger. She watched the man embrace the female before he ran back through the rain to his truck and drove away.

The woman watched the truck leaving, one hand waving and the other clutching the package. She was about to turn when their eyes met. Echidna held her breath, and was relieved when she entered the gallery.

"Hello." The salesclerk behind the counter glanced up at Camille's entrance. "I can't tell you how excited I am, Annelise," she gushed to the woman Echidna had seen out front.

"I'm sorry I couldn't get the brochures to you sooner, Louise," Annelise said. "I always seem to have car issues when I need to get to and from the island on schedule."

"Murphy's Law." Louise reached into the box, taking out a handful of brochures. "These look great! I can't wait for tomorrow night's opening. Even my boyfriend is looking forward to it. He's invited several of his friends. It's going to be fun."

Camille browsed through the store, eavesdropping. The woman with the baby stroller was browsing in the corner. The child was drifting off to sleep and she watched the tiny pink arm twitch before dropping the toy car on the store's carpet.

Louise approached Camille and pressed a brochure into her hand.

"Tomorrow night's the opening at seven thirty. The exhibit goes on for eight weeks."

"Actually nine," Annelise replied. "The exhibit ends before Labor Day."

"If you get a chance," Louise continued, "Bainbridge is only a short ferry ride away."

Camille nodded politely. Louise went back to the counter.

"What time would you like me to be at the gallery?" Louise asked.

"Get there when you can," Annelise said.

Camille looked at the advertisement in her hand. The paper was dark blue with yellow letters, announcing Petrakis Gallery's spring/summer opening exhibit.

"Petrakis," Camille whispered.

Annelise handed Louise another pile of pamphlets and resealed the box. She caught Camille staring at her and smiled briefly before returning to her conversation.

"I'll see you tomorrow, then," Annelise replied. She hiked the box back up under her arm. She spun around and crossed to the front door.

Camille watched from the store's corner. She kept her eyes on Annelise, making note of her every move. Annelise looked up and met eyes with her once again. She smiled and walked out the door.

Echidna stood still, watching. The smile meant something. The woman didn't recognize Echidna's true self. It took her a few minutes more before she realized with surprise that the look was flirtatious.

"Thanks for your patience, Jane."

Camille heard small talk behind her.

"I'll be right back with your order," Louise said. "Miss. If I can help you with anything, let me know. Miss?"

It took Camille a moment before realizing she was being addressed. She looked over her shoulder. "Just looking," she answered. "Thank you."

Louise disappeared behind a curtain leading to the back storage room. The mother wheeled the stroller next to the counter. She stepped away to look at the art on the shelf.

Camille saw the infant's toy car discarded on the carpet. She picked it up. Camille crept over to the stroller and gazed at the sleeping child. The red pulsing lights stirred her hunger. She could smell that delicious scent. This creature possessed powerful magic, and it was what Echidna needed.

Echidna glanced at the distracted mother before looking down at the sleeping child. She whispered her spell and felt the air about her shimmer and her body's illusion shift once more.

Breydon reached carefully into the stroller and unbuckled the child. He lifted the sleeping thing from its bed.

Louise came back from the storage room with a package wrapped in brown paper. She put it on the counter, immediately addressing the African American man holding a struggling puppy in his arms.

"Sir, sorry, but you can't bring dogs into this store," Louise said. Her tone was curt and rude. "Unless it's a service animal."

"Don't worry," Breydon said. He flashed his most charming smile, his amber eyes twinkling. "I'm leaving."

Breydon left. The puppy continued to struggle, barking in his ear.

"Shut up, maggot," Echidna hissed in the concealed infant's ear.

When the mother's panicked cries were heard, Echidna was already cutting through the crowd out front. She pressed the child tighter to her clothed chest.

No one paid attention to the gangbanger carrying a whimpering blond puppy.

❖

Echidna stirred from her sleep. She felt refreshed, renewed, and stronger, all from the unpolluted blood of a child. As she slithered from her nest, she saw the toy car on the dirt floor.

Echidna picked it up and turned it over in her hands. She went out of her cave and stood on the edge, bent down and traced a circle in the dirt at her feet, then placed the blue car in the center.

"Car of my enemy becomes this car of mine," she hissed into the howling wind. She closed her eyes and visualized the truck she'd seen in front of the gallery. "I name you A545QRT."

Echidna picked up the toy, cupping it in her palms. When she opened her hands, the car was a red truck. Her eyes focused on the vehicle in her hand. She lifted the toy to the dark moon.

"In the darkness of night, when there is no moon, they will come for you," she chanted. "Hidden from sight, they shall visit soon and will come for you. Nightmares to haunt you while you sleep, and dreams that make the bold men weep. My Fury shall find you wherever you be and swiftly bring revenge for me!"

The movement inside her started slowly, pushing its way out of her body. Two shadowy hands tore free and dug the jagged edges of their claws into her inner thighs. They scratched up her legs as they tried to pull the body out from her womb. The skull of a bat protruded from her flesh. The six serrated teeth interlocked like pointed mountain peaks. Its pointed ears were sharp and plastered against the head. A thin wiry body freed itself, trying its bat-like wings for the first time. A set of gangly legs hung down with clawed feet, each with three long, razor-sharp talons curling at the end.

The creature turned on its mother and roughly shoved its gnarled hands back into Echidna's body. She screamed, feeling the claws taking hold. The sharp fingers pulled out, tightly clasped onto another solid shadow. Within moments, the two Furies were fully grown and hovering over the ground. Their wings beat ferociously, and they howled with the rage of being born.

Echidna pushed herself up by her elbows. She panted heavily. She looked at her children, Torment and Havoc. They were pure energy, dark, and for the moment, strong. Echidna knew they would fade with daylight even if the storm continued to rage.

"Go!" Echidna gave her command. "Find the truck and destroy my enemy."

The Furies screeched in acknowledgment. They flew out of the cave and into the night's storm.

CHAPTER ELEVEN

Annelise left the Red Dragon restaurant feeling relaxed. All business was complete; there was nothing left but to let the opening happen. She had no further responsibilities for the evening. The tapas plates and the large glass of Cabernet had also helped.

"I was hoping the rain would have at least lightened up by now." Annelise glanced at her watch. It was 7:45. There was still plenty of time for walking onto the 8:30 ferry.

"I think it's gotten worse."

Yvonne offered Annelise her arm. In her hand she carried a stack of brochures wrapped in plastic, closed with a rubber band.

Yvonne was a handsome woman. Her compact body was naturally athletic. Her gray hair had darker streaks and was cut short on the sides. Her hazel eyes were deep-set. The crow's feet were usually present as she smiled often.

Arm in arm, the women walked briskly to Yvonne's metallic green Prius. Annelise put the brochure box on the backseat.

"If the storm is worse," Yvonne said, "that usually means it's almost over."

"It's been raining so much lately," Annelise said. "I actually saw two locals using umbrellas." Annelise buckled her seat belt as Yvonne started the ignition.

"What's up with you?" Yvonne asked.

Annelise shrugged. "I guess I'm just a little anxious about the opening."

The car was still in park. Yvonne turned in her seat, her arm resting on the curve of the steering wheel.

"Why this one?" Yvonne asked. "You've had many gallery openings before this, and you do get a little crazy about it, but not usually until the night of. Why the nerves all of a sudden?"

"I don't know," Annelise said. "Maybe I don't want to jinx it."

"No. That's not it." Yvonne narrowed her eyes. "There's something else."

"I don't know what you mean."

"You've met someone."

"No." Annelise coughed. "No. I haven't."

"Then you're interested in someone." Yvonne steered the car into traffic.

"I've only seen her once, briefly, and that was today."

"So there *is* someone."

They drove a few moments in silence.

"I don't know anything about her," Annelise said. "I was at Louise's gallery on First Avenue earlier today, and she was there. Just a harmless flirtation and I was on a schedule," Annelise said with a sigh. "That was that."

"You're all charged up for someone you didn't even meet?"

Annelise smiled at the absurdity. "There was something about her. I don't believe in fate or destiny, but the way she was looking at me…it made me feel like she knew more about me than I knew myself."

The sirens ahead grew louder. Yvonne pulled the car to the side. Two ambulances with lights flashing raced past the paused line of cars. In a moment the Prius continued onward.

"And so this woman of mystery has you completely bewitched, all from a casual glance in a gallery? That must have been one helluva look."

"For all the good it does me."

"Maybe you'll meet again," Yvonne suggested.

"Maybe," Annelise resigned with a sigh. "Stranger things have happened."

The cars in front of them slowed. The red taillights glistened eerily through the heavy rain.

"Must be an accident up ahead," Yvonne said.

"That would probably explain the ambulances," Annelise replied. She glanced at her watch. "There's still time to catch the ferry."

At the bottom of the road was a four-way stop. As the cars crept closer, they saw a police flare set up in the middle of the crossing. An officer dressed in a bright yellow rain slicker was directing traffic from the center.

The cars inched forward. The wrought iron fence to an old graveyard came into view. A fire truck was pulled up diagonally in front of the gates. Floodlights brightly lit the area, casting ghostly images on the tombstones and mausoleums.

Annelise shifted in her seat as the Prius approached the accident.

"Why is it," Yvonne mumbled aloud, "that whenever there's an accident, people feel the need to crawl by and gawk?"

Annelise sat up in her seat. Her back went rigid, her eyes opened wide, and her breath raced through her chest.

"Yvonne," Annelise said. "Pull the car over."

"What are you talking about?"

"Pull the car over," Annelise commanded, reaching for the door's handle.

"What do you mean pull over?"

"Now," Annelise shouted. "Now! Do it now! Pull the fucking car over now!"

Yvonne put on her signal. The Prius was barely stopped when Annelise unhooked her seat belt, threw open the door, and leapt out. She crossed the road, darting past the four cars ahead.

Annelise stopped abruptly on the corner. Her breath caught in her chest. Her knees threatened to buckle and she felt bile churning her stomach. Her eyes were glued to the collision.

A red truck had crashed through the cemetery gate, knocking down a six-foot section. The front end smashed into a large mausoleum. Annelise stared at the red truck's tailgate.

"Oh fuck, no." Annelise's wail grew louder until she was shouting. "No. No. No! NO!"

Annelise spotted two of the yellow slickers and took off toward them, ignoring Yvonne's confused, pleading calls. One of the officers saw her approaching and stepped in front blocking the way.

"Stop right there, miss," the officer said.

"That's my brother's truck," Annelise said. "Is he okay? Is my brother okay? Adrian? Adrian!"

"Is Adrian your brother's name?" the office asked, trying to calm her down.

"No," Yvonne snapped. She came up from behind Annelise holding an umbrella. "She's doing her best Rocky impersonation."

The officer stared at Yvonne before turning back to Annelise. "Are you sure that's your brother's truck?"

"Are you kidding me? Of course I'm sure!" Annelise rattled off, "Red 2008 Nissan pickup, standard bed with a black tarp on the back. There's a string of those, what the hell do you call them…those brown Hawaiian nuts, ah…Kukui nuts hanging from the rearview. The license number is…damnit!" She clenched her eyes shut. "A545QRT. Now where the hell is my brother?"

"Take a deep breath," the officer advised. "What's your brother's full name?"

"Adrian Dmitri Petrakis," Annelise said. Her heart was pounding, but her breathing was slowing down. "He's my twin. Forty-eight years old. Is he all right? Was he hurt? Where is he? Adrian? Adrian!"

The officer reached out to gently take hold of Annelise's arm. "Ma'am, I need you to calm down. Wait right here, and I'll find out what I can. But I need you to stay calm. Can you do that for me?"

Annelise took a deep breath. She nodded. After a moment, the office returned to Annelise. "Your brother lost control of his vehicle," she said. "Does he have any problems with alcohol or drugs?"

"What?" Annelise said in shock. "No. He doesn't do drugs! And he wouldn't be drinking and driving. Where is he?"

"I'm sorry," the officer said. "He was unconscious when the ambulance arrived. He was alive, but unconscious and not responding. They're taking him to Harborview Medical Center. I'm sorry."

"Annelise." Yvonne was gently tugging at her arm. "Annelise. Take a deep breath. It'll be okay. I'm sure Adrian is going to be all right."

Annelise didn't react.

"Annelise," Yvonne said, more urgently.

Annelise closed her mouth, swallowing hard. She nodded.

"Let's get you out of this rain. I'll take you to Harborview. Okay? Let's go."

Annelise remained still.

"Come on," Yvonne urged.

Annelise allowed herself to be led back to the car.

CHAPTER TWELVE

Adrian boarded the ferry at 8:15 and went upstairs to the concessions seating area. He sat in a booth by the window, staring out into the dark and waiting for Annelise to text him.

The boat signaled its departure from Edmonds, and the safety announcement started. There weren't many walk-on passengers and Adrian started searching for his sister.

"If she missed the damned boat," Adrian bemoaned, "I'm going to be really pissed off."

He made a final lap around the deck before heading over to the passenger's exit ramp.

"Oh shit!" Adrian said. He looked out at the darkened coastline.

The storm had caused a power outage. At least generators lit the ferry terminal holding pen and passenger pickup areas. The boat docked, and Adrian filed off to the closed donut shop to wait for Lily.

When the last car left the pickup area, Adrian checked his phone. There were no messages from either Annelise or Lily, and the screen read 9:15; he had been waiting for over thirty minutes.

Where the hell are you?

Adrian sent the text message to his sister. His chest felt tight. Instinctively he knew something wasn't right; his twin-tuition started to nag at him. He glanced around and saw nothing but a line of cars parked in the holding pen, waiting to board the next ferry.

"Come on, Lily," Adrian complained. "This is not the time to flake out."

He tucked his arms across his chest. "I knew it," he mumbled. "She missed the boat."

As if on cue his phone vibrated in his hand.

I'm at Harborview! read Annelise's text. *Are you ok? Where ARE you?*

"The hospital?" Adrian muttered. He pressed the number to speed-dial his sister. After the third ring, he went to voice mail.

"What the hell is going on?" Adrian shouted into the phone. "What are you doing at the hospital? Are you okay? Is Yvonne okay? Call me!"

He disconnected the call.

Adrian started pacing under the two yards of immediate cover. He searched the road for any signs of Lily's car, wishing he had some other contact for her than the gallery phone.

The phone rang in his hand.

"Sorry, it took me so long to call you," Annelise said. She was catching her breath and sounding calmer.

"What's going on?" Adrian demanded.

"Are you okay?"

"Yeah, I'm fine," Adrian replied. "I'm a little wet and cold standing here waiting for you in Kingston, but I'm fine. What are you doing at Harborview?"

"Yvonne drove me here," Annelise explained. "There was a wreck. I thought you were dead!"

"Why?" Adrian demanded. "What would make you think that?"

"Yvonne was taking me to the ferry." Annelise paused to catch a breath. "We were almost there when we passed a wreck. All I could see was that it was a red truck and completely totaled. It was your truck and…"

"My truck?" Adrian said. "Oh my God! It was Marcus. Remember, Marcus was dropping me off at the ferry? What happened to my truck? Is Marcus hurt?"

Annelise said, "I saw the wreck and thought it was you."

"What happened!"

"He must have skidded on wet pavement and lost control," Annelise explained. "He crashed through the gate at that cemetery."

"Oh my God! Is he okay? Is he alive?"

"He's alive," Annelise said. "He was pretty badly hurt and is in surgery right now."

Adrian spun around and started jogging his way back to the ferry terminal. He stopped as the departing horn sounded.

"I just missed the ferry. I'll be on the next one and will Uber it to Harborview. I'll be there in about an hour."

"Adrian," Annelise said. "Adrian, listen to me. Don't bother. His family is on their way. They won't let you in to see him. There's nothing you can do right now."

"Fuck!"

"Adrian." Annelise's voice was calming. "Listen. He's in the best hands he can be in, and there's nothing else to do but wait. You stay there, go on over to my house and try to get a good night's sleep. I'll wait until his family shows up and give them my number. I'll have them contact us as soon as they know something."

"I'm heading back," Adrian said. "The power is out across Kingston."

Annelise said, "There's a flashlight right inside my door, and the hurricane lamp is on the kitchen table. Stay there."

"No," Adrian argued. "I'll get on the next ferry. If you want to stay the night, you can. I think I should be there for Marcus."

"There's nothing you can do," Annelise argued. "Visiting hours are almost over, and since you're not family, they aren't going to let you in. Try to get some sleep. I'll call Lily and guilt her into rushing over to pick you up."

Adrian stomped his foot with each word. "Wait a minute. He was driving my truck. How bad is my truck?"

"Be glad it's insured," was all Annelise could say. "I have to go. His family is arriving, and I want to talk to them before they get too hysterical."

"Call me as soon as you know anything!"

"I promise," Annelise said. "I love you, bro."

"I love you, too."

Adrian hung up the phone. He looked across the water. Seattle still had power.

"Fuck!"

He reached into his pocket and took out his vaporizer. He took a large toke, exhaling as a set of headlights came down the road. The lights were too high up to be Lily's small Miata. Adrian dismissed the lone vehicle for ferry traffic. He put his hand to his eyes, shielding them from the brightness.

"Turn down your lights, asshole," Adrian mumbled. "Overcompensate much?"

A low-toned horn rapidly sounded twice. Adrian turned to see an oversized black truck creeping forward to the front of the closed shop. The truck's dark color and tinted windows made it difficult for him to recognize either the vehicle or the driver. He cautiously put the vaporizer back into his pocket and his hand closed around the backpack's handle.

The truck's window lowered with a mechanical hum. The interior remained dark. A shadowy figure sat behind the wheel.

"Are you going to get into the truck, or are you going to stand in the rain?" A low voice rumbled from the truck's cab. "Come on, pretty boy. It's wet out there, and I'm getting cold."

"Fuck," Adrian whispered. "Just what I don't need."

Reaching up for the door's handle, he used the built-in step to climb into the large truck.

Adrian closed the door and settled into the seat, keeping his eyes straight ahead. He buckled his seat belt and placed the backpack between his legs.

"Relax. Annelise tried Lily first but she couldn't be reached."

"Look," Adrian kept his face turned away, "I've had a really bad night, and I'm not in the mood for any bullshit. I appreciate you picking me up, but please, I need a little break here."

"No problem."

The truck pulled out onto the main road.

"Your sister explained what was going on," Zack said after a few moments. "I'm sorry about your friend. Is he going to be all right?"

"Don't know," Adrian said. It came out sharper than expected.

"Sorry."

Long, awkward moments of silence followed, interrupted by the grumbling of Adrian's stomach.

"You hungry?" Zack asked.

"A bit," Adrian answered. "I'll get something to eat when I get to Annelise's place."

"You do know the power's out there, right?"

"I can see that," Adrian said. He sat up in the seat and pointed out the front window. "And you're about to miss the turn. It's right here. Coming up. And...you missed it."

"Calm down," Zack said. "I did it on purpose."

"Why the hell did you do that?" Adrian demanded. "Are you kidnapping me?"

"You wish." Zack laughed. "The power's out. Annelise isn't going to have electricity for some time."

"We are quite accustomed to island life, thank you," Adrian replied. "And she is well equipped with flashlights and hurricane lamps."

"And I have a generator and a working stove," Zack answered. "I'm done eating and there's plenty leftover. From the way your stomach's been growling, I thought you might want some dinner."

Adrian sat back, staring out the windshield.

"I can turn around, if you'd rather," Zack offered. "It's completely up to you."

They drove another half mile in silence.

"What did you have for dinner?"

"Blue-cheese burgers I made on the grill." Zack rattled off, "Baked potato, and a salad of fresh greens."

"You grilled in this weather?" Adrian sounded doubtful.

"I have a patio with a large awning," Zack answered with a broad smile. "And I'm not afraid of a little rain; I don't melt."

Talking about food made Adrian's stomach rumble on cue.

"Annelise lives closer," Adrian said, trying hard not to sound like he was making an excuse. "Thank you, but you don't need to drive all the way out to your place only to turn around after I eat and drive me all the way back here. It's silly."

"It's really not a problem," Zack said. "And if you'd like, you're welcome to spend the night."

"What?"

"The power will be out for a while," Zack repeated. "I always keep a guest room set up. It really is no problem. This way you can take a hot shower, charge your phone back up, and try to relax. It'll be better than being alone in a cold, dark house."

Adrian looked out the window. "I really do appreciate you picking me up. It's been a fucked-up night."

"Glad I could help," Zack said. "Besides, I never have issues picking up pretty boys in the rain. Generally speaking, of course."

"Either way, I appreciate it."

The truck pulled onto the private road leading to Eagle's Nest Farm. It slowed down, meandering on the road through the trees. The house was brightly lit from the outside. A floodlight shone down from the top corner of the apse above the front door. Another two lamps were directed to the sides, casting light on both staircases. From under the house, in the storage area, works in progress remained dark, staring out from shadows and under drop cloths.

"Sorry 'bout the house," Zack said. He parked the truck. "I wasn't expecting company."

Adrian grabbed his backpack and got out. Following Zack, he jogged to the stairs and carefully climbed the steep wooden steps.

"Feel free to kick your shoes off," Zack said. "Make yourself comfortable."

The main room looked as it had the one time he had been here before, except the lights were on in the kitchen. A dim nightlight lit up the hallway toward the bathroom.

"In case you don't remember, the bathroom is two doors down," Zack called from the kitchen, "if you want to shower or wash up. The guest room is the next one down."

"I'm fine for now," Adrian said.

"What do you want to drink?" Zack said from the kitchen. "I have water, milk, wine, iced tea, and beer. Do you want something stronger? Name your poison, I got everything."

Adrian balanced on one foot trying to wrestle the sneaker off the other. Zack stood in the living room, waiting for an answer.

"A vodka anything would be great."

"No problem." Zack waved toward the sofa facing the sliding doors. "Make yourself at home. There's not much of a view right now, but the couch is comfortable."

Adrian made his way to the sofa and sat down. The curtains were open, and he looked out the glass doors. Beyond the reflections in the glass, he saw a deck stretching out into the darkness.

"Aren't you worried about people seeing in?" Adrian asked.

"Not at all," came the reply. "You can't see it now but the deck is too high up for anyone to see in, unless they climb a tree. If watching a sixty-year-old man wandering around his home gets someone off, then by all means go for it."

Adrian smiled. Over the fireplace was a painting. Two squat half-burnt dark blue candles sat on pedestal holders to either side. The oil painting was a yard high and framed handsomely in stained oak. The picture was of a minotaur sensually resting on a throne.

The creature sat at an angle; relaxed, comfortable, and waiting. It stared straight out from rich, earthy brown eyes. The horns curved upward from either side of the blackened bull's head. Smoke flowed around the silver ring strung from the septum of his nose. Below the head was a male human body, with broad shoulders and rippling arms. Meaty hands with thick fingers hung off the edge of the throne; the right hand loosely held the hilt of a trident, the blade's three prongs pointing down. The minotaur's torso had patches of dark hair curling across the chest and down the center of the outlined stomach. A harness with thick leather straps crossed over the chest. The creature wore a leather kilt, the pleats falling open over a thick set of muscular legs. Between the animal's feet was a cauldron overflowing with golden coins.

"Here ya go," Zack said. "Dinner with a vodka-soda on the side."

Zack set a glass down on the table. Next to it he placed a square plate stacked with a large hamburger and a steaming baked potato. On the other side of the plate was a small pile of greens covered in blue cheese crumbles and sliced strawberries.

Adrian took a healthy bite. "This is good."

"Thanks," Zack said. He sat down at the other end of the couch. "Hope the drink isn't too overpowering. I figured you could use a strong belt by now."

"I'm not much of a drinker," Adrian said. He swallowed another bite before taking a large sip. "But tonight's an exception."

Within a few moments, the plate was emptied and the beverage was half gone. He sat back into the couch with a heavy sigh.

"Must have been hungry," Zack said. "There's more, if you'd like it."

"No. Thanks," Adrian said. He leaned back into the sofa cushions, reached into his pants pocket, and took out the vaporizer pen. He was about to take a toke before catching himself.

"I'm sorry," Adrian said. "Do you mind if I..."

"You don't strike me as the smoking type," Zack said with slight surprise. "E-cigarettes don't bother me, feel free."

"It's not tobacco," Adrian confessed. "It's a pot vape."

Zack raised both eyebrows. Adrian took a hit and held it out as offering.

"Oh," Zack said. "It's been a long time. How do I do this?"

"Inhale until the lights flash on the end. That's it. Who did the painting?"

"That painting?" Zack blew out the vapor. "Wow. That's smooth. My brother Hayden painted that a few years back."

"I really like it," Adrian said. He took another toke. "There's something raw and masculine about the subject."

Adrian turned back around to offer the vaporizer to Zack.

"Yes," Zack said. "Hayden does good work."

Zack leaned forward, handing the vape back to Adrian. His empty hand fell to Adrian's knee. Zack's grip was strong.

"Thanks for that," Zack said. "Let me go get a towel for you, so you can shower. Then you can head off to bed when you're ready."

Adrian stood up and walked over to the fireplace. He leaned one arm against the mantel and gazed up at the minotaur. There was something bewitching about it. He felt as if he were kneeling in audience before this mighty king. Adrian looked into the eyes, noticing how realistic they were, capturing light in tiny pinpoints with golden stars around the rounded brown eyes. He found himself torn between a deep-rooted respect for the artist, and a twinge of childish envy at the talent.

Adrian returned to the couch. He finished off his cocktail and leaned back, sinking into the cushions. He returned to study the painting, his eyes slowly taking in the masculine chest, the leather harness, and the penetrating stare.

"Zack and Hayden?" Adrian mumbled. "What kind of names are those?"

CHAPTER THIRTEEN

*T*he oceans rose up in rebellion. The monstrous godlike giant Typhaeon stood on the cavern's edge watching the storm rage at his command. His long arms reached into the blackened sky, stirring the storm. Serpents writhed off the edges of each hand instead of fingers, hissing into the sky and stoking the wind's fury. He was the first child of the Earth Mother, and thick bark covered his face, chest, and legs. Two huge wings sprang from his back, beating and creating hurricanes. The Titan's eyes burned, peering through the clouds and seeing the great battle in the distance. From the secret lair hidden among the mountain peaks, Typhaeon, the strongest of Gaia's Titans, continued waging war against his brother's children, the Olympians.

The waters crashed along the coastline, as violently as the thunder tore among the heavens. Typhaeon's brother, Oceanus, was overthrown by their nephew. The rebellious Poseidon possessed a new weapon, one of greater strength. His Trident controlled the waters and all within it, giving him complete power. Poseidon was sending out his scouts, minions, and armies to all parts of the world to hunt down the last of the Titans.

The heavens exploded with destructive thunder. Bursts of lightning flashed through the dark clouds as Typhaeon's brother Cronus defended his throne against his own son, the Usurper, Zeus. Bolts of fire burned a blazing path across the skies. Cronus used his magical sickle to reflect the lightning and strike at his foe. The skies illuminated with fire and lightning as son battled father for power.

With his monstrous height, Typhaeon could see the world in its entirety below him. Mountain ranges were torn, leveled to the ground *from the great battles of the Titanomachy. Fields once rich with bounty were now burned black with destruction. Forests were razed as the war raged from all sides, forcing the ground to split and burn. The mortal populace hid themselves in caves, sacrificing in vain to be spared from the war among the gods.*

The Earth Goddess Gaia, Mother of All Living, helped carve out strongholds among the mightiest mountains. She built sanctuaries for her children to hide, regroup, and plan their attacks against the Olympians. Only Gaia could open these hidden refuges, for only she knew the deep secrets of the Earth. Their mother hid Typhaeon and his equally powerful sister/wife Echidna in the last of the secret mountain fortresses, on the farthest island of the world.

Typhaeon lowered his hands knowing the end was near. Defeat was inevitable. For the first time their future was uncertain. Echidna was still weak from giving birth. Neither she nor the child should be moved. His wife lay curled in the nest toward the back. She finished ripping this child from her body not long after reaching the refuge, her birth pain howling buried under the mountain. Her human body curled atop the dragon's hide, and her thick tail swept the ground in her sleep.

As Typhaeon approached, the child stirred at Echidna's teat. Two of the three canine heads lifted from their suckling. Their eyes not even open yet, they sensed their father's movement. Echidna woke when her child stirred, and smiled. She rolled to her side, letting the three-headed puppy feed more easily.

"How goes the attack?" Echidna said. Her voice was still scratchy with sleep.

Typhaeon said nothing, settling next to his sister. One hand reached out, allowing the snakelike fingers to caress the underside of her chin. The other hand scratched behind the ears of the central head of his newborn son.

"These Olympians are strong. We shall strike down the godlings and prevail," Typhaeon whispered. "You take care of our child."

Echidna saw the concern in the bark covering her brother's face.

"Do the oceans still rebel?" Echidna asked. She curled her head into his hands.

Her tail wrapped protectively around the baby hound.

"No." Typhaeon hesitated to answer. "Atlantis was destroyed. The last fortress of Oceanus has fallen."

"*Atlantis destroyed?*" *Echidna whispered the unthinkable.*

Typhaeon looked at his love with sadness. The fires burned dully in his hollowed eyes. He knew he would not dilute the truth for her. Their lives were joined at the beginning of time. There were no illusions now.

"*The godling has a new weapon,*" *Typhaeon said.* "*It is stronger than even Lapetus could forge.*"

"*No weapon can penetrate Atlantis's dome,*" *Echidna said.* "*The Titan home is protected by magic. Powerful magic; magic that is even older than us. It cannot have fallen.*"

His silence betrayed him.

"*How?*" *Her eyes filled with blood tears.*

"*Poseidon struck with a weapon of immense power,*" *Typhaeon solemnly explained.* "*It holds great strength, commanding all the oceans, all the waters of the world, and all those that reside in them.*"

Echidna reached down, hugging her child close to her breast.

"*Why were the Cetus not released?*" *Echidna asked.* "*Or Leviathan? Only Oceanus controls the Depth Monsters. What of the Kraken?*"

"*All of them were released,*" *Typhaeon answered. His face was empty, worn and defeated.* "*The Cetus was easily tamed by this... Trident. Leviathan fought valiantly but was eventually subdued. Only the Kraken seemed immune. Oceanus rallied the Merfolk armies. They were turning the tide when betrayal struck.*"

"*Metis.*" *The name hung maliciously between them.*

"*I knew she would be our ruin,*" *Echidna said.* "*What was the price for her betrayal? Power or posterity?*"

"*She is to be Zeus's queen.*"

"*Betrayal of her own father for the price of the Usurper's bed.*" *Echidna's bitterness dripped from every word.* "*For all her prophetic gifts, she could not have made a graver mistake.*"

"*Wise or not, it is done,*" *Typhaeon said.* "*And the Underwater Kingdom has fallen into Poseidon's hands. When Oceanus bent his knee, the godling struck the city. Atlantis was destroyed and sunk beneath the waters.*"

Echidna looked up into Typhaeon's eyes. The fires that raged were now dulled, glowing embers. His strength was sapped. One by one their monstrous, godlike siblings were defeated. They were murdered or enslaved; or worse, thrown into Tartarus. The prison of the gods was built for one purpose: the eternal, tormenting punishment of those condemned there. Tartarus was impenetrable except for the cries of the damned begging for death to release them. Death never came to Tartarus; eternity mocked them instead.

Echidna reached her hand out for her lover. The serpents entwined with her human fingers. Despite the war raging outside the cave, she felt safe here with him. Hesitantly she asked what she already instinctively knew.

"Cronus?"

At the mention of their brother's name she felt his hand tighten and release. A chill pierced her scales, running her blood cold.

"Our King is defeated," Typhaeon answered. "If not, it will not be far in coming. He will be banished to the Throne of Time, forever to sit completely still. At midday, he will turn the Sand Clock over and resume watching time pass."

Echidna's tears ran at the thought of their brother's fate.

"Do not worry, my love." Typhaeon tried to comfort her. "We are safe here."

"If the oceans and the skies can be defeated," Echidna asked, sincerely frightened, "how can we be safe here?"

"Do not doubt our mother," Typhaeon said. "Gaia knows ancient magic, and this lair is hidden deep within the earth. Only she knows of our location, and our mother will not betray us. Even if the outside world falls tnto the Olympians' hands, we are safe within our mother's arms."

Echidna looked for comfort in her lover's words. They sat heavily, churning inside her.

"Can't we escape somewhere else?" Echidna asked. "We can leave these lands to the Olympians and go far away. We can find our way into Egypt and feast among the Canaanites."

Typhaeon reached up to caress her hair, knowing how it calmed her.

"My love," Typhaeon whispered. "Could you leave your children here to the Usurper's wrath? Never to see them again?"

"They are hidden well," Echidna defended. "My magic will protect them until they are grown. Then they shall seek revenge on this world we leave behind."

Even as she spoke Echidna knew she could never abandon her children. Hydra, Chimera, the Gorgon triplets, and the other creatures she ripped from her body; they were hidden now and would survive this war. She could never abandon them to be destroyed. She looked down at the child nuzzled against her body. This one was too young to take on such a journey, and she was too weak herself.

A great attack struck the mountainside. The cavern began to shake. The rock walls rattled and giant stones fell from the roof. The floor buckled beneath their feet.

Echidna curled her body to protect the baby monster.

A high-pitched wailing of pain emitted from all sides, filling the inner space. The shrill grew louder until Typhaeon was forced to his knees from the pain. The shriek split the back rock, and an opening was formed.

Typhaeon was knocked backward, his body slamming against the cavern wall. The lair was filled with the cries of Chaos, causing disruption to all those that heard her harsh bitter wailings.

Echidna was thrown backward, hitting the cavern floor. Her ears were ringing loudly. She looked around helplessly, seeing their destruction unfurl before her eyes.

They were betrayed! There could be no doubt. Only Gaia knew where they were, and only she could have allowed access. A bolt of lightning flashed into the cave and exploded against the rocks. The light became blinding until Zeus, the Olympian King, stood before them. He summoned another bolt and hurled it at the back of the cave. The wall shattered and the last fortress was breached.

Typhaeon broke out from under the falling rocks with a deafening roar. He stepped back until he was standing on the mountain's edge. The Titan unfurled his massive wings, summoning hurricanes with every pulsing beat. He held his thick arms out before him, serpents writhing at the end of his hands. Snakes sprang up from the ground. Their bodies twisted around the limbs of the Olympian, curling around his ankles and wrists. They pulled him down, binding him tightly to the cavern floor. Typhaeon took hold of the nearest boulder. He held it in his hands until the stone became a sphere of burning lava. The Titan hurled it at the Usurper. Zeus met it with a lightning bolt and together they exploded, sending debris flying through the cave.

A giant eagle swept into the cave from the outside storm. It gave a war cry as it plummeted down, talons fully extended. It took a firm *hold of Typhaeon's wings, the sharp claws tearing through the skin. The raging hurricane lost its power. The great bird flew back up, taking firm hold of one of Typhaeon's arms.*

The Titan fought against the eagle. The snakes from his hands bit at its claws, trying to release his arm. The bird pulled him back, leading him to the edge of the precipice. He swung his tree trunk arms into the eagle's chest. The bird's talons released Typhaeon, leaving him teetering on the edge. Zeus hurled another lightning bolt. It landed at the Titan's feet, setting him further off balance.

Typhaeon swayed as the cliff crumbled beneath his weight. His arms waved wildly and his torn wings beat with a desperate fervor. With a final hopeless grasp at nothing, the last of the rebellious Titans fell back and teetered off the mountain.

Zeus sent a merciless attack of thunderbolts to follow. They crashed into the sides of the cliffs, sending boulders and rocks hurling after the fallen god. The Olympian reached across to the mountain peak and ripped its crown from the earth. He hurled the summit down until it crashed onto the Titan, forever locking him within its constraints.

A dark shadow swept through the cave like a cyclone. It spun black until stopping by the nest and shimmering into a form. The wraith became a man with eyes black as coal and hair to match. The phantom became solid and Hades stood next to his Olympian brother. The Brooding One scooped the puppy into his arms.

Seeing her child abducted, Echidna coiled her body, hissing and ready to fight. The spiked tail swung low, knocking Hades off his feet. Echidna lunged at him, digging her claws into the back of his leg. She raised her head and buried her fangs into his flesh. The blood poured into her mouth.

A hand grabbed hold of her hair. It wrapped itself in her curls and yanked back with great force. Her mouth was ripped from the Olympian's thigh and her body was hurled across the cave. She crashed into the walls and fell to the floor.

Zeus was on her in an instant. He grabbed her by the throat, squeezing and choking until her breath was a series of short coughs and gasps. Her hands pounded on the Olympian's arm. She tried to swing her tail but found it held by the Brooding One. Echidna hissed, spitting venom at her captor's face.

Hades pounded on the ground with his fist. A giant crevasse formed, splitting the cavern floor until a swirling vortex formed in the belly of the chasm. It inhaled violently, causing the loose stones and gravel to vibrate, getting sucked into the oblivion. Zeus stood above the maw holding the struggling Echidna in his hands. The claws cut into his flesh as the God of Thunder held her tightly by the throat.

"Foul worm," Zeus seethed. His voice rolled richly throughout the cave. "For your treason I condemn you to Tartarus."

Echidna was hurled down into the vortex. Her arms flailed as she fell, fingers grasping at the air. The speed of her fall ripped at her scales, tearing at her flesh. Her screams echoed louder, mocking her as she plummeted down into blackness. She had no idea how long she fell into the void. There were no ways to follow the passing of time. Only the blackness was there, endlessly biting her with its sharp fangs. Her voice grew hoarse from yelling until it gave way, and she no longer made a sound. She hit solid stone at the bottom of the pit. Her bones broke upon contact, staying together by the immortal bag of skin holding them.

The Wraiths of Tartarus stood around her broken body. The hooded black robes hid their faces except for the glowing red eyes. Festering hands reached out from the sleeves and clasped a heavy collar about her neck. They connected it to a large chain, the links rattling as they unfolded the length. The end link was locked onto a hook set into the wall.

For millennia, she lay on the floor, unable to move and not caring to try. Her body slowly healed itself, reconnecting bones and letting soft tissues rejuvenate. She was left with emptiness, defeat and darkness; Tartarus allowed for nothing else.

The Titanomachy was ended—the Olympians had triumphed.

Echidna woke from her haunted memories. Her hands flew to her neck to see if the collar was there, or if it too faded with the dream. She let out a sigh of relief when her fingers felt nothing, her hands falling heavily to her side. Slowly she uncoiled her body.

Tartarus was another place, another time, and no longer part of her life.

Echidna looked into the dark sky. The storm was subsiding, leaving only light rains with a gray cloud covering. Her sharp eyes searched for any signs of the Furies, knowing they dissipated before sunrise. Magic worked differently in this world, with its limitations.

She slithered back into the cave. The male was presumably dead, leaving the woman vulnerable for attack. If Annelise had no knowledge of her lineage, then all the worse for her. An idea took form in Echidna's mind. She rooted through the debris and rotting flesh before finding the gallery's brochure. She studied the glossy pamphlet. Louise's words came back to her.

"Bainbridge is only a short ferry ride away."

"She'll be there," Echidna whispered. She tapped the print at the bottom: *hosted by Petrakis Gallery.*

She studied the address again, committing it to memory. There would be a lot to do before the gallery opening.

Echidna would need to conserve her strength.

CHAPTER FOURTEEN

*H*e started the spin slow, crouching low to the ground. His right arm curved at the perfect angle, pulling into the curl. The wind whistled as he slowly started to stand. He spun around once more, leaping, building momentum. The open field transformed into blurry green streaks as his speed increased. The discus would sing to him, whisper at the exact moment to let go. He would know; he always knew.

That was why Apollo was Champion.

The spin pulled him to full height. He rolled his shoulders forward, leaning into the curve, readying for release. His biceps tightened as his forearm locked around the discus.

A sharp sting pierced his ankle, sending pain shooting up his calf. It was enough distraction. The discus was already prematurely leaving his grasp, and Apollo was aware of his failure. The pain in his leg flared.

"Hycinthius," Apollo called out. "That throw shouldn't count. Something stung me."

His fingers touched the wound. Blood trickled from two small marks in the flesh, directly below the bone. Pressing his fingertips to the wounds, Apollo drew the poison out, discarding it into the tall grass around his feet. The green blades turned brown where the venom landed. The wounds healed, and he turned to look for the culprit.

The snake slithered backward, retreating until its body was coiled onto itself. The zigzag black pattern ran from its triangular head down its reptilian back and to the edge of its tail.

The God of Light still felt annoyance. It would not cause him illness or death, only discomfort, and that was enough. He was an Olympian, *and it would take more than simple serpent's venom to bring him down. He brought his sandaled foot down with full force. The reptile's head was pulverized into the ground.*

"Cursed serpent," Apollo hissed at the writhing body. "I tire of your foul, sly behavior and cunning ways. You have plagued me for the last time."

He wiped his sandal on the grass.

"Hycinthius," Apollo called to his companion. "How bad was the throw?" He looked up with a playful smile. He looked around, seeing nothing but waist-high stalks of grass.

It was then Apollo noticed how quiet the field had grown.

There were no sounds. The breeze stopped, and the glade was perfectly still. There was no sign of his best friend and lover.

Apollo tossed the hair from his eyes. He scanned the field, seeing no traces of his companion.

"Hycinthius!" Apollo called out. There was no answer. "Hycinth?"

The god moved, his legs trudging through the high grass. He called his friend's name again.

"Where are you?" the god shouted. "If you're hiding, I'm going to find you. When I do you'll be sorry."

Apollo's blue eyes sparkled with the sunlight. He started to jog across the field. When he saw the plastered-down section of grass, his pace slowed.

Red splashed across the tops of the grass. It was blood, still wet, running down the stalks. Slowly, he crept forward.

It was then he saw the bloodied head of Hycinthius.

Next to him lay Apollo's discus.

The Sun God fell to his knees. His strong arms reached under Hycinthius's shoulders, pulling the lifeless man into his lap. Blood ran from the cracked skull. The god's eyes fixed on the bloodied discus, shouting out his sorrow.

His grief changed to anger. He lifted his head to the sun-filled sky, letting his pain erupt with an animalistic howling.

With trembling hands Apollo laid his beloved on the ground. His palms and fingers were covered in blood. He released an anguished cry before shaking his hands. The blood flew off his fingers across the field, and every blade of grass it touched immediately fostered a new stalk. The stem shot up from the center, developing into bunches of dark lavender leaves. The red continued to flow, spreading over the entire field as smoothly as a wave washing onto a beach. Budding purple flower clusters sprang up in its wake.

Apollo turned his pain-stricken face toward the blackened clouds. He let go with another tormented, deafening howl.

The anguished sound rolled across the field.

Adrian's eyes bolted open. He sat up in bed, his heart pounding. His heart hurt. His face was covered in tears. He fought to catch his breath.

Adrian leaned against the headboard. His heartbeat slowed. He picked up his phone: 4:43 a.m., and four text messages delivered. He wiped his eyes with the back of his hand. After only four hours' sleep, he stifled a yawn before reading the text messages.

You have nice sister. The first text was from Marcus's mother. *We at hospital now.*

Marcus out of surgery. The second message was also from her. *Unconscious.*

Marcus sleep for a while. He'll be okay. No need for you to come tomorrow, he'll be sleeping. We will text you when something changes. Marcus lucky to have friends like you and your sister.

The last message was from Annelise. *M will be all right. I'm at your house. Exhausted. Going to bed. I'll check on M before coming home.*

Adrian reached down and picked his shorts up from the floor. They were still a little damp from being caught in last night's rain. He dropped them again and grabbed his boxers instead, slipped them on over his waist, and took the vaporizer from the nightstand. He opened his backpack, rooting through until he took out the pencil case and sketchpad. Quietly, he padded out through the hallway and into the living room.

Zack's bedroom door was closed. The rain had stopped and the house was silent except for two ticking clocks. The curtains on the glass doors were open.

Adrian sat on the couch, sinking into the cushions, gazing out the door. He braced his feet on the coffee table, balancing the sketchpad on his knees. Carefully, he selected one of the two drawing pencils. His hand moved across the paper several times before the pencil ever touched down. The pencil captured the vision on paper. The outlines of the dying athlete being held by his lover slowly took shape. The field sprang up around the couple, the stalks bending away from the bodies. Adrian used the pencil's edge to shade in the discus and draw in the darkened bloodstain.

Adrian paused to look over his work. He toked off the vaporizer.

"That's a very handsome picture."

Adrian opened his eyes. Zack was standing in the doorway of his bedroom. He turned the pad over in his lap.

"How long have you been standing there?"

"About ten minutes," Zack answered. "I was enjoying watching you draw. You reminded me of my brother. He liked to get up in the early morning and work. He said the light was better for drawing."

Zack leaned against the open doorway. He was naked except for a pair of gray cotton shorts.

"Mind if I join you?" Zack asked. He didn't wait for an answer. He took a seat in the chair, crossing his right leg over his left knee. The lighting revealed more gray strands in the goatee and trimmed chest hair. His blue eyes twinkled in the early morning light.

"I hope the bed was comfortable," Zack said. He leaned his head back and closed his eyes.

"The bed was fine, thanks," Adrian replied.

"I wouldn't have thought you an early riser."

"I'm not usually," Adrian explained. "Couldn't sleep. There's too much on my mind. What time is it, anyway?"

Zack stretched his neck to look at the wall clock in the kitchen.

"It's five thirty," he said. "How long have you been up?"

"God," Adrian mumbled. "About forty-five minutes. I hope I didn't wake you."

"You didn't," Zack replied. "I like the early morning. It's quiet, and like a fresh start for anything you want to do."

The older man let out a stifled yawn, letting the muscles ripple across his stomach.

Adrian could hear his own low breath starting to rattle with excitement. He felt himself getting hard, and reached down to adjust the front of his cotton boxers. Adrian froze, one hand still on his crotch as Zack stirred in the chair. He frantically moved the sketchpad to cover his erection.

"Sorry," Zack said. He opened his eyes and shook his head. His stretched his arms, arching his back. "I must have dozed off for a second."

He looked over at Adrian fidgeting on the sofa. "You okay?"

"Yeah."

"Can I see what you're working on?" Zack gestured to the sketchpad in Adrian's lap.

"Sure."

Zack leaned forward. He sat back in the chair, looking at the drawings with a smile. "This is beautiful," he said, not looking up from the paper. "And you did all this this morning?"

"Yeah." Adrian snorted. "I did."

"What inspired this?"

"A dream," he answered. "I woke up, and it was still very clear in my mind."

Zack held the drawing out before him.

"You can see the pain in this one's face," Zack said. His finger moved around the grief-stricken Apollo, without touching the drawing. "Is this a discus?"

"Yeah," Adrian said. "It was part of the dream."

Zack stood up to yawn. The outline of his penis was visible against the cotton material. "Sorry."

"What?" Adrian replied, startled.

"That I'm a bad host. I should be making coffee," Zack said.

"Don't bother on my account," Adrian said. "I'm hoping to go back to sleep for a little bit. That is, if I can. I didn't sleep well."

"I'm sorry," Zack said. "I thought you said the bed was comfortable?"

"No, no," Adrian said immediately. "The bed was great. I just don't sleep well in strange beds, that's all, and there's a lot on my mind."

Zack came back with a glass of water in his hand. He sat down in the opposite corner of the couch. He picked the picture up and leaned it on his lap to continue viewing it.

"I like the way you have the light breaking through the edges of the cloud clusters."

"Thanks," Adrian said. "I was thinking about calling it *Mourning*."

"That works." Zack looked up. "It's very good."

Zack closed the pad, replacing it on the table, and sat back with the glass in his hand. His right arm stretched across the back of the couch. His fingertips rested inches away from Adrian's.

"Did you hear from Annelise?" he asked. "Is your friend going to be okay?"

"Yes. Thank you," Adrian said. "I got a couple of texts from Marcus's mom and one from Annelise. He's out of surgery, and they said he should be all right."

"Good," Zack said with a heavy sigh.

Adrian leaned forward to pick up his vaporizer. He took a large toke and held it out as an offering to Zack.

"No thanks," Zack said. "I'm still a little tired from last night."

"Amateur," Adrian joked. "I'm hoping it'll make me sleepy and I can get back to bed."

"How are you doing?" Zack asked. "I mean with everything going on? You okay?"

"Me?" He took another toke. "I've committed to helping Annelise out tonight for her exhibit opening. I can't leave her in a bind now. She'd be screwed. Besides, there's nothing I can do there. Marcus will be unconscious anyway." Tears were running down Adrian's cheeks.

Zack took Adrian into his arms. He pressed Adrian's cheek against his chest, cradling the back of his head. Adrian threw his arms tightly around Zack's bare torso. He broke out into sobs.

"Shhhhh," Zack soothed. "It'll be okay."

The strong hands gently rocked him, making small, tight circles on his back. He pushed his face far into Zack's solid chest.

"It's okay," Zack repeated in a whisper. "It's okay."

Adrian tried to catch his breath.

"May. I. Have. Some water," Adrian said. "Please."

Zack reached for the glass on the table.

"Thanks," Adrian said. He drank it in two large gulps.

"Come here." Zack opened his arms, motioning with his fingers.

Adrian allowed the strong arms to close around him. He nuzzled farther into Zack's chest, the trimmed hair brushing against his face.

Zack smelled of the forest. The scent of wood mixed with his natural musk, smelling of tree bark after a rainfall. Adrian pressed his palms against Zack's back. His fingers traced the sinewy muscles along the spine, gently massaging as they crept down Zack's back.

Adrian turned his head, brushing his lips against the flesh. Gently he kissed the front base of Zack's neck, giving short kisses up under his chin. His mouth traced over the goatee until meeting Zack's lips. Adrian pulled back for a brief moment before kissing him full on the mouth.

Zack's lips tasted sweet. Adrian pressed harder, trying to part Zack's lips with his tongue.

"Adrian." Zack interrupted, breathing heavily. "I'm not sure this is the right time for this."

"I know what I'm doing." Adrian continued kissing Zack's neck. "I *know* what I'm doing."

Zack was about to say something when Adrian covered his mouth with his own. The edge of his tongue traced the space between Zack's lips, teasing until Zack's desires gave in and he succumbed to passion.

Zack's strong hands pressed firmly against Adrian's back, pulling him tightly against his body. His palms rubbed across Adrian's shoulders and spine, then his hands made their way to the waistband on Adrian's boxers. Zack maneuvered them both until Adrian was on his back with Zack lying on top.

Adrian felt Zack's lips teasing the skin on either side of his neck.

Zack let out a low growling moan as Adrian slid his hand between the gray cotton shorts and the muscular roundness of Zack's ass. He lifted himself, allowing Adrian to push them down and off. Zack took one of Adrian's nipples between his finger and thumb, giving it a quick pinch before covering it with his mouth. Adrian leaned his head back with a moan of pleasure.

"Wait a minute," Zack said. His breath came in heavy panting. "Come with me, pretty boy."

Zack pushed himself off Adrian's body. He stood next to the couch, offering his hand. Adrian took it. Their lips met. Zack stepped away, leading Adrian to the bedroom.

They stood at the foot of the bed. Adrian lay down on top of the sheets. Zack climbed over Adrian's body, propped up by his strong arms, leaning down to kiss Adrian's mouth. Zack's lips made their way down the center of his chest. Zack teasingly licked across the sensitive skin of Adrian's stomach, his goatee teasing Adrian's skin into gooseflesh.

Sensually massaging Adrian's legs as he went, Zack slowly climbed up the Greek man's body. The legs were covered with coarse hair, and the crotch bristled with the scent of natural musk. Zack reached down, wrapping his hand around Adrian's cock, and positioned it at his open mouth.

Adrian's moan served as encouragement. Zack spread Adrian's legs with his knees, repositioning himself to tickle the inner flesh of Adrian's thighs. As he worked Adrian's cock with his mouth, Zack's hand slid down.

The erotic shocks running though his body made Adrian buck his hips, pushing deeper inside Zack's throat. One hand grasped Zack's shoulder, while the other took firm hold of Zack's head. Adrian became lost, his orgasm mounting, building faster.

"I'm getting close," Adrian warned in short gasps.

Zack began to stroke himself.

Adrian's head tilted back. His heart felt like it was going to explode. Every muscle in his body became rigid. Adrian's mouth hung open, a short gasp escaping.

Zack lifted his head as the first hot shots of cum rained down on Adrian's chest. His body convulsed. His breath was shallow and his heart raced. His hand wildly stroked his cock until his body exploded.

Adrian opened his eyes to see nothing but the royal blue of sky stretching out before him. Looking down, he saw the gauze of clouds passing underneath, and the graphic patterns of the earth far below that. The height was dizzying, but the vertigo did not bother him and he watched the world pass below without issue.

The golden chariot traveled on the clouds, using them like road patterns. Two large wheels with seven open spokes allowed the cart to methodically glide along the sky's path. Four brilliantly white horses pulled the chariot along, bridled in pairs. The reins vibrated tightly in his hands. As the black hooves of the large steeds struck the clouds, rays of light shot out across the heavens, illuminating the earth below.

The chariot drove higher as the ground below turned rockier. It climbed above the mountain peaks. Still, the horses galloped higher, and soon only the crest of Mount Olympus broke through the clouds. The powerful white steeds galloped toward their home.

A large black stripe divided the flat plateau into two long strips. At the far end standing side by side were two gigantic stables, one gold with the doors flung open, while the doors were shut on the argent silver building. Standing between them was a lone figure, waiting to greet the chariot.

The white horses raced down the strip, slowing as they went. As they approached the open stable doors at a walk, the waiting figure raised his arms. At the signal's release, the silver doors were flung open and another chariot came careening out. Pulled by a pair of charcoal black horses, the chariot raced by with a large crescent moon emblazed on the front panel. The driver looked like Annelise, and she nodded as the chariot shot past.

The lone figure strode over to the side of the heavily panting horses. The man was tall with a thick cap of white hair. His muscular chest was bare, except for the snowy curls of hair thinly laid across, and the strong arms had not yet softened with age. A pale blue tunic was worn over his waist and hung down above the knees. Sparks of lightning flashed in the piercing blue eyes, and a warm smile lit up Zack's handsome face.

Adrian opened his eyes, still grasping for breath. Beads of sweat covered his face.

Adrian stared at Zack, still kneeling between his knees and panting. He looked into the blue eyes, searching for any explanation of the vision that just appeared. Zack crept toward him, remaining on all fours and looking at Adrian with a smile.

"What's wrong?" Zack asked.

"Who the hell are you?" Adrian asked.

"First," Zack said, "tell me what you saw."

CHAPTER FIFTEEN

*A*nnelise looked about the wood. The forest was still, disturbed only by the random sounds of owls calling, insects crawling, and the stirring of other nocturnal creatures. Moonlight broke through the treetops.

A white doe led her across the field and to the lip of the forest. The magical creature darted between the trees, disappearing from sight. Annelise rode her horse to the field's edge, dismounting and following the majestic animal into the thicket. As an expert huntress she felt at home in the forest, and entered without hesitancy.

She crept through the woods, her hounds scurrying after their prey. Cloth leggings covered her lower half, with a lightweight skirt around her waist. She wore a leather breastplate that connected behind her neck. A conjoined sun and moon insignia was embossed on the leather. She held a wooden crossbow, ready to fire at a moment's notice as she moved through the woods. The trees thinned out ahead. She approached, using the tree trunks as camouflage to spy on the drinking doe.

The moss flooring led to the lip of a large rounded lake. The surface was smooth with a pearly glow from the full moon's reflection. Steam rose in ghostly strands like spirits from a watery grave. Across the water, the white doe stood drinking.

Annelise remained still behind the edge of trees. She raised the bow and was taking aim when the doe lifted her head.

The moonlight illuminated the animal. The doe stood on her hind legs. The creature shimmered for a moment, appearing to melt in the light, revealing a beautiful woman. She glowed with an ethereal light. Her pale arms delicately lowered to the sides of her curvaceous hips *and legs. The face was rounded with long strands of auburn hair. She reached up, brushing the hair behind her, causing the full breasts to lift over a lean body.*

The wood nymph walked into the lake. The water line crept up her body. She stopped when the water was at her waist and dove under the surface. When she reappeared a short distance away she stood, lifting her hands to pull her hair away from her face. Drops of water ran down her breasts, the pale skin glistening in the moonlight. Taking a deep breath, she dove under once more.

Annelise watched from the safety of the forest. She leaned the bow against a tree. Her eyes searched the water for any signs of the wood nymph's reemergence. The ripples from the dive reached the edge of the lake. Annelise grasped the trunk and leaned forward for a better view, careful not to step clear of her covering.

The nymph's body broke the surface of the sacred waters. She turned until facing Annelise directly. The stare was so cold, so intent, that Annelise immediately crouched down. She watched the nymph gracefully swim toward the shore, her head above the water and eyes focused in her direction. The nymph slowly ascended from the water.

The nymph's naked torso gave way to a dragon's body the size of a small elephant, the hide covered with gray reptilian scales. A large serpent's tail swung behind. The creature stood on shore, the cold moonlight revealing the nymph's true self.

Annelise felt a scream building in her throat. Her stomach churned with bile and she turned away, crawling back to her feet and running from the oasis. The branches scraped her, and she dodged her way through the brush skillfully as any deer.

She screamed as her shoulders exploded with pain. Something took hold of her wrists. Her arms were covered in coarse hair and changed to a snow-white color. She doubled over in pain. Both sets of fingers melded together, becoming black hooves, and Annelise found herself leaping through the forest with a fearful doe's grace.

From behind her came the distant sound of barking dogs. The random howls quickly united the pack, who were closing in on her scent. The white doe ran faster, weaving through the tree trunks. It wouldn't matter; Annelise had trained the dogs, and there was no escape.

The doe leapt over a fallen tree and landed on soft ground. Her hoof twisted and Annelise felt the bone snap. She stumbled, rolling on the forest floor, listening as the pack of dogs drew closer. She tried to run only to have her leg buckle underneath her weight, and Annelise knew her only choice was to stand and fight.

The three black hounds found her. Seeing her leg damaged, they circled around the doe. They snarled, showing their sharp fangs.

The lead hound barked once and leapt for her throat.

Annelise woke with her heart pounding.

It took a moment for her to remember where she was.

She leaned against the headboard and gazed over at the clock on the nightstand: 7:43.

"Oh shit."

Annelise swung her legs out of bed. She reached for the phone to check on both Marcus and her brother.

"Thank God he's stable," she muttered. She read the three texts from Marcus's mother, then she sent a text to Adrian.

I'm awake. Marcus is okay. Sorry for last night but Lily wasn't available. Hope you and Zack at least played nice. I'll be on the 10:30ish ferry to Bainbridge. I'll text you when I'm close. Use my car and pick me up.

Annelise went to the bathroom to wash her face and threw on her brother's bathrobe. Her mind replayed the dream. There was something about the nymph.

As she waited for the coffee to brew, she sat on the coach and looked over the drawing still mounted on the easel. It showed real promise, and she made a mental note to push Adrian to let her exhibit the picture. She drank her first cup of coffee before starting to get ready for the day.

The shower felt good as it pelted her skin. Annelise was shampooing her hair when the connection dawned on her.

The nymph's face from last night's dream; she *had* seen it before. It was in Louise's shop and belonged to the woman Annelise had noticed browsing. She thought back as she washed lather from her body.

The woman in the gallery and the nymph from her dream were the same.

Annelise got dressed. Her mind replayed the dream once more.

It's frightening how the mind can turn something so attractive into such a monster.

CHAPTER SIXTEEN

A drian woke up to the smell of brewing coffee. Morning light was already filling the room. Adrian looked around. A closet ran along the opposite wall, giving way to the master bathroom. Light filtered through a set of closed curtains covering the glass sliding doors that ran along the right wall. Mounted on the wall and tucked into the left corner, a television stared back with a blank screen.

The bed was an oversized king with a cherrywood frame and large canopy poles. Mounted atop each pole was a carved and stained teardrop embossed with a lightning bolt. Adrian rolled onto his stomach, the blanket falling away. The headboard was also cherrywood, and in the center was carved a flying eagle. The feathers were stained dark, except for the bird's head and the collar of feathers around it.

"You really are a pretty boy," Zack said from behind.

Adrian looked over his shoulder. He pulled the blanket up and rolled onto his back. "When you say it that way, it doesn't sound so condescending."

Zack was standing at the bedroom door holding a breakfast tray in front of him. He wore the same cotton shorts as the previous night. He placed the tray over Adrian's legs before taking a seat by Adrian's feet.

Adrian reached for the cup of steaming coffee. A plate of waffles with strawberry compote filling the small squares waited, with a set of silverware tucked underneath the plate's side. Three strips of bacon lay on a smaller plate next to it.

"Aren't you going to eat?" Adrian swallowed coffee and returned the mug to the tray. Adrian began cutting into the waffles.

"No," Zack answered. "I've been up for about an hour and already ate. I didn't want to wake you. I do think we should talk when you're through."

"What about?" Adrian said, crunching on a piece of bacon.

"Last night."

"Oh," Adrian said. He shrugged his shoulders. "That was fun."

Zack blushed and looked at the floor. "That's not what I'm talking about."

"You mean that little vision I had?" He shrugged again.

Zack reached over and put his hand onto Adrian's knee. "Your 'little vision' *does* have something to do with it."

Adrian continued eating.

"I told you last night we'd talk about it after you had a good night's sleep," Zack said.

"What about?" Adrian said.

"There's a reason I was in your vision last night," Zack started.

"Aside from the fact that we just had sex?" Adrian cut him off.

"Didn't you feel a strong connection, Adrian?"

"There was something there, but…"

"Adrian!" Zack snapped. "Listen to me for a minute."

"All right," Adrian said. "You have my attention. Go."

"Let me ask you this." He paused. "Have you been having a lot of erotic dreams lately?"

"Yeah. So? I figured they were because I've been in a sexual dry spell. Until last night. What does that have to do with anything?"

"This is going to sound odd," Zack tried again. "But I'm willing to bet they've had a mythological theme to them. Greek mythology."

"Yeah," Adrian said. "I guess so. So what? My name's Petrakis, I'm Greek."

"It's not that simple."

"I'm guessing with you nothing ever is," Adrian replied. He got out of bed.

"Adrian!" Zack's voice bellowed through the room. It was commanding and rolled with a thunder's echo. "Sit down and let me talk to you."

Adrian grabbed his clothes and shimmied the boxers up, then stepped around Zack and sat back down on the bed.

"I'm trying to tell you there's a reason for all of this," Zack said. "Both you and Annelise have a special lineage."

Adrian briefly paused.

"I knew the moment I saw you two," Zack continued. "It was confirmed when I shook your hands. I still wasn't sure if you knew it yourselves."

"And you have this special ability to see this unique lineage in people?" Adrian said.

"Yes," Zack answered. "So do you, if you let me show you how to tap into it."

"Is this a kink thing?" he asked. "Are you into some role-playing game and want me to be a part of it?"

"No," Zack said. "It's more of a heritage thing. You're descended from the Greek gods."

"Okay then," Adrian said. "The Greek gods."

"The Olympians, to be specific," Zack clarified. "After meeting you and seeing your artwork, I'm guessing Apollo. Annelise would be Artemis."

"Because my sister and I are twins," Adrian responded. "And Greek, and both names start with an *A*, that must mean we are descended from Greek gods."

Adrian reached over and patted Zack's knee. "Thank you. That clarifies so much and everything makes sense now." He stood and took a step away from the bed. "I'm going to get dressed. Then I'm going to call the one cab on this island, and hopefully shortly thereafter, leave. Thanks for the hospitality."

"Adrian!"

The voice thundered through the room. Adrian slowly turned back around.

"Sit down," Zack said in a commanding whisper. "What I have to say is important and you will give me the respect of listening to everything I have to say."

Without a word, Adrian sat down.

"Now I'm going to ask you trust me for a minute." Zack sat next to him. "Don't say anything smart-assed. I'm going to lean over and put my hand over your eyes."

"Fine."

"Okay," Zack said. "I'm going to put my hand behind your head and the other gently over your eyes. I'm not going to put any pressure on you, but you may feel a little heat."

Adrian closed his eyes, feeling Zack's hands palming the back of his head, gently keeping it stable. The other hand slid down in front of Adrian's eyes. Zack's hand grew warm, the heat feeling good on Adrian's face. After a moment, both hands were removed.

"Count to ten," Zack instructed. "Then open your eyes and look at me."

Adrian counted aloud.

"Eight," he rattled off. "Nine. And one more makes ten."

Adrian opened his eyes. He looked at Zack, seeing a solid, glowing sphere of red surrounding his head and shoulders.

"What the fuck?" Adrian said.

"Let me guess. You're seeing a red halo around my head."

Adrian nodded.

"I knew it!" Zack slapped his knee in delight. "What you're seeing is the recognition we have for one another. The stronger the lights, the more that person is aware of their true heritage. If it's a dull light or blinking, it usually means that person's lineage has become diluted and they have less chance of becoming aware of whom they really are. The stronger the light, the stronger their connection to the gods."

"And everyone that has this 'lineage' has this halo thing?"

"Well," Zack said with a shrug, "anyone or anything that has a divine connection to the immortals."

"And you have this bloodline as well?" Adrian scoffed. "Isn't that convenient. And whose child are you, prey tell?"

"I'm a descendent of Zeus," Zack answered.

"Zeus? The King of the Gods. Well. No delusions of grandeur there, eh?"

"I'm sure you noticed all the eagle references around my place," Zack said. "All the lightning bolt symbols? The thunderstorm tattoo on my arm?"

"That could mean you're a patriotic ornithologist who happens to be a Harry Potter fan, for all I know."

"It could," Zack answered. "But it doesn't."

"You're not even Greek," Adrian said. "You're...I don't know what the hell your background is, but you are *not* Greek!"

Zack acknowledged the point with a nod. "My family is originally from the lower part of the United Kingdom," he explained. "But that doesn't matter. Somewhere in my distant past, someone in my family was Greek. And whoever they were, they had this very elusive, very recessive, and very strong gene in their DNA."

"So you're saying all this," Adrian made a quick motion with his hand at the wyre-lights, "is genetic? It's inherited."

"As far as I can tell," Zack said.

"And how did you find out that you were a descendant of Zeus?"

"I met someone who recognized it in me," Zack answered. "Like you did. And also like you, I thought she was crazy."

"She?" Adrian sounded surprised. "So this isn't something brought about by sex?"

"Not at all," Zack answered. "Although usually a series of erotic dreams preludes becoming aware. For me, it was a friend of my parents. She saw it in both my brother and me."

"The same brother that drew the minotaur picture?"

"The same one," Zack confirmed.

Adrian nodded. "What do any of you have to do with Greek gods?"

"Okay." Zack shook his head. "I'm going to start all over. The Greek Olympians were the first pantheon to have human physical traits. They often had liaisons with humans and, as you can guess, had many offspring."

"Demigods," Adrian said. "I do know something about mythology."

"Take it down a notch." Zack shook his head. "The gods' offspring had children of their own. Some stayed within traditional lines and others did not. The powers got passed down through genetics and DNA over the years. Some people got more than others; some only a little, and most of them don't even know they possess any gifts at all. It's like any genetic trait, except this one is a little more special and a lot more elusive. Is this making any more sense?"

"Now you're saying I'm a demigod?" Adrian scoffed. "Which is it, god or demigod?"

"I'm trying to tell you," Zack was getting exasperated, "that your powers will start to emerge more now that you're aware."

"I'm not aware of anything more than you doing some cheap magician's trick to make a light shine around your head."

"Like I said," Zack replied, "that's only the first one. You have other abilities, aside from your artwork, which will develop and start to come to the forefront now. If you learn how to use them, they can be quite powerful and helpful in life."

"I owe my drawing to this?" Adrian asked. "What's next, can I fly? 'Cause there has been a lot of dreams about me flying."

"Not quite so blatant as that," Zack answered. "They start off subtly, almost unknown to others—like your artwork. Then they'll develop as you become more accustomed to things."

"I get it," Adrian shot back. "I'm a member of a special society, and now there are people out there that will be able to recognize me. Oh gee, this sounds like fun. What happens next? Do you turn yourself into a bull and rape Europa?"

"You want to act like a petulant child, then fine. Out to my porch. Now!" Zack commanded. "Give me two more minutes of your time and then I'll gladly take you back to your sister's."

"Two minutes," Adrian replied.

Zack led Adrian from the bedroom, out the glass sliding doors off the main room, and onto the deck. Four chairs, their backs leaning forward to rest against the table, still dripped from the evening's rain. A large gas grill sat covered by a protective tarp. The deck hung over a short yard with a rich ocean of pine trees beyond.

Zack roughly took Adrian by the shoulders, facing him toward the woods. He reached his arm over Adrian's right shoulder and leaned in close, whispering in his left ear.

"Look." Zack pointed toward a tree standing separate from the others. "On the left, four branches up. Do you see the eagle nesting there?"

It took Adrian a moment to spy the large bird standing by a nest.

"The Pacific Northwest has a lot of eagles," Adrian said. "Big deal."

"You don't notice how it is staring down at you?" Zack asked.

"Are you kidding me with this?" Adrian turned his head. "You have one more minute, and then I'll walk if I have to."

"Fine." Zack's face tightened. He looked up at the sky.

"Do you see those clouds?"

"Yeah," Adrian said. "They're finally starting to break up. Apollo may be a sun god, but I can't take that much credit."

"Shut up!" Zack commanded. "Watch the clouds and don't say a word."

Zack took a deep breath and slowly let it whistle out his lips. A dull roll of thunder echoed from a storm gathering miles away. Instantly, the few slivers of blue sky were blocked as the clouds grew and became knitted together. They turned darker shades, and flashes of lightning weaved through them. Thunder crashed as the storm unraveled.

The eagle leapt into flight and circled overhead. It flew higher in a spiral, until it disappeared into the darkening clouds. Lightning exploded behind as a deafening crash of thunder sounded. A bolt of lightning cut downward and hit the branch holding the eagle's nest. It burst into flames.

"Holy shit!" Adrian exclaimed.

"Close your eyes and count to three," Zack commanded.

Adrian did as he was told. When he opened his eyes the clouds were clearing. Blue streaks were woven between the drifting clouds. The large bald eagle was sitting calmly on the branch, the nest unharmed.

"That's a pretty good trick," Adrian said.

Zack stood up, removing his hands from Adrian's shoulders. He took another deep breath and let out a slow, solid whistle. The flat note went on for ten long seconds before he stopped, the sound echoing through the woods. Adrian slowly turned around. Their eyes met.

"Evohe!"

A single bolt of lightning shot down from the clearing sky. Zack raised his hand and caught it as easily as catching a Frisbee. His eyes never left Adrian's as he held the flaming rod in the palm of his hand. Zack slowly held it up between them.

"Is this a better trick?" Zack sternly said.

Adrian took a step back.

Zack took aim at the clouds. He let the electric arrow fly into the sky and disappear. Slowly, he turned to Adrian.

"I'll take you to Annelise's now."

Zack went back into the house. Adrian went back to the guest bathroom and stepped inside. The mirror over the sink was made of black glass. Even in the dim reflection he could see the red lights circling around his head.

"What the hell did he do to me?" he muttered in a huff.

Adrian got dressed. The clothes were still a little wet, but he didn't care; he just wanted to get away. Adrian threw his things back into the backpack.

"Your sketchpad and vaporizer are on the table," Zack said. "I'll meet you outside."

He walked out the front door. Adrian stopped and took a deep breath. His shoulders felt heavy, tired. He slid the sketchpad into his pack and swung it up to his shoulder.

They drove the twenty minutes to Annelise's house in complete silence. Zack pulled the black truck into the drive.

"Thanks for picking me up last night," Adrian mumbled.

Zack kept his eyes forward, not saying a word, still visibly upset.

"Fine." Adrian hopped down from the truck and slammed the door. "Fuck you."

Chapter Seventeen

Outside the pickup area of the Bainbridge Island ferry terminal, Annelise paced. As her blue Crosstrek pulled up, Adrian waved from behind the wheel. He gave her a strange look when she got in.

"What's the look for?" Annelise asked. "You okay?"

"Yeah." Adrian wiped his eyes with his fingers. "Sorry I'm late. I didn't get your text until a little bit ago."

"No problem. Just overly anxious about the opening tonight."

"I sent a text to Marcus's mother after getting the ones from last night. I haven't heard anything more."

"I managed to reach her during the crossing," Annelise said. "He's doing as well as can be expected."

"I should have gone over there last night," Adrian mumbled.

"There's nothing you can do."

"How bad is my truck?"

"Was." Annelise corrected him. "I'd call the insurance company."

"Shit."

"Please don't tell me the power's still out?"

"When I got home this morning, the power was fine."

"This morning? That explains it."

"Explains what?"

"My dream last night," Annelise said with a laugh. "It was quite erotic. Well, at first. But I must have been picking something up from you. Do tell."

"There's nothing to tell."

"I'll make a deal," Annelise bargained. "Tell me what happened and I'll tell you my dream. Spoiler alert: I get butchered at the end of it."

"That does sweeten the pot," Adrian replied. "Fine. Zack picked me up last night."

"I figured," Annelise said. "I was the one that called him."

"Since the power was out," Adrian said, "Zack took me back to his place to eat dinner. He has a private generator."

"I'm guessing you guys fought again."

"Not at first," Adrian said. His tone softened. "We got along well. Very well. Then this morning…"

"What happened?" Annelise asked.

Adrian tried to think of the right way to explain. He glanced over and saw the red lights blinking around Annelise's shoulders. "Has Zack ever mentioned any kind of Greek theology, or even mythology to you?"

"No," Annelise replied. "Only in the carving he does. He likes to keep within that theme. So do a lot of artists, so what?"

Adrian paused.

"Did he hurt you?" Annelise asked.

"No. He was trying to impress me with some sort of magic trick," Adrian said. "Now I'm seeing red lights."

"You mean like eye floaters?" Annelise said. She sighed with relief. "Everybody gets those. They're nothing serious."

"No. Nothing like that." Adrian tried again. "Remember when we were kids and saw fireflies for the first time?"

"When we went to Greece."

"Yeah," Adrian confirmed. "That's sort of what I'm seeing, except in red. They were around him, and after looking in the mirror, they were around me."

"Do I need to take you to a doctor? Are they still there?" Annelise asked. "I don't see anything."

"They were there earlier," Adrian said. He looked into the rearview mirror. "I saw them in this weird mirror Zack has in his bathroom. I don't see them now."

"I've been to his house. I know the mirror you're talking about. It's decorative, nothing more." Annelise shrugged. "Maybe he was trying to impress you."

"Maybe," Adrian said. "I'm sure you're right and he was doing some stupid magic trick. My eyes don't hurt or anything like that, except I'm pretty tired."

"I think we could both use a nap before tonight."

"Now," Adrian said, "tell me about your dream. How badly do you get slaughtered?"

Annelise recounted her dream about secretly watching the bathing nymph, and how her own dogs ripped her apart for it.

"What did you eat for dinner last night?" Adrian asked.

"This monster had the same face as the woman in the gallery," Annelise said. "Don't you think it's odd?"

"If you say she was hot," Adrian said, "then maybe she was rooted in your subconscious and this is how it played out?"

"Maybe." Annelise shrugged. "Either way, I'll probably never see her again."

"If she had your dogs attack you, I'm not so sure why you would want to."

"Wait a minute," Annelise said. The car pulled into her driveway. "Did you and Zack...last night or this morning?"

"Last night. Why?"

"And the eye thing?" Annelise continued. "Last night or this morning?"

"This morning."

"Okay. I'm blaming it all on you," Annelise said. "I had the dream last night because of you having sex."

"I don't see how."

"I'm guessing my subconscious picked up on you having sex."

"Because that makes so much sense," Adrian replied.

"I have no other ideas," Annelise said. She threw him a cautious sideways glance. "I guess I should tell you that he'll be at the exhibit tonight. So I'm begging you, play nice tonight. Please. You're both adults and don't need me to babysit."

"He'll be mixing with the artists," Adrian said. "I'm the help, I'll be hanging with the riffraff out of his way."

"Zack isn't displaying his art tonight. He's the person I roped into helping you."

"Fuck it. I'm not doing it," Adrian said.

They got out of the car and entered the front door of the house.

"The hell you're not!" Annelise said. "Listen here. You will be perfectly polite and I will not have either of you fuck up my exhibit opening. Do I make myself clear?"

Chapter Eighteen

When Adrian and Annelise entered the gallery at 6:30, Lily was behind the front desk. She stood up as the two siblings entered.

"Wow!" Lily gave an appropriate whistle. "Don't you two look nice."

"Thanks." Annelise wore a pair of black slacks that outlined her legs. An admiral blue sleeveless blouse made her brown eyes sparkle. A thick black belt wrapped around her waist. Draped over her arm was a smart black half-jacket.

Lily flirtatiously laughed. "It's rare I get to see this one all dressed up and looking so good."

"Please," Adrian joked. "I look like a mime."

Lily came out from behind the desk. She placed both hands on Adrian's shoulder and pecked him on the cheek.

"All the handsome ones are gay or married," Lily bemoaned.

The front door opened, and Zack strode into the front foyer. Adrian could smell his cologne, a mixture of musk and moss. Lily's smile grew as she stepped between the men, linking each of their arms in hers.

"Two handsome men." Lily smiled.

Annelise waited at the door for the three of them. "When you guys are done with your little meet and greet, join me in here and I'll give you assignments."

"And it begins..." Lily whispered to Adrian. "As if we both haven't done this how many times before?" She followed Annelise.

"What does that mean?" Zack asked.

"Annelise gets very Type A when she has gallery openings," Adrian explained. "It's like a light switch; with a simple flip she goes from calm to hyper-tense. It is rather fun to watch her get uptight. I call it sibling schadenfreude."

"Getting defensive when stressed," Zack muttered. "Is that's a family trait?"

"You know, for Annelise's sake I think we should keep this formal and professional." Adrian extended his hand. "Strictly formal and professional."

Zack shook Adrian's offered hand. "If that's what you want," he said. "That's fine. I understand. Are you handling things any better?"

"The blinking lights around Annelise disappeared," Adrian said. "If that's what you mean."

The halo reappeared around Zack's shoulders.

"And they're back again. Did you do that on purpose?" Adrian asked.

"They'll come and go," Zack said. "You didn't give me a chance to show you how to ignore them. By tomorrow they should be gone completely, unless you want to see it."

"I don't want any part of any of this crap," Adrian said. "In fact, after tonight, I don't even want to see you again."

Track lighting lit up painted scenes from the Pacific Northwest in the main gallery. Subtle beams highlighted baskets of different-colored beads skillfully woven into flowers. Tucked below was the name of the piece, its creator, and the price. Oversized blocks were used as pedestals for displaying art pieces. Upright cocktail tables were scattered throughout the room. Adrian led Zack to where the others waited.

"And now that you two have joined us," Annelise called out, "on the back porch are two refrigerators stocked with champagne. There are trays of glasses. Take what you need, and when it gets low, let Adrian know."

Annelise clicked the remote in her hand. The introduction to Dvorak's "Song to the Moon" began to play.

"The music will be set on satellite radio, the classical station, so there are no issues there."

"Annelise," Adrian said. "Calm down. We got this."

Annelise opened her mouth to answer when her cell phone rang.

"I have to take this. Adrian, explain the routine to Zack. Hello..." Annelise strode back into the entrance foyer.

"Now that we have a minute's break," Adrian said. He took the vaporizer from his pocket.

"And I'm right behind you," Lily said. She followed Adrian onto the porch.

"I think it's all quite self-explanatory." Adrian waved at the refrigerators and the trays of glasses. He put the vaporizer up to his lips and inhaled.

"That's a lot of champagne, isn't it?" Zack asked. "For an opening this size?"

"Maybe," Adrian said. "But this way at least one or two bottles come home with me."

"And one for me," Lily replied.

"And if there's one left over," Adrian said. "One is yours. The payment for tonight's help."

"I'll take it."

Adrian took the vaporizer back from Lily's hand. He took another drag before offering it to Zack. He shook his hand.

"Believe me," Lily assured him, "this will definitely help with tonight's crowd."

"Lily?" Annelise called out from the gallery. "Adrian? Where are you guys?"

"Quick," Lily said in a frantic, hushed voice. "Put it away, Mom's coming."

Annelise called again.

"I'll go," Lily said. "Take another minute. You know I'll be finding you for more later."

Lily opened the screen door and darted back into the gallery.

"Alone again," Zack said.

"Yup." Adrian looked away.

"Can't we just relax and talk?" Zack said.

Adrian shrugged. "We're talking now, aren't we?"

"Can't you be serious for one minute?"

Adrian spun around to face him. "You seem like a nice guy..."

"I *am* a nice guy."

"A nice guy that happens to be into some weird shit that I don't need to get involved in."

"What I'm trying to tell you," Zack said, "is that you don't have a choice in it. You *are* involved in it. It's like being gay—you can acknowledge it or not, you can try to deny it, but it is always going to be there."

"Then I'll deal with it."

Zack put a hand on Adrian's shoulder. "Let me help you understand what you're going through."

Adrian roughly knocked Zack's hand away. "Will you stop and let me deal with it on my own!"

Zack stepped back, surprised.

Adrian pushed past Zack and returned to the gallery. The music was playing the overture of Handel's *Judas* from the hidden ceiling speakers. He took his place next to Lily. After a few moments, Zack sauntered to her other side.

"There you guys are," Annelise said. "Did Adrian give you all the instructions?"

"Crystal clear," Zack answered.

"Okay then," Annelise said.

"Adrian." Annelise watched as Lily led Zack back to show him where the bathrooms were and walked over to her brother. "Everything okay? Between you and Zack?"

"Yeah. Sure. Don't give me that look," Adrian said. "I said it's all right and it'll be all right."

"It *will be* all right is not the same as it *is* all right," replied Annelise.

"I said it's no big deal," Adrian growled. "Back off."

"I know you better than that." Annelise grabbed his arm. "You're my brother and I love you, and I'll help you deal with whatever you're going through…tomorrow. But tonight, you and Zack need to keep this shit out of my gallery."

"Annelise," Adrian said. "You're uptight because it's the opening. You do this every time and it always goes off without any problems. Do us both a favor and calm your ass down. I'll deal with my shit. You deal with yours. This is Bainbridge Island; what is the worst that can happen?"

CHAPTER NINETEEN

The ferry was easy to navigate. Camille followed the brochure's map and walked the short distance from the terminal. She passed shops that would remain open for another hour or so, depending on the ferry foot traffic.

She felt empowered by the toddler, its blood replenishing her. Echidna felt prepared to do battle with this Annelise Petrakis, one on one. It would be easier for Echidna to make her move now that the male was out of the way. And the woman didn't seem to be aware of her powers; it shouldn't prove too difficult.

Echidna was hungry.

She used the Concealment to appear as Camille, and walked leisurely down the path until she saw the gallery. She started for the gallery's front door.

"Excuse me," said a voice from behind her.

Camille recognized the thin, auburn-haired gallery owner from Seattle.

"Weren't you in my boutique yesterday afternoon?" Louise asked. "My store is on First and Pine, downtown Seattle? I could have sworn it was you."

"It was I." Camille's French accent sounded pleasant.

"Thank you for coming to see my exhibit."

"Yes, I liked your work. I was there when the other woman," she pointed to the gallery's door, "Ms. Petrakis, came in with the brochures."

"Oh." Louise's face changed. "Were you there then when the child was kidnapped?"

"A child was kidnapped?" Camille repeated. "That is horrible."

"It must have happened after you left," Louise went on. "Something went wrong with the security cameras for two hours. That's when it happened. The police think it isn't a coincidence."

"What happened?" Camille asked.

"The police aren't sure. The only other people I remember coming into the store at that time were the mother and child, Annelise, you now, I guess..." Louise counted off on her fingers. "And this African American guy that came in when I was in the back. I saw him leave the store but he was carrying a puppy, not a child."

"That is awful," Camille said.

"I know. I feel so bad," Louise said. "It happened in *my* store."

"Louise, we should probably go inside," a man said impatiently from behind her. "You *are* one of the contributors."

"I'm sorry," Louise said. She raised a hand to her companion's shoulder. "This is my boyfriend, Peter."

Camille snapped her hands under her arms, disregarding Peter's extended hand.

"I do not shake hands," Camille said. "I do not like germs."

"Okay," Peter said.

Peter leaned forward to open the gallery door. He gently gave Louise a shove through.

"I hope you enjoy the exhibit," Louise called back over her shoulder.

Camille waited before entering. She walked through the foyer and entered the main gallery. About thirty people were milling around the room, browsing along the perimeters or standing at one of the cocktail tables, chatting about the artwork.

The moment she entered, the hackles on Echidna's neck stood. Her senses tingled and she searched the room for danger. There was another spattering of wyre-lights, pulsing weakly around Annelise's shoulders; she posed no threat. Echidna searched through the human herd, her eyes scanning the room for anything hinting at danger. A gray-haired man came bustling in from the porch with a champagne tray balanced on his shoulder. He turned away and disappeared into a crowd anxious for their drinks.

It was undeniable. The lights glowed dark red around his head.

This foe knew his bloodline, his power, and was a threat. Her eyes remained acutely focused, waiting for the crowd to clear. The rest of the room blurred and faded from her vision.

"Excuse me." A waiter startled her.

The room came back into focus. Camille blinked. She turned to see Adrian standing before her. Torment and Havoc had failed her! Adrian was a replica of his sister; the same dark hair crowned the olive skin. The same rich eyes stared back with the same impish twinkle.

It was the halo glimmering around him that caused her golden eyes to deliciously narrow and her jaw to hang slack. The lights were stronger than yesterday; they were even stronger than his sister's. Time was against her now. It wouldn't be long before either of the Greek twins grew aware of the powers.

"Would you like a glass of champagne?" he asked.

"No. Thank you," Camille said.

The man smiled and started forward. He stopped and turned sharply around to study her face.

"Is everything all right?" Camille purred.

"Yeah," he replied. "All good."

Echidna watched him push through the crowd before he disappeared within its center. Her mouth watered with hunger and her stomach ached with the pains it brought. She could smell his scent lingering in his path and took a step. It was the sense of danger that brought her to a halt. He had survived her Furies' attack, yet he was the lesser of the two threats present this evening.

Get the girl, her mind told her. *You can attend to the others once you've feasted on her blood.*

The sound of a glass tinkling rippled through the crowd, bringing conversation to a halt. As a single unit, the audience turned to face the small dais by the far wall. Annelise was commanding attention by gently rapping on a glass flute, Yvonne and Louise a step behind her. Lily stood to the side.

"Excuse me," Annelise said. "Thank you for coming tonight. My name is Annelise Petrakis. Welcome to my gallery."

She paused for light applause.

"Tonight's exhibits focus on local artists from around the Puget Sound area…"

The sound of her voice faded in Camille's ears. She watched

as Annelise introduced the artists and explained about the evening. The speech was short, ending with the same smattering of applause. Annelise stepped down to talk to waiting potential clients.

"Dark-eyed owl," Echidna whispered. "Beautiful bird with olive feathers, your brown eyes shall find what I have lost."

Camille's lips silently moved in the ancient language. Her eyes remained focused on Annelise, and her hand crept slowly to her chest. The nimble fingers fished an apple pendant from her cleavage. She tightly wrapped her fist around the golden charm.

"Fruit of Discordia." Echidna cast her spell. The pendant started to burn in her hand. "Sister to Strife and Chaos, I call to you. Cloud her mind with fog. Let her become lost in the mist, and let mine be the voice of her reason to lead her free."

The pendant seared the palm of her hand. She welcomed the pain. The apple cooled just as quickly and Camille tugged it from the chain. It snapped free easily.

Camille moved through the crowd toward Annelise, careful not to bump into anyone. Her unblinking eyes remained focused.

Annelise was busy chatting with the few people surrounding her. Three women talked with her eagerly, while a man waited his turn patiently. Next to Annelise stood a taller, handsome woman with gray hair.

"Look at me," Camille whispered. She would have to lure Annelise away from the crowd.

Annelise glanced up. Their eyes met briefly. Color flushed her cheeks and Annelise smiled, continuing the conversation with those around her. It was only an instant before she looked up again. This time she sought Camille's eyes. The taller woman at her side craned her neck to see what captured her friend's attention. She leaned over and the two of them whispered.

Echidna patiently waited for Annelise to look up a third time. A flirtatious smile crossed her lips. She waited until Annelise's stare remained fixed, before allowing Camille's smile to widen.

"Go." Camille whispered the command.

The apple fell off the edge of Camille's extended palm. It rolled across the floor, swerving to avoid being stepped on by other guests. The pendant tripped its way until bouncing against Annelise's shoe. She looked down and bent to retrieve the tiny golden fruit.

Annelise stood, examining the pendant in her palm. She looked around. One of the three women at her table pulled her attention away, and Annelise absently put the pendant into her jacket pocket.

There was nothing to do but let the spell take hold. The longer it stayed with Annelise, the stronger the curse would become. Camille nodded and smiled when Annelise looked up once more. Echidna waited for Annelise to be locked into conversation, assuring she would leave without being followed. She could sense Annelise's eyes following her as she drifted to the far end of the room.

Camille slowly walked about, pretending to look at the art. From time to time she looked back over her shoulder at Annelise. Every time the Greek woman found herself free, Camille was careful to duck out of sight, prolonging both the chase and temptation. After fifteen minutes of playing cat and mouse, Camille waited for Annelise to be intercepted by another guest. After making sure the gallery owner's eyes were on her, Camille sauntered out of the gallery.

Camille waited outside. Another ten minutes passed and several people left before Annelise appeared at the gallery's front door. She talked to a few people on the front porch, subtly trying to look around. When Annelise saw Camille standing a few yards off by herself, her face lit up.

"Hello," Annelise said.

"Bonjour," Camille responded.

"Are you French?"

"Oui. I was born in Paris."

"It's a beautiful city," Annelise said. "I love the galleries there. I've been several times. My name is Annelise."

"I'm sorry," Camille said. "I don't shake hands, I have a little cold. My name is Camille."

"Oh," Annelise said, withdrawing her arm. "I understand. It's a pleasure meeting you. *Enchanté.*"

She laughed. Camille smiled politely.

"You look familiar," Annelise said. "Have we met before?"

"We saw each other yesterday," Camille said. "At your friend's boutique. We were not introduced."

"I remember seeing you there." Annelise brushed her hair away from her neck.

The tall woman came out of the gallery.

"Camille," Annelise said halfheartedly. "This is my friend, Yvonne."

"Nice to meet you." Yvonne stuck out her hand.

Camille turned up her nose and stared at the hand.

"Yvonne," Annelise said softly, "Camille has a cold and doesn't shake hands."

"So," Yvonne tried to start a conversation, "are you enjoying the exhibit?"

Camille's closed lips smiled tightly. She nodded.

"Yvonne did the watercolors you see tonight," Annelise said.

Camille looked into the handsome woman's eager face. "Those are so cute."

Yvonne blinked as if she'd been slapped across the face. "Thank you," she answered. "Annelise, can I speak to you a minute? Alone and inside."

"Will you excuse me?" Annelise asked Camille. Color flushed her cheeks.

"It's all right," Camille said. "You have a gallery to run."

Annelise looked at Camille with hopeful brown eyes.

"I'll be here for a while yet," Camille assured. "We may talk later."

"Thank you," Annelise whispered. "I look forward to it."

Camille smelled the disruption circulating around Annelise and enjoyed watching it isolate her. The magic was working faster, and with stronger results. That would mean it would probably burn through quicker as well. Over the next thirty minutes, Camille went into the gallery just long enough to capture Annelise's attention before walking back out into the cool evening's air.

The party was winding down when Annelise came outside. "Sorry," Annelise said. "I've been trying to find the time to come back and chat more, but it's been one hell of a night."

"When a gallery opening is that busy," Camille said with a smile, "that's called a 'good thing.'"

"It's not just that," Annelise said. "It seems that for every one good thing that has happened, two more go horribly wrong. I'd say it's the full moon, but there isn't one tonight."

"Your friend did not seem too happy with me," Camille added.

"Yvonne?" Annelise dismissed her with a wave of her hand. "She's nervous about tonight's exhibit."

"Is she your girlfriend?" Camille asked.

"Not anymore." Annelise smiled. "Not for several years now. We're still good friends; except for tonight, evidently."

Camille's smile brightened. Yvonne came out the door.

"I'm gonna go," Yvonne said.

"If you can wait a minute," Annelise said, "I'll say good-bye."

"I can go," Camille murmured.

"Don't," Annelise said. "Yvonne can wait."

"Don't bother," Yvonne growled. "I don't want to miss my ferry." She pushed between them and stomped around to the back of the gallery.

"Don't you think you should go after your friend?" Camille asked. "She seems upset."

"She'll be fine," Annelise said.

"Are you sure?"

"Definitely."

They watched the Prius pull out of the parking lot and turn toward the ferry dock.

"If you don't immediately have to catch a ferry home, I have a crazy idea," Annelise suggested. "Would you like to get a drink? I know a nice patio bar a short walk away."

"But this is your party," Camille said with a chuckle. "You cannot leave it."

"All the buyers have already left," Annelise said. "The only people sticking around are the ones staying for the food and alcohol."

"You are teasing me, I think." Camille laughed.

"No, really," Annelise said with enthusiasm. "It's only a five-minute walk if we cut through the alley behind the gallery. Then it's across the street and down the pier."

Camille smiled.

"I'll run in and tell them I'm leaving," Annelise said. She paused. "On second thought, I don't want to go back in there. All of my friends are being assholes tonight. My assistant can lock up."

"Are you sure?" Camille was already turning away.

"It'll be fine," Annelise replied. She took a step forward to catch up with her.

"A little overwhelming for an opening night?"

"I don't want to dwell on it," Annelise confessed. "It's sufficient to say that anything that could get screwed up, has."

"I am not sure how to take that."

"Not you, I'm sorry." Annelise sighed. "Yvonne has nerves, and my assistant, Lily, is being hypersensitive. My brother is going through his own issues."

"Brother?" Camille asked. "The waiter with your smile? Of course."

Annelise laughed. "Yeah, that's Adrian. he's my twin."

"Twins." Camille's voice rang with delight. "Greek twins."

"It runs in my family. We're the only ones born in several generations, though."

"How fortunate that you two have each other."

The blue Crosstrek was parked in the far back corner of the parking lot. A wooden fence tightly formed the boundary of the gallery's property. A latched, narrow gate was in the corner of the fence. Annelise walked between her car and the fence. She leaned against the car's hood, facing Camille.

"After our parents died," Annelise explained, "we only had each other. We're very close."

"That is, I think," said Camille, "the nature of a sibling."

Annelise nodded. "Let's go."

Annelise reached out for Camille's elbow. Her fingers touched the back of Camille's hand. Annelise became immobile as Camille's image melted away. Standing in her place was a reptilian monster. Camille's plump face disappeared into the curls of black hair. A crone's complexion emerged, serpent's eyes burning. The human torso transformed and grew until it towered two feet above the car roof. Clawlike fingers hung off scabbed, sallow fleshy arms. A green-scaled body emerged. A long tail smacked on the ground behind the creature.

Annelise was paralyzed with fear. Her heart pounded. A scream choked in her throat. She was trapped between the monster and her car. The thing reached out with broken, clawed hands, grabbing for her throat.

CHAPTER TWENTY

Adrian made the rounds along the back of the room. The guests were keeping him busy, and there hadn't been a moment to stop in over an hour. The music was playing a simple piano version of Pachebel's *Canon in D*, and the evening so far hadn't been too bad.

Adrian stopped to look at one of Yvonne's watercolors. It was well done, but she used too many bright colors to represent Seattle light. Only in a dream would downtown be so full of pastels.

Entering the gallery with another tray of drinks, Adrian scanned the crowd. He turned his head quickly to follow the retreating figure of a handsome man.

"Oh, bloody hell," he whispered. "It's Zack."

He went in the opposite direction.

What kind of game was Zack playing? Gods, powers, and blinking lights, it was too much to comprehend.

He rebalanced the tray on his shoulder.

Adrian saw red light burning around the shoulders of a woman. "Excuse me."

The woman blinked. A chill ran through his body, causing the glasses on his tray to rattle. The red light burned around this woman.

"Would you like a glass of champagne?"

"No, thank you," the woman said, speaking with a French accent.

Adrian felt the hackles on his neck prickle and itch. He could feel himself growing defensively angry, not knowing why.

"Is everything all right?"

"Yeah," Adrian snapped. "All good."

The sound of a glass tinkling rippled through the crowd, bringing the conversation to a halt. Annelise stood in front of the dais, gently wrapping her hands around a glass flute. The other two artists stood behind her.

"Excuse me," Annelise said. "Thank you for coming tonight. My name is Annelise Petrakis. Welcome to my gallery."

As the crowd turned as one unit, Adrian took the opportunity to sneak around the French woman. With the crowd occupied, Adrian snuck out onto the porch; it would be a perfect time for a break. He caught Lily's attention as he went. She subtly nodded with a smile.

Adrian saw Zack already on the porch and paused in the doorway. He debated on going back when Lily appeared behind him and pushed him through.

"Now for a break while she speaks," Lily said.

"How long will she speak?" Zack asked.

"Depends. But we have time for another toke."

She jabbed Adrian with her finger.

"Is everyone being a bitch tonight, or are they only being bitches to me?" Adrian asked. He dug the vaporizer from his pocket and flicked it on.

"I think it's just you," Lily teased.

"It's not you," Zack assured them both. "I can feel it, too. There's something in the air."

"Sometimes it's like the hairs on your neck stand up," Lily said. "And you just know that somehow, somewhere, something isn't going to go well."

A round of applause sounded from inside the gallery.

"And that would be our signal," Lily said. "The work continues. Smile, song, and away we go."

"They'll be drinking for another hour or so," Adrian said. "Take another tray and then you can sit out for a while. I'll make the rounds inside."

"Okay," Zack softly answered. "I'll do two more rounds and then hang out here."

As he made his way through the crowd, Adrian noticed that Annelise and Yvonne were huddled together in a corner.

Yvonne finished speaking and stormed away from the table.

"Everything okay with you and Yvonne?" Adrian asked as he approached his sister.

Annelise looked up. With an overly exaggerated eye roll she huffed an exhausted breath. "Fine."

"Why'd she storm off?"

"I pointed this woman out to her and said I was interested," Annelise explained. "Yvonne also thought she was attractive. Now she's saying I embarrassed her in front of a potential client."

"Did you?" Adrian asked. "You do that when you flirt sometimes; talk others down to make yourself look better."

"I do not," Annelise said. "And I don't need dating advice from you."

"Everything seems to be going well." Adrian changed the subject. "Are you sure you're all right?"

"Yeah," Annelise snapped. "Sorry. I'm just…in a mood."

"I'd say." Adrian nodded. "Maybe Mercury is in retrograde or whatever that is. Zack said he felt something was out of whack tonight. Maybe he's right."

"Whatever is going on between you and Zack," Annelise suddenly said, "you just need to keep it to yourselves." She turned and stormed away.

Adrian remained still, his mouth hanging open in surprise. He shook his head and tucked the empty tray under his arm.

Lily rushed by, knocking into him. "Your sister is absolutely bat shit cray-cray."

"What happened?" Adrian asked.

"She's being a bitch. First she bit my head off for no reason. Then started bawling me out like it was my fault. I need some air." Lily darted off through the crowd and out the back door.

Adrian was about to start after Lily when he felt someone grab hold of his arm.

"Great," Yvonne said, disgruntled. "You're out of drinks, too. Just when I need one."

"Et tu, Yvonne?"

"Your sister is unbearable." Yvonne shook her head.

"You know how she gets at these things," Adrian said.

"Yeah, I know," Yvonne snapped. "I was with her for how long? But tonight she's in rare form. She chewed me out because I wasn't here when the exhibit began."

Adrian shrugged. "You weren't that late. Nobody else was here except us. Louise was later than you were anyway."

"Tell your sister that," Yvonne complained. "I can't help the ferry schedules. She was just looking for an excuse to scream at me."

"What was the real reason?"

"She and I both saw this really hot woman," Yvonne said. "Annelise saw her go outside and twat-blocked me by introducing a client so I couldn't follow. When I got out there, they were already talking. Then Annelise started her little games, putting me down in front of this woman."

"You know it's nothing personal," Adrian said. "Several people seem to be having issues with her tonight."

Yvonne exhaled sharply. "I think the best thing I can do is let her calm down. I'm going to leave. I've had enough for one night. I'm going home."

"I hope you at least made some decent sales. You know she'll be fine in the morning. All apologetic like, 'I'm so sorry. Forgive me. You know how I get.'"

Yvonne smiled. "You're a good man, Adrian. Why do we put up with her?"

"I have no choice." Adrian winked. "You're just a glutton for punishment."

Yvonne leaned in and gave Adrian a hug. "I'm sorry to hear about Marcus," she whispered.

"Thanks." Adrian smiled. "Let her sleep it off, and wait for her call tomorrow."

Yvonne left the gallery. Adrian waited until she was out of sight and let his shoulders drop.

"One issue fixed," he mumbled to himself. "Ninety-nine more to go."

Zack was already comforting Lily when Adrian walked out onto the porch.

"There's still a handful of people in there," Adrian said. "One of us should be in there before Annelise notices."

"Yeah." Zack gave Lily's shoulders a reassuring squeeze. "One of us should."

"I came out of the bathroom," Lily said. "Annelise was standing in the lobby. I teasingly said, 'Hell of a night, eh?' and she whirls around and starts yelling at me."

"It's not you," Adrian said. He put a hand on her shoulder. "She's just being a megabitch tonight."

"Fuck you, Adrian," Annelise said from behind them.

"Annelise," Adrian replied. "Calm down."

"Don't tell me what to do," Annelise snapped back. "You just said I was a megabitch."

"That's only because you're acting like a megabitch," Adrian said. "Get over your big bad self."

Annelise narrowed her eyes. "I came out here to find out why my help isn't in there doing their job."

"Help?" Adrian snapped. "I'm doing you the favor."

"Some favor." She spun around and stormed into the gallery.

"Are you okay, Lily?" Adrian asked.

"Give me a minute," Lily said with a sniff. "I'll be right in."

Adrian went inside with another tray of drinks. Annelise was nowhere to be seen.

It was almost 10:00 p.m., and there were seven people dawdling behind. Adrian cleared a table at the front and arranged ten glasses of champagne in a circle. Lily and Zack came back in after a few more minutes. Lily disappeared up front. Adrian and Zack started picking up the empty glasses and discarded remains from opposite ends of the room.

"No," Lily said. She was shaking hands with the remaining drunk couple. "Annelise had to take care of a personal issue. Thank you so much for coming."

She politely ushered them out.

"Done," announced Lily. "Everyone's gone and the door is locked."

"Where's Annelise?" Adrian asked.

"Don't know," she answered with a shrug. "Don't care. She'll be back, eventually. And if she's not, I have my keys."

"Give me a hand getting the porch cleaned off," Adrian said.

"I'm a delicate flower," Lily said. She continued cleaning up. "Zack's already out there, get him to help you. I'll finish up in here."

He grabbed a bag of trash and started for the door. Zack was already putting the empty flutes into the plastic crates. He looked up as Adrian walked onto the porch, immediately turning back to his task. Adrian stepped around him to lock the refrigerator door.

"Where's Annelise?" Zack asked.

"Don't know," Adrian said.

"If you need a ride back to her place, I can give you a lift."

"I don't think that's a good idea," Adrian replied. "Besides, I can see Annelise's car."

The car was parked in the far, dark corner by the wooden fence. Adrian saw someone standing, talking to Annelise. His blood began to race. "You don't know when to quit, do you?"

"What's your problem now?"

"Can't stop with those fucking lights," Adrian said. "They're all over her car. Hope you enjoyed your joke."

Adrian pointed out to the corner of the lot. Zack looked in the direction. All color ran from his complexion.

"Stay back," Zack commanded. "No matter what you do, don't get involved. You're not ready."

"Ready for what?" Adrian's eyes grew wide with shock. He saw Annelise turn around and something tall and monstrous step from the shadows. The body of a dragon with a human female torso stood there swaying like a serpent. He watched as it took Annelise by the throat.

"Get the hell away from my sister!" Adrian yelled.

"Adrian, wait!"

Adrian leapt off the porch. He took off running across the parking lot. As if in slow motion, Adrian watched the monstrous beast sink its fangs into her neck.

The monster pulled her bloodied mouth away from Annelise's flesh. The creature saw him running toward her and threw Annelise to the pavement. It coiled back onto the monstrous body, arms extended and her spiked tail vibrating with anticipation.

Adrian charged forward. As he got closer, the creature grew in height.

Adrian felt a blast of heat rush by his head. A glowing rod of fire hit the pavement by the creature's feet and exploded. Sparks flew. A second burning arrow flew past and hit the creature's scale-covered body.

Adrian looked back to see Zack, his head lowered and a storm blazing in the shadow covering his blue eyes. His hands were by his sides, with orange-red flames glowing around them. Both feet firmly planted, Zack raised his arm, launching another firebolt.

The monster coiled itself on its haunches. The tail swung out from behind, batting the bolt away. The fire collided with the parking lot fence, ripping a hole through the wood. The beast raised its head and opened its mouth, screeching. Adrian and Zack covered their ears. The monster darted through the fence and disappeared into the alley.

Zack ran ahead, jumping through the fence in pursuit of the monster. Adrian went straight to Annelise, unconscious on the pavement. She was bleeding from several places. Adrian ripped his shirt off and pressed it against the wound. He sighed in relief when he finally found her pulse.

It was slow, but it was there.

"Annelise!" he cried out. "Can you hear me? Annelise!"

She didn't move.

"Somebody!" Adrian shouted, tears running down his face. "Somebody help!" He saw Lily coming out onto the gallery's porch.

"Lily!" he shouted. "Call 9-1-1, Annelise has been attacked!"

Lily disappeared back into the gallery. Zack came back through the broken fence. Dirt and grime covered his face. His shirt was torn in several places, and he was out of breath.

"Is Annelise all right?" Zack asked, bending down at their sides.

"I don't know," Adrian said. "I can feel a pulse, but it's weak. She's lost a lot of blood. Lily's called 9-1-1."

Sirens wailed in the distance.

"Adrian," Zack said. "I need you to listen to me. You can heal her, but I need you to listen to me and do it now."

"How?" Adrian cried.

"You're descended from Apollo, the god of healing."

Adrian started to interrupt.

"Close your eyes and open yourself to channeling your power. We don't have much time. Do it. Now!"

Adrian moved his hands and placed them over his bloodied shirt at her neck. His eyes closed. Adrian concentrated.

A warm glow started from the center of his chest. The intense heat spread through his body, running into his arms and pouring out through the palms of his hands. His fingers felt as if they were burning, but he could not tear them away. It raged through his blood and into every muscle. The fire extinguished and for a brief instant, the edges of his fingers turned numbingly cold.

Adrian was about to take his hands away from Annelise's throat when he felt the needles pricking his fingertips. Tiny sharp pins felt like they were being pushed underneath his fingernails. He let out a cry. His hands remained in place as the stinging sensations traveled up his arms. Both palms were pushed away from Annelise's body and Adrian was thrown backward onto the pavement. His pressed his hands into the ground as hard as he could. The poison drained from his fingers and sank into the earth.

The sirens sounded close. Adrian looked up to see the flashing lights entering the parking lot. He rolled onto his stomach and pushed himself up to all fours. Adrian heaved the contents of his stomach as the ambulance pulled up. He vomited again, rolled to his side, and blacked out.

CHAPTER TWENTY-ONE

A nnelise opened her eyes.
      She was lying on a cold, flat surface. She pushed herself to a sitting position and stood up in the middle of a hallway. Her eyes adjusted to the light emanating from the walls. There was endless darkness above her, and the floor was constructed of smooth slabs of silver-gray hematite.

A chill hung in the air. Annelise rubbed her arms and found she now wore a simple tunic. The peplos hung down to her knees and tied behind her neck, leaving her arms, back, and lower limbs exposed. Her hair hung loose to her shoulders.

The hall stretched in either direction, with nothing but a burning red light in the darkness. Annelise cautiously padded her way left toward the glowing light in the distance.

Each step was arduous; her feet felt strapped to weights. She pushed forward, forcing herself to get closer to the glowing ruby in the distance.

The glowing red came from a burning sconce hung on the hall's left side. As Annelise approached, she saw it lit up a mosaic on the wall opposite, bathing the tiles in what looked like blood. The picture detailed a procession of twenty women carrying jugs to and from a riverbed. Some women stood patiently, waiting, while three of them were kneeling on its banks. The others walked away, unaware the water was running out the bottom of their canisters. They then reclaimed their place in line, creating an endless cycle.

The details were unbelievably fine. Annelise reached out her fingers to brush over the cool tiles. As she touched the painted droplets of water, they changed colors, becoming blood red. Annelise clutched her hand to her chest, scalded. She examined her fingers, studying every inch for damage. When she found nothing wrong, she stepped away from the picture and continued down the hall.

Annelise saw another glowing red light in the distance. Another sconce, this time on the right side, lit up another mosaic on the opposite wall: a naked man tightly strapped upside down to a table in an open field. Two vultures tore at this skin; the first had its beak deeply stuck into an open stomach wound. The second tore at the calf muscle from one of the bound legs.

Annelise forced herself to continue. It felt like she was walking against a strong current. She continued until the end was in sight. The hallway ended at a great doorway. The frame was thick, made of heavy ebony wood. A round marble was set inside the perimeter, pulsing dark red. A willow tree burned at the center, its long branches swaying across the polished surface.

Hesitantly, she reached out for the glowing sphere. The tree branches lashed out, wrapping their willowy whips around her wrist. They pulled her palm against the door until a single branch reared up and penetrated the pad of her fingertip with its edge. Blood beaded to the surface and the tree branch swept it into the glowing globe. The door swung open, and a strong wind from behind her shoved her into the room. She fell onto the cold gray-silver floor. The door shut, sealing itself.

Annelise looked around the antechamber.

A huge statue of a naked man crouching down on one knee with the literal world balancing on his shoulders dominated the room. Each muscle was exquisitely carved. The hands tightly held the huge sphere resting on his shoulders.

Atlas.

The Titan's eyes stared through Annelise. A red fire burned in the empty eye sockets, and the mouth hung open in a twisted, eternal cry of anguish. A pathway led under the statue's body.

Annelise crept along the path. She kept her eyes on the colossal statue above her, half expecting the Titan to come to life. Once she crossed under him, Annelise sighed in relief. On the wall in front of her was a duplicate of the previous door. The red sphere pulsed, and the willow tree danced within its fires. Annelise put her hand toward the red sphere. Again, the tree became alive and took its entrance fee in blood.

Annelise stumbled forward and through the door. She found herself in another hallway. The passage stretched into impenetrable darkness with the exception of a red light, glowing in the darkness. There was no sound other than the soft slap of bare feet against cold stone. A chill hung in the air.

Annelise approached the burning ruby light. Hesitantly, she turned to examine the tiled wall.

The mosaic was the same as the first picture she came across. The Danaides were endlessly waiting in line, all trying—and failing—to fill their canisters from the river. Annelise fell to the floor, her palms braced against the stone. She began to lose feeling in her fingers and toes. The numbing sensation moved through her.

Annelise felt the cold creep past her ankles and start up her calves. She pushed herself to her knees. She felt sharp pins running under her skin.

"It is only in your mind," Annelise told herself. She repeated the words like a mantra.

"It's only in your mind," Annelise continued. "You are in control of your body. Tell it to stop."

The pain slowed and faded. The numbing began to ebb back down her legs until only the tips of her fingers and toes were tingling. Annelise opened her eyes when it completely stopped.

She looked down the hall behind her. The door had disappeared into the wall.

Annelise looked in the other direction. If there was going to be a way out, it would be somewhere on the path ahead. She would have to search each section of the wall.

Annelise took a deep breath and tightened her resolve. There had to be a way out of this, and eventually she would find it.

CHAPTER TWENTY-TWO

Echidna flew through the hole in the wooden fence, barreling down the alley. Her concealment shattered when Annelise touched her. She had not expected an attack. The wound reminded her what pain was, and bitter memories flooded back. The bolt held powerful magic, and the strike sapped most of her energy and strength. If not for the blood of Annelise, she would have been even more severely wounded.

There was no other choice but to flee.

At least she'd managed to drink from Annelise. The Olympian's blood was not as strong as she'd hoped, but the power was enough. The Discordia invocation had worked fast and struck hard. The spell had made Annelise susceptible. She could not physically imprison Annelise in Tartarus—only an Olympian could do that—but Echidna was a Titan, and she could cause a soul severe torment by keeping it hostage.

Echidna paused in the shadows. People from the small bars nearby were looking toward the gallery. She could not risk exposure or capture. Humans would never take the Mother of Monsters for study. Sirens wailed through the night, and the flashes from the ambulance lights sent the bars' patrons running toward the gallery. Echidna seized her opportunity in the brief stillness that followed; there was nothing but darkness between her and the water.

A firebolt flew past her head. It hit the side of the fence with a blinding flash, sending wood flying in every direction. The broken sides burned, sparks spreading to the patches of grass along the bottom. Beyond the wooden fence, a forgotten section of trashed land ran up to the bluff's edge, disappearing past a short metal fence.

Echidna turned to see the one called Zack coming toward her. His hands glowed, recharging their electric fire, readying another attack. She clapped her hands together twice. A ball of fire the size of a cue ball appeared in her hand. It grew to the size of a grapefruit before she hurled it at the Olympian.

Her attack took him by surprise. He hit the ground, rolling out of its way. The fireball exploded in the air, sparks of shrapnel flying out like a starburst. Through the thick smoke and small puddles of fire, Echidna could see the Olympian down on his stomach, winded and coughing on the ground.

She did not wait for the smoke to clear. Seizing her chance, Echidna darted through the fence opening, shattering the fragile remainders on either side as she barreled through. The pain from her side wound throbbing with each step, Echidna fled down to the edge and hurled herself over.

She hit Puget Sound with a stinging splash, sending up a large geyser of water. The Mother of Monsters allowed her weight to pull her to the bottom. Lack of air burned her lungs briefly, before the skin of her neck transformed into gills. A membrane crossed the amber eyes, letting the watery surroundings come into focus. The saline stung, cleansing the large wound at her side. The cold water provided relief to the scorch marks burnt onto her scales. She crawled across the sandy bottom.

Echidna clawed her human hands deep into the bottom, crushing the crustaceans caught in her fingers. She packed handfuls of the mud into the wound. Her flesh pulled sustenance from the pulverized sea life and from the dark earth's energy. When her wounds subsided from agony to merely a steady, throbbing complaint, Echidna started across the muddy floor.

Schools of fish broke their ranks, dispersing in panic, to get around her. She caught what she could with her hands, devouring them for the small nourishment they provided. The wounds began to heal and the pain slowly faded away.

Echidna closed her eyes and let her senses reach out. This sonar located her lair, and the dragon's body turned instinctively in its direction. Propelled with the aid of her tail, she moved in great strides, disturbing the water and the muddy floor as she crossed. When light broke dimly through the surface, Echidna's senses became more acute and she reached out for the safest place to exit the water.

Her climb up the side of the cliff was excruciatingly painful. She swallowed her howling rage, channeling her energy instead to return to her lair. Echidna pulled herself over the ledge outside her cave and fell to the ground, panting heavily.

A high-pitched screeching cut through the air from beyond the clouds. Echidna held her breath and snapped her eyes open. The film across her eyes retracted, her normal, sharpened sight searching the dark, clouded skies. The sound echoed again. Her blood chilled and her body constricted with fear. She had heard that cry only once before, and the sound echoed in her memory forever.

Echidna would never forget the shrill sound of the Usurper's pet eagle. That sound brought back memories of Typhaeon's assassination.

If the eagle found her, the Usurper would know where her nest was hidden. That high-pitched shriek foreshadowed her death.

Closing her eyes, Echidna inhaled deeply. She held the breath tight in her lungs. She puckered her lips and slowly let the poisoned wind leave her body. It channeled away from her, churning until it twisted into a howling storm. With the last bit of air she released the squalling wind, setting it free. Should the bird came near the lair, the wind cyclone would at least keep it at bay.

This was not the world she once knew. She had spent millennia plotting her revenge on a world that no longer existed. There had been a time when mountains would tremble before her and the winds were at her command. She was a Titan, a goddess; one of the firstborn of the Great Mother, Gaia, and Uranus, Ruler of the Universe. Echidna's strength was terrible, and she had been worshipped and revered.

No gods existed in this world. It was cold and corrupted by the magic of science. Even the strength of a Titan was not powerful enough to keep her two Furies, Torment and Havoc, from fading in the morning sunlight. The Olympian powers were not what they once were, either, but they were powerful enough still to hunt her into extinction. The storm would eventually fade and the eagle would be able to find her lair. It was only a matter of time.

Her powers would take too long to replenish from this night's work, and she did not have much time to react.

"If Heaven shall enter the World of Night"—Hecate's prophecy came back to Echidna's ears—*"Even the mightiest can die."*

There was only one place where she could take their advantages away from them. She needed to lure them into the Underworld. Magic would be more readily available to her deep in the earth. The mortals would lack knowledge of their surroundings and how to harness their powers in a strange world. Both would work to her advantage.

The Land of the Dead was full of predators, and those without the knowledge necessary to avoid them would soon fall as their prey.

Echidna smiled. She might have been wounded in the battle, but she knew how she could win the war.

Echidna moved to the front of the cave, lifting her tail. Angling her hindquarters, she released her foul scent into the air. She dragged her tail on the ground, clearly marking the territory as she made her way back inside the cave. When the storm cleared, the scent would be enough to draw the eagle to her lair.

The Mother of Monsters stood in front of the cave drawing. She opened her arms and arched her back, chanting her prayers. The stick figure flinched and peeled itself from the stone. It strode over the crudely drawn wheel and took firm hold of the crank at its center. The Wheel of Destiny turned slowly at first, speeding up until it became a spinning blur.

The emptiness gnawed at the core of Echidna's stomach and she felt her body being pulled firmly forward. She opened her mouth, letting the spinning void around her flood her lungs.

Her mind raced with how to plan her attack as she was drawn into blackness.

CHAPTER TWENTY-THREE

M r. Petrakis?" a scrub-clad doctor called out.
Adrian stopped his pacing and looked up. His body cramped.
Zack stood up from his plastic chair in Harrison Memorial Hospital's waiting room. He stepped behind Adrian, gently placing a hand on his shoulder.

"That's me." Adrian bolted over to the doctor. "I'm Adrian Petrakis. How is Annelise?"

"She lost a lot of blood," the doctor answered. "We gave her a transfusion and sewed up her shoulder. That surgery was a success."

"Thank God," Adrian said, relieved. "When can I see her?"

The doctor continued. "She's breathing on her own, and her vital signs are good, but she has lost a lot of blood. She's still unconscious, but we are doing everything we can."

"She's going to be okay, right?"

"She's not out of danger yet," the doctor said. "That was quite a deep gash at the base of her neck, and it appears—well, it looks like there's an infection of some sort. We're not quite sure from what. Can you tell me what happened to her?"

Zack's hand gave Adrian's shoulder a gentle squeeze.

"Someone attacked her." Adrian repeated the same story he told the police. "He wore some kind of monster mask and was really tall. When he heard me yell and saw me running toward him, he dropped Annelise and took off. By the time I got there, he was gone and my sister was just lying there, bleeding on the ground."

"Mr. Petrakis, you need to stay calm."

"When is she going to wake up?"

"Mr. Petrakis," the doctor said, "we don't know right now. We'll need to run more tests. We should know more in the next forty-eight hours. Right now, she's in a coma." He shook his head. "There's nothing you can do right now. Go home and try to get some sleep. That's the best thing, for yourself and your sister. Go home. I promise we'll call you if there is any change."

Adrian was silent. He felt like his heart was tearing in half. "Thank you, Doctor."

The doctor turned with a nod and walked away.

"Adrian," Zack said hesitantly. "Are you okay?"

"No," Adrian said quietly, "I'm not. I'm tired. I'm scared, and I'm worried. So no, Zack, I'm not okay. In fact, I'm very far away from being okay."

"Mr. Petrakis?"

Adrian looked up to see a nursing assistant looking around the waiting area. She held a plastic bag in her hand. When she saw Adrian's raised hand, she came over to where he was standing.

"Mr. Petrakis," the woman said. She held out the bag. "I didn't think you'd want to leave your sister's personal belongings behind. I packed up her clothes, jewelry, wallet, and her other personal items. I thought you'd rather keep them for her."

"Thank you."

The woman turned to leave, but stopped. "I should also tell you that when we were taking her jewelry and clothes off, her pendant broke off the chain. I put it in a small baggie for you. It's inside with the other items."

"Thank you."

"I should take you home," Zack said. "I think the doctor is right... you need to get some rest."

"I'll sleep here," Adrian said, shaking his head. "I want to be near Annelise."

"I don't think that's such a good idea," Zack replied. "You heard what the doctor said. There's nothing you can do, and you won't get any sleep in these plastic chairs."

Adrian looked around the waiting room and bit his lip.

"Let me take you back to Annelise's house at least," Zack offered. "Or you can stay here if it makes you feel better. I can stay with you, or

I can get blankets and pillows, or I can just stay home. Whatever you need."

Adrian nodded, attempting to blink away tears.

"Do you want to stay here?" Zack asked.

Adrian didn't answer.

"Do you want me to take you back to Annelise's? Or I can drive you back to Seattle to your own apartment if you'd rather."

"No," Adrian muttered. "I think I should stay close." He wiped his eyes. "You're right, I can't stay here for the next two days. Take me to Annelise's. I'll stay there until we know something more."

Zack patted Adrian on the back before leading him out into the parking lot where his black truck was parked. Zack opened the door for him while Adrian climbed into the passenger's seat.

"I'm texting Lily," Adrian said. Zack climbed into the truck. "I'm letting her know what the doctor said."

Zack drove out of the parking lot. They didn't speak. Adrian sat looking directly out the passenger's window, silently crying.

"Zack," Adrian said quietly, "can I ask a favor?"

Zack looked over. "Anything."

"Can I spend the night at your place?" Adrian's voice was soft. "I don't want to be alone right now. I don't think I can handle it."

Zack reached over and put his hand on Adrian's leg. He gave it several reassuring pats. "Of course."

"Do you think Annelise is going to be all right?" Adrian asked.

"I know what you know," Zack answered. "The doctors said all of her signs were good. We'll know more soon."

"I know what *they* told me," Adrian said. "I wanted to know what you thought."

Zack glanced over at him. "I don't know," he answered softly.

"I want to know what the hell that thing was," Adrian said. "Why did it come after Annelise? And why do I feel that this is all tied into the same bullshit you were telling me this morning?"

"I think we should wait until we get back to my house," Zack said with a cautious sigh. "We'll be there in five minutes. I think you'll need a strong drink first."

Adrian reached into his pants pocket and withdrew the vaporizer. He inhaled deeply.

"I think I'm ready to start listening now," Adrian said. "I'm about as relaxed as I'm going to get."

Zack turned the truck into his driveway.

"What do you want to know?" Zack gave in. "It'll be easier if you just start to ask questions."

"What the hell was that thing that attacked my sister?" Adrian asked.

"Well," Zack replied, "I'm not really sure. Let's say it was something evil. What do you remember about it?"

Adrian stopped to think.

"Only what I told the police," he answered. "I know it wasn't some psycho freak in a mask."

"Good," Zack said.

"Why the hell is it coming after Annelise?" Adrian took another toke off the vaporizer. "And what does this have to do with all the Greek god shit you mentioned this morning?"

"It *is* tied together," Zack said. He parked the truck under the house and turned off the engine, then shifted to face Adrian directly.

"How?" Adrian insisted. "How are they tied together…and why?"

"Okay," Zack said. "From what I can tell, that creature was some sort of ancient monster."

"That much I got," Adrian interrupted him. Echidna's shadowy form flashed through his mind. "I figured that out when I saw the dragon's body…and spiked tail."

"I'm not sure what it was," Zack replied. "I don't know. All I can tell you is that it is something evil that is drawn to those of us that have this kind of power."

"How do you know?" Adrian insisted. "Have you dealt with this kind of thing before?"

"Yes and no. Like the gods themselves, these creatures don't die. They fade and become something else. I have dealt with spirits and entities before, but this was something more malevolent than anything I've ever seen."

"Why?"

"I don't know why," Zack answered. "Like I said, from what I can tell, this creature is more ancient, more powerful, and more deadly than anything I've come across."

Zack got out of the truck and closed the door. Adrian quickly followed, his mind racing with questions.

"How did you throw those thunderbolts?" Adrian said when they reached the top of the stairs.

Zack smiled. "I wasn't sure if you saw that or not."

"How could I not?" Adrian asked. "They flew right by my head."

"Those—well, being able to do that is one of my powers," Zack admitted. "Like healing is one of yours. That's how I knew you could save Annelise's life."

"Some good that did me."

Zack opened the door. "You saved her life. You do know that, right? If you hadn't started healing her immediately, she would have died. And believe me, if I'm right about what I suspect that thing was, Annelise's death would have only been the beginning of her suffering."

"What does that mean?" Adrian walked in and threw himself onto the sofa.

"A lot," Zack said. "There's so much more in our world than what we can see. Think back to your mythology; there's always a grain of truth somewhere in those stories. More often than not, there's more truth than we know or give credence to."

"So you're saying there are giants, and gremlins, and ghosts?"

"Yes," Zack replied. "But not necessarily in the same way we think of them. Giants are now just people that are much taller than the average person. Gremlins are little spirits that didn't have much power to begin with and are usually simple mischief-makers. I think ghosts are self-explanatory."

"And all these monsters are floating around out there? Why can't we see them?"

"They exist on different levels. There are a lot of parallel worlds that overlap. Sometimes they have minor effects on each other, sometimes they have a lot more," Zack explained. "Most people don't see these creatures because they aren't trained to, or they wouldn't believe what they were seeing because they've been told such things don't exist. It's the way these things have evolved and developed, a kind of illusion for human eyesight. The same way that your mind is pushing you to remember a man in a mask instead of the monster that was actually there. When I mention the creature, you get a quick flash of it in your mind. I'm willing to bet that your memory of what you saw is fading quickly now...until I mention it again."

Adrian thought, trying to summon the memory of the hideous creature attacking his sister. Only brief flashes of a human's face and a blurred body came to mind. He tried to keep the images, but they faded almost instantly.

"If you ask Lily what she saw, she'll tell you what you reported to the police; she saw a man in a mask. People don't *want* to see the unexplainable. That doesn't mean these things don't exist." Zack continued, "You and I are different. We have a stronger recollection than the average person not just because of our background, but because we were there experiencing it. Since you're only newly aware of it, the power to see through the illusion is still weak." He hesitated. "And something caused that creature's illusion to shatter. That thing has some powerful magic...but so did whatever shattered her illusion. We might not have even seen her true form had that not happened."

Zack walked around the back of the sofa. "Would you like that drink now?"

"Nope. Still good," Adrian replied, his nerves raw. He toked on the vaporizer.

Zack poured himself a large tumbler of Scotch and sat down in the rocking chair.

"Look." He tried again. "I know you want all the answers now. That's not how it works. There's lots of stuff I don't understand." He took a deep breath. "I'll start at the beginning." Zack drank the rest of the liquor and held the glass's rim by the tips of his fingers. "Okay," he said. "This is what I know. The ancient Greek gods had lots of offspring. Like any other hereditary trait, certain powers and talents get passed on with each generation, sort of like blond or black hair, and green or blue eyes. There seems to be a reclusive recessive gene that rarely gets passed on, and that's the one that gives us certain abilities. It's very rare, but when it does occur, it can be extremely dominant."

Adrian kicked off his shoes, making himself at home. Leaning back into the cushion, he put the vaporizer to his lips and took another deep inhale.

"What are we?" Adrian asked. "Mutants? X-Men?"

"Not quite, but similar in a way." Zack continued, "It's a recessive gene trait that gives us more than the usual talents. It's also what allows us to heal faster, become more in tune with our artistic abilities, and also, in most circumstances, recognize this gene in other people."

"And that's why I now see these lights around you and Annelise?"

"Wyre-lights," Zack informed him. "I call them wyre-lights, but yes, that is why you see them. And what I told you earlier is true, you will grow accustomed to them and you'll learn to see with a sharper set of eyes."

"When you put your hands over my eyes yesterday morning," Adrian asked. "How come I only started seeing them after that?"

"It was only a matter of time before you started seeing them on your own," Zack explained. "I only helped you develop the ability faster because I thought you were ready. I thought that you would let me help you. If I rushed you and I was wrong, I'm sorry."

"So who was the other woman at the party?" Adrian asked. "Pandora?"

Zack looked at him curiously. "What woman? You had me on the back porch refilling glasses most of the night. I didn't see the majority of the guests."

"She was this French woman," Adrian said. "I caught her zoning out when I offered her a drink. She had these, what did you call them, wyre-lights around her."

"Did you know this woman?" Zack sat up, very interested. "Have you ever seen her before?"

Adrian thought a moment. "No."

"When did you see her? What did she look like? Was she at the party later on? Did you see her talking to Annelise at any time?"

"She was dressed in a red skirt and a white top." Adrian paused to remember. "She had black curly hair and had a French accent. That's all I got."

"Did you see her talking to Annelise at all?"

"No," Adrian answered after careful thought. "I was kind of busy, and I wasn't really paying attention."

"The lights around her," Zack asked. "Were they strong?"

"What?"

"Did the wyre-lights pulse, or were they solid? Were they bright or dull?" Zack asked insistently.

"I don't know." Adrian struggled to remember. "Solid and bright, I think? I don't have much experience to go on, remember?"

"She was at the party," Zack muttered half-aloud. "She was stalking...Annelise. When you spoke to her, did you touch her at all? Brush her skin or touch her hand or anything like that?"

"No," Adrian said. "She kept her hands folded under her arms. I thought she was being a pretentious snob. Why? Is that important?"

"She must have lured Annelise into the corner of the parking lot," Zack muttered aloud. His voice seemed far away. "Annelise must have touched her, and that's why her illusion was shattered." Zack looked at Adrian. "That's how I knew who you and Annelise were when we first met; we shook hands, and I picked up on it."

"How come I didn't?" Adrian asked.

"You probably did somehow," Zack replied. "You weren't aware of what you were experiencing."

Adrian thought back to their first meeting. The erotic daydream when they first met came rushing back to his mind; the image of Zack massaging his shoulders, and their passionate kiss replayed. It had been so real...he remembered feeling flushed from it.

"Wait." Adrian sat up. "Annelise and Yvonne had an argument, and they got nasty with each other. Both of them were pissed off."

"Anything else? Wasn't Lily complaining about Annelise, too?"

"Right after that," Adrian said. "We were all on the back porch, remember?"

"Divide and conquer," Zack muttered aloud.

"What?"

"It makes sense," Zack said. He shook his head. "The creature started poisoning Annelise earlier. She must have used the French woman's skin as a costume."

"It was wearing someone else's skin?" Adrian made a face. "That's disgusting."

"She must have used some sort of magic to get Annelise pissed off at everyone else."

"This is all too much for me," Adrian said. "I'm tired. My head is pounding and I can see the sky getting lighter through the curtains. I need to get some sleep."

"I agree." Zack was distracted, still lost in thought. "The guest room is still set up. You know where the towels are, so if there's anything you need, help yourself."

"Try to get some sleep," Zack suggested with a yawn, and went into the kitchen.

"Zack," Adrian timidly called after him. "Can I sleep with you tonight? Nothing sexual, that's the last thing on my mind right now. I…I don't want to be alone. Do you mind?"

"Sure." Zack nodded.

After a quick shower, Adrian climbed into bed behind Zack.

"Thank you," Adrian whispered. He gently pecked Zack on the nape of his neck and rolled over onto his side, turning his back to him.

Zack turned over and draped his arm over Adrian's side. He let Adrian curl into his shape. It wasn't long before Adrian's breath became regular and he was in deep sleep. Zack lay there for several moments longer. Slowly, he withdrew his arm and slid from the bed.

Zack pulled on a pair of gray shorts and snuck out of the bedroom. His body was exhausted, but his mind was racing. He poured himself another tumbler of Scotch and paced the living room floor. He opened the curtains of the glass doors and stepped out onto the back deck.

The sun was already peeking through the lower tree branches. Zack could feel the heat rising. He closed his eyes and took a deep breath, letting out a whistle. The air around him went still. A giant eagle flew down from its nest in the treetop. It hopped on the deck before folding its wings.

"Find the creature's nest," Zack said. "Look in caves along the coastline, and search the forests. Be aware for any magical concealments and watch for traps. My faithful Aetos, when you find the lair, come back at once."

The eagle raised its head and flew off.

Zack went back inside, going over to the fireplace. He put both hands on the mantel and looked up into the painting of the minotaur. The black eyes stared back from the demigod's face.

Zack quickly found the small box of matches he kept on the mantel. He struck a match, letting the warm glow illuminate the picture with flickering light. He lit the blue candles on either side of the painting and braced himself against the mantel with both palms. He took a deep breath, closed his eyes, and lowered his head in reverence.

"Brother," Zack said solemnly. "I need your help."

The minotaur's head slowly turned until the black eyes were

looking directly at Zack in the candlelight. The strong arms moved from the sides of the throne, the black bands around the biceps restricting the strong muscle. The silver buckles of the leather harness glinted. One dark crimson nipple poked out from the leather strap crossing the broad chest. The demigod uncrossed his thick animal legs, placing both hooves flat in front of the throne.

"Why have you called?" The voice was a low, deep baritone.

"Something has attacked," Zack explained. "Something I don't understand."

"The Earth was raped," the rumbling voice explained. "Tartarus has been opened."

"Tartarus?" Zack asked. "That still exists?"

"What the gods create, nothing can destroy."

"How could anything have survived that prison after so many centuries?"

"Sealed from the world and sustained by the eternity of the curse that placed her there."

"Her?" Zack felt his heart skip a beat. His chest tightened and he held his breath. "What was released?"

He could feel sweat breaking across his brow.

"The Mother of all Monsters," the bull-headed god answered. "Echidna, the last of the Titans, is free."

CHAPTER TWENTY-FOUR

A drian woke with a start. His hand slammed into the empty space next to him, and he sat up in a strange bed. At first glance, he didn't know where he was; then the room came into focus. The events of last night returned to him, and he remembered coming back to Zack's. The nightstand alarm clock read 10:42 a.m. Adrian leaned over the side of the bed and took out his cell phone. There were two text messages from Marcus. He opened them.

The first message was a listing of what was wrong.

Broken tibia on left, broken right collarbone with badly sprained forearm. Two cracked ribs, black eye, bruised face, and missing tooth.

The second message was a picture showing the damage. Marcus was propped up in a hospital bed, his left leg in a cast resting on a trapeze hoisted above by a pulley. A sling held the cast on his right arm, his left hand raised in a peace sign. The left eye was swollen shut. Marcus managed to smile through it all.

Underneath it read: *You should see the other guy. Where the hell are you?*

Adrian smiled. He texted back: *Stuck in Kingston. Not been a good weekend for friends/family. I'll be in touch ASAP. Sending love.*

Adrian slid out of bed and pulled on his shorts. With a stifled yawn he padded his way to the closed bedroom door. He reached for the doorknob and paused when he heard voices from the other side. The first was definitely Zack's, but the other was deeper. Adrian could only understand a few random words. He pressed his ear to the door carefully. The muffled words continued and then silence. A moment later he heard a coffee grinder and knew the conversation was over. Hesitantly, he walked into the main room.

Adrian looked around, seeing only Zack puttering in the kitchen. Zack turned around, a frying pan in his hand. "Morning," he said. "Sleep okay?"

"Yes," Adrian said. "Thanks."

"Coffee is brewing," Zack said. "Milk is on the table. I wasn't sure if you wanted breakfast or lunch. I can make eggs and bacon or I can grill two chicken breasts. Neither one will take much time."

"How long have you been up?" Adrian stood in the open doorway of the kitchen.

"About an hour or so. Is something wrong?"

"No," Adrian said. "I just thought I heard voices before I came out of the bedroom."

"You did." Zack opened the refrigerator door and took out a package of bacon.

"Did they leave?" Adrian asked.

"Not exactly," Zack answered.

Adrian watched him frying bacon, waiting for him to say something more.

"Look, I'm not in the mood to play games," Adrian started. "Can you level with me and tell me what's going on?"

"It's not that easy," Zack said. "There's a lot more going on here than you realize; a lot more than even I realized. I'm having trouble understanding it, never mind trying to explain it to you."

"Why don't you at least try?"

Zack met Adrian's eyes. "I'll tell you what I've learned," he said. "But let's eat first. Have a seat and let me finish here. I'll have pancakes up in a minute."

Adrian sat on the couch, crossing his arms, waiting for Zack to finish. When Zack came over with two plates of food, Adrian realized how hungry he was. He shoveled a few bites into his mouth while casting sideways glances at the rocking chair and waiting for Zack to speak. After several more bites, Adrian pushed the plate away and settled back into the couch.

"What attacked Annelise wasn't just a simple little evil fairy. It's much more than that." Zack took a sip of coffee. "I consulted with someone and was given more information about what we're up against."

"Just tell me!"

"We're up against a god."

"So if you're descended from a god," Adrian said, "and I'm allegedly descended from one, don't we outnumber this bitch?"

"It's not that easy," Zack said. "We are talking about one of the most ancient and primal deities ever to exist. Somehow she escaped her prison and has come back."

"What prison?" Adrian asked. "Who is she? And what did she do to be put into prison in the first place?"

"She was imprisoned before humans walked the Earth."

"What are you talking about?"

"When the world was created there were only two forces," Zack explained. "Heaven and Earth, Uranus and Gaia. Chaos was the first of their offspring and, being unisexual, Chaos impregnated itself, creating horrific spirits that roamed the world, destroying all in their way. The next offspring of Uranus and Gaia were the Titans."

"Okay," Adrian interrupted. "I know enough about the Greek myths to remember the stories of Cronus, the Titans, the Olympian gods, and most of the heroes and monsters. So what the hell broke out of prison?"

Zack took a deep breath and paused before answering.

"It is Echidna, the mother of all living evil. She's a goddess in her own right. She and her brother, Typhaeon, were the first Titans, and nothing like their later, more human siblings. Echidna is mother to several offspring including creatures like Chimera and giant pythons."

Adrian said nothing as the hideous monsters from his dreams and drawings flashed through his mind.

"I don't care if she's Mary, mother of Jesus Christ," Adrian said. "There's only one of this thing, and two of us. We need to hunt down this French bitch and kill her."

"You don't understand," Zack said. "First of all, the French woman was only an illusion used to conceal Echidna's true form. The truth is, she could be anywhere in the world by now. And there's the little thing of her being practically immortal."

"'Practically' is not definitely," Adrian answered. "That's good enough for me. Let's kill her."

Zack smiled. "It's not that easy."

"How did she get here in the first place?" Adrian asked.

"There are Universal portals that naturally exist," Zack explained. "Most of those were destroyed or shut down many eons ago."

"She got here somehow," Adrian persisted. "That means at least one still exists. Let's find this Enchilada thing and kill her."

"Her name is pronounced E—keyed—nah," Zack said with a smile. "You should know the name of what you're up against."

"Echidna. Whatever. How did she get here?"

"Remember that oceanic drilling a month or so ago?" Zack asked.

"The one that caused that major underwater earthquake," Adrian responded. "I remember."

"They were more accurate than they knew when they called it the death of Mother Earth," Zack said. "They dug too deep and somehow sent a tremor into a different ethereal plane. With Gaia so weakened, Tartarus became vulnerable, and somehow, Echidna broke free."

"If she got out she can be put back in," Adrian argued. "There's got to be a way. Everything can be killed, right?"

"That's kind of my point," Zack insisted. "The gods didn't die. Their attributes were passed to their offspring, and those powers have been diluted."

"Aren't there other portals to wherever she is?" Adrian pushed on. "The way she got here was by accident. It couldn't have been the only one left in the universe."

"There are other portals," Zack answered. "With enough magic and very pronounced craftsmanship, they can be opened. They are rare and only lead to and from the Underworld. She could be anywhere in any world. For all we know she might have returned to her nest, content with the damage she's already done. Who knows? We'll have to wait until she makes herself known again."

"There's got to be a way to find her." Adrian put the coffee cup down and stood up. "I can't stand by and do nothing while Annelise lies sleeping in a coma."

Zack leaned forward, putting his coffee mug on the table. "That's it. Your sister is the key," he said. "Annelise is trapped, literally."

"I don't like the sound of that," Adrian said.

"No," Zack said. "That's what is going to help us find her. Assuming Echidna resurfaced when the drilling broke through, then she's only been back in this world for a month or so at most. Unless she's feasted on a lot of very strong descendants of the gods, her magic can't be that powerful."

"How many 'very strong descendants' are there?" Adrian asked.

"As I said before, there could be millions of descendants running around the world. The numbers that would be considered 'very strong' are much fewer. And even fewer of those few descendants ever realize their true potential."

"Get to the point," Adrian said. "Are there enough in this area?"

"I don't know." Zack pounded the arm of the chair for emphasis. "There's no way of telling. It's not like there's a club with a membership roster. I live a pretty secluded life on the island. I don't meet a lot of new people. Wyre-lights aren't popping up around everyone's shoulders. That's not the point I'm trying to make."

A loud, high-pitched sound came from the back of the house. Adrian looked up to see a larger-than-average golden bald eagle swooping across the deck. It flew out of sight before returning, gracefully landing on the deck's edge. The bird folded its wings and peered through the glass at the two men, cocking its head. It resumed its frantic chirping.

Zack stood up and went to the sliding door. He opened the door, stepping out onto the deck. He reached into a metal box tucked into the deck's corner, withdrew a dead rat by its tail, and tossed it in the air. The eagle stretched and caught the rodent in its sharp beak. The majestic bird chirped a few more times and flew away back into the trees.

"You have a trained eagle?" Adrian asked as Zack came back inside.

"What? Oh no," Zack replied. "That's Aetos."

"You have an eagle as a pet?" Adrian asked. "Is that legal?"

"Aetos is not exactly a pet," Zack explained. "If you know what a familiar is, that's closer to what he is to me. It's easier to say that he and I know each other and have built trust between us."

Adrian gazed out the glass doors. The eagle was sitting on a tree branch.

"He's already found Echidna's nest," Zack said.

"Really? How? Where is it? Let's go kill her!"

"The nest is deserted," Zack explained. "Aetos followed traces of her magic until he found where she was hiding. She put a tornado elemental in place, keeping everything away until she could escape.

Aetos found it along the shoreline cliffs of Myrtle Edwards Park. It was pretty heavily scented and not difficult to find once the wind elemental dissipated."

"Where did she go?"

"If she's abandoned her nest," Zack said, "that's not a good sign."

"Maybe she just went out," Adrian suggested.

"No," Zack answered. "It doesn't work that way. She's a magical creature and needs to have a lair to regenerate and recharge. There's only so much she can do in this world until she reaches a certain level."

"A certain level?" Adrian asked. "What is she, a third-level druid with chaotic powers? If she's weak, then that's the time to attack. Why wait until she builds up resilience? For that matter, how does she build up resilience?"

"By eating," Zack answered bluntly. "Like you, she's not used to how her powers and magic work in this world. That can be our saving grace. She'll have to find others with the magical bloodline in order to regain any real strength."

"Yeah," Adrian said. "But you said there could be hundreds of us around."

"Yes. That's the problem. And we have no idea as to how many she's found."

"How do we find her?" Adrian demanded.

"That's another issue," Zack said. "We'll have to go check out her nest. Hopefully she left something behind, a trace."

"What's a trace?" Adrian asked.

"If we can find something that has her essence on it," Zack explained, "we can use it to find out where she is. We need to find something she touched or marked. Hopefully she was careless and we can find something in her lair."

"My head is starting to hurt," Adrian said. "How can we use that against her?"

"We don't," Zack answered. "You do."

CHAPTER TWENTY-FIVE

"What do you mean, 'I do'?" Adrian said.

"We need to use your powers," Zack explained. "When we find something of Echidna's to use as a trace."

"My powers?" Adrian scoffed.

"Yeah," Zack insisted. "You're descended from the god of prophecy, vision, and healing, among his other attributes. But we need to have some sort of object that absorbed some of the monster's energy."

"Like what?" Adrian asked.

"Something she kept near to her," Zack listed. "It could be anything."

Adrian snapped to a sitting position. "You know, when the nurse gave me Annelise's belongings, I didn't think anything of it."

He retrieved the heavy dark blue plastic bag he'd brought in last night. The hospital's name was clearly printed on the side. He dumped its contents onto the table and quickly sifted through the miscellaneous items. He found the plastic zipper bag with the apple pendant inside.

"I thought it was odd when the nurse mentioned it," Adrian said. He held up the baggie by the plastic zipper top. "Annelise rarely wears jewelry except for a couple of rings our mother left her. I've never seen her with a necklace. I just thought it was some sort of gift from a client or one of the artists there last night, so she felt like she had to wear it or something."

Zack leaned in and scrutinized the baggie.

"Please put that down on the table," he said. "And go stand by the mantel."

"Why?" Adrian asked.

Zack disappeared into the kitchen. Adrian could hear a drawer opening, and Zack reappeared and stood in the kitchen doorway with a black cloth draped across his open palm.

"I'll explain it all in a minute. Please put the baggie down on the table and stand by the mantel."

Adrian felt his patience giving way. He dropped the baggie onto the table and stood up. He marched over to the mantel, folding his arms tightly across his chest.

Zack used the black cloth to pick up the baggie. Holding it safely in his palm, Zack folded the material around the pendant and put it on the mantel in front of the painted minotaur.

Zack sat back down in the chair, motioning for Adrian to return to the couch.

"Is that what you needed?" Adrian asked. He nodded toward the cloth-wrapped baggie. "Is that what you were asking about?"

"I think so," Zack answered confidently. "If you had such a strong reaction so quickly, I'm guessing that thing is full of dark magic."

"Reaction?" Adrian gazed back at the wrapped baggie.

"As soon as you held it up I saw the wyre-lights around it," Zack said. "I'm surprised you didn't. Maybe that's because it was already working on you."

"How?"

"It's an Apple of Discordia," Zack explained. "Remember the story of Paris and the Golden Apple? Its sole purpose is to cause chaos and disruption to anyone that touches it."

"Let me guess how it works," Adrian replied. "By causing them to pick fights and start arguments for stupid reasons?"

Zack nodded.

"Add that to Annelise's natural gift to be overly angsty on opening nights, and it explains why she picked fights with Yvonne, Lily, and me."

"Exactly," Zack confirmed. "I'm willing to bet Echidna somehow threw the apple in Annelise's way."

"And if the nurse at the hospital gave it to me," Adrian concluded, "then Annelise must have had it on her for several hours."

"That would be long enough for it to have a strong hold on her," Zack said.

"So how do we use it to find this monster Titan thing?"

"'We' being the very important word there," Zack answered.

He went back to the mantel. At the far end sat a squat oil burner in the shape of a Greek urn. He retrieved the small brass burner, along with the box of matches and the wrapped apple pendant, and placed all three items on the table. Sitting on the chair's edge, he leaned over the small collection. After removing the lid, Zack lit the oil floating in the brazier's shallow bottom. The liquid shimmered in flames.

"This is going to be quick," Zack explained. "I'm going to drop the pendant into the flame and I need you to relax your mind and tell me what you see."

"Why does it have to be me?" Adrian asked. "Can't you do it?"

"You're the god of vision," Zack repeated. "It's your sister that is under the enchantment. Only you can trace the spell."

"I don't know what I'm doing," Adrian said.

"Yeah, you do," Zack insisted. "You just don't know it yet."

Zack picked up the black cloth. He undid the folds until the plastic baggie was exposed. Making sure his skin never touched it, he used the cloth to open the zipper top. Squeezing the ends together he forced the baggie open, turned it over, and let the apple drop into the flames of the brazier.

The pendant hit the oil. The flames became green, with a dark emerald center. A low-grade whistling emerged from the magical fire.

"It won't last long," Zack instructed. "Look into the center and tell me what you see."

Adrian looked into the wildly dancing flames. Dark sharp angles rose up, forming burning green mountain peaks with dark centers. The points became the jagged turrets of a castle as the picture flashed in the fire. The building loomed above the ground, uninviting and foreboding.

"I see a tall building," Adrian called out. His eyes became transfixed on the green fire. "It's huge and dark surrounded by mountains. There's nothing around it but wasteland, swamps, and a single wide shadowy road that leads to it."

"What else?" Zack encouraged him.

Adrian strained his eyes, trying to see more details. The castle's silhouette imploded and crumbled back into the brazier. The fires burned dark before transforming into another shape.

"I see Annelise," Adrian said. He readjusted his position on the sofa's edge, leaning closer to the fire. "She's walking, slowly, looking around. I think she's trying to find something."

"Any idea of what?"

"I don't know," Adrian replied. "She's just walking and looking around. Wait."

Something stirred in the magical fires burning around his sister's image. Two small almond shapes rose on either side.

"Something's moving," Adrian said. "They look like seed pods on their sides."

The oval beads slowly shimmered in the dark. Suddenly, they flashed open.

"They're eyes!" Adrian called out. "They're watching her. They're watching her!"

The fire suddenly withdrew into the brazier and disappeared. Only the pendant remained, sitting in the oil at the bottom. The apple was burned black.

Adrian sat back on the couch, panting. A light perspiration had broken out on his forehead and cheekbones. "What the hell was that?"

"From what you said you saw," Zack answered, "it was the Dark Palace."

"And where is that?" Adrian said.

"The Underworld."

"You say that so easily," Adrian said. "Do you mean, like hell?"

"The Underworld has had many names depending on who is ruling it at the time," Zack explained. He sat back down in the rocking chair. "What you see there also depends on who is doing the looking. To a devout Christian, it would be fire and brimstone. To the Greeks, an Underworld with the River Styx, a ferryman, and the Dark Palace."

"And that's where we need to go?"

"First of all," Zack said firmly, "*we* aren't going anywhere. It's too dangerous and you're not experienced enough. I'm going alone."

"No way!"

"Adrian," Zack said. "This isn't some sort of game. This is the Underworld, and you have no idea what you're up against."

"From what you said," Adrian snapped back, "neither do you. It's my sister, and I'm going."

"It's not a good idea." Zack spoke slowly. "You're not going."

"It's not really all your choice, now is it?" Adrian lowered his voice.

Slowly, Zack's arms became stiff and held at an angle from his body, palms facing outward. The light in the room seemed to be sucked away, tiny brief currents flashing around his body. The hairs on his arms stood up. He lowered his head, keeping his lightning-filled eyes locked on Adrian.

"I said no." Zack's voice rolled like thunder.

Zack seemed to grow in height, towering high in the room. All light ceased to exist other than the natural aura running rapidly around his body. Dark clouds gathered across the high wooden ceilings, thunder rolling from within them. Flashes of lightning speared randomly across the roof.

Adrian's eyes grew wide with awe, his mouth hanging open. The light rippled down Zack's arms and across his naked chest.

"Listen." Zack's deep voice thundered. "You are not ready. You will stay here, and that is it!"

Adrian leapt to his feet, driven by a force beyond his control. He took a deep breath, his body filling with an immense heat that burned through him like wildfire, igniting every nerve. Pure energy flashed out of every open pore. The light shone brightly, dwarfing the storm's lightning and punching holes in the thunderclouds. The raw power made Adrian feel as if he were a giant. Each muscle expanded, becoming large and tight. His feet pushed beyond the floor and down into the very root of the earth. Renewed vigor flooded through his veins. He looked Zack in the eyes.

"She's my sister, and I'm going!"

Zack was forced a step back. The lightning stopped. The thunderclouds dissolved, and he briefly stumbled before falling back into the chair.

Adrian felt his knees buckle beneath him. He fell back onto the couch and lay sprawled, panting against the cushions of the couch.

"Well," Zack said through heavy, short breaths. "I'm guessing you're more in tune with your power than I originally thought. That feeling of twitching going through your body will stop in a few moments. You eventually get used to it until you don't feel it anymore. I'd almost forgotten what that was like."

"What the hell was it?" Adrian gasped.

"A brief glimpse of Apollo," was the answer.

"I'm going with you." Adrian returned to the argument.

"After that display, I'm not going to argue with you anymore," Zack said. "But there's a lot you still need to learn."

Zack stood and walked over to the mantel. He kept his back to the couch, bracing both hands on the edge in front of the two blue burning candles. He lifted his head up to the Minotaur.

"Great Brother." Zack spoke reverently. "It is time."

He stepped back until he was standing next to Adrian. The Minotaur once again became animated within the borders of the painting. Its bull's head turned and the black reflective eyes focused on the two men. The demigod shifted on its throne and, using the Trident clutched tightly in its left hand, pushed itself to a standing position.

The Trident was made of dark silver metal. The three prongs were grouped together to form more of a triangular pattern. The center prong stood out more than either of the other two. All three were capped with what looked like razor-sharp arrowheads.

A dull yellow glow surrounded the Minotaur's hand. The color intensified along with the light's strength and brightness. The creature's entire palm was illuminated in gold. The reflection expanded until a translucent door appeared on the outside of the painting's frame. As easily as if pushing open a window, the Minotaur moved his hand forward and the doorway swung outward. A set of stairs made of light unfolded from the top of the mantel, ending at Zack's feet.

"If you think I'm going first, you're crazy."

Zack smiled. Without hesitation he stepped up and began to climb. The Minotaur moved aside and Zack entered the painting. He embraced the Minotaur for several long moments. They broke the hug, keeping their hands on each other's shoulders, and pressed their foreheads together. The two held the position for another minute before Zack disappeared behind the throne. The Minotaur slowly turned its head to Adrian, waiting.

Adrian swallowed his fear. He stepped into the painting.

The Minotaur drew a tight counterclockwise circle with his palm. The stairs folded onto themselves and disappeared. The open translucent door shut and the golden light around his hand dulled and became extinguished.

Zack's home disappeared from view.

Adrian stood still, too intimidated to move. The great beast focused his black eyes on him. Adrian closed his eyes but could feel the demigod's stare. When he opened his eyes, the Minotaur was still staring, and Adrian could see the benevolence within the eyes. The Minotaur opened his muscular arms and wrapped them around Adrian.

The demigod's body radiated immense heat. The coarse hair of the chest, arms, and legs scratched Adrian's skin. The strong hands slid up his back. The Minotaur broke their embrace, allowing his hands to move to Adrian's shoulders. Their eyes met, and Adrian felt exposed and vulnerable. The demigod lowered his head until their foreheads touched.

"Do you fear me?" The god's voice rumbled low.

Adrian wasn't sure if the Minotaur spoke or if he heard the rich voice only in his mind. The intense smells of animal musk and leather filled his nostrils. His blood warmed as it raced through his veins. He took a breath, barely waiting a moment before answering.

"I am hesitant of you," Adrian answered. "I do not fear you."

"Do you swear to finish this quest, no matter what?"

"To swear to an uncertain thing is a foolish act," Adrian slowly replied.

"You show thought before action," the Minotaur said. "The true seeds of wisdom, and the first important steps of your journey."

The Bull God lifted his head away from Adrian's forehead, breaking contact. Smoke curled out of the bull's nose and around the silver ring that hung from its septum. It snorted and jutted his head for Adrian to go behind the throne.

Adrian walked around the great throne. There was a small space behind and a closed door on the back wall. Adrian strode over, opening it without hesitation.

CHAPTER TWENTY-SIX

Beyond the Minotaur's throne was a perfectly square chamber. The room was filled with only stark white and pitch black. The tiles on the floor alternated the two colors like a giant chessboard. The walls on either side were reflectively white while the ones in front and behind were polished black. A lantern hung in each corner. The ceiling was dark, glowing pinpoints of light creating the constellations of gods, monsters, and heroes. Toward the far end of the room two pillars stretched to the ceiling; the left one iridescent white, the other column dark ebony.

Adrian found himself clothed. His sandaled feet softly padded on the tiles as he crossed the room. A leather kilt was fitted around his waist, the long pleats hanging down to just above his knees. He wore a light blue mesh shirt. Over the shirt he wore a sleeveless leather vest. The emblem of a blazing sun was embroidered over the chest.

Finely lined designs drawn on the walls with crushed amethyst stones glinted in the dim lighting. The wall behind him showed a giant skull with its mouth gaping open. One of the teeth was a door, barely distinguishable from the others. On the right wall was drawn the tarot card of the Fool: a figure walking forward with a blindfold over his eyes, about to step off the edge of a cliff. On the opposite wall were two detached hands, hovering at the base of a roaring fire. The fingers pointed toward the flames. A glowing infinity symbol hovered over the fire. Eyes gazed out from the center of the flames.

Adrian crossed the room to the giant pillars. Zack stood in front of the black column on the right. He wore a similar leather tunic and sandals. His shirt was a darker blue. The emblem on Zack's tunic was an eagle with its wings fully spread, clutching lightning bolts in its talons.

"Where are we?" Adrian asked.

"The Temple of the Minotaur," Zack answered. "He is a Sentinel of the Crossroads and can open a portal to the Underworld."

"Why do I feel that his questions were tests?" Adrian asked.

"Because they were."

"What would have happened if I didn't pass?"

"The Minotaur would have impaled you on the Trident," Zack answered. "Then he would have ripped you apart with his bare hands."

"You aren't serious."

"Adrian," Zack said. "I tried to tell you, this isn't a ticket to Disneyland. This isn't a game. If something goes wrong here, there's no replay. If you die…you're dead. There are dangers here beyond anything you can imagine. Believe me, it's better to be ripped apart by the Minotaur than to fall into the hands of anything that might be potentially waiting for us."

"Then let's find Annelise and get the hell out of here."

The Minotaur stepped in front of them.

"Your armor is made from the skin of the Giant Pallas." The Minotaur's deep voice rumbled. "The hide is magic and will protect you well."

The Minotaur sauntered over to the black column behind Zack. He planted his hooves firmly on the ground, snorted deeply, and raised the Trident in his hand. He grunted and tapped the weapon's shaft three times at the column's base. A panel appeared at the base of the column. The Minotaur removed two weapons, giving each man a javelin.

The weapon was forged from an extremely lightweight, silver-colored metal that felt to Adrian like it was an extension of his arm. It vibrated in his hand, its power running into him. The razor-sharp points glinted in the dim lighting. On the flat part of the blade was an engraving of the sigil Adrian had painted in his drawing of Bellerophon: an image of the radiant sun and crescent moon conjoined into one face.

The demigod strode over to the white column, again tapping the floor by the pillar. Another panel appeared at the column's base.

The Minotaur retrieved a strung wooden bow and gave it to Adrian. Less than a yard high, the bow was carved from a durable blond wood and decorated with an array of sunbursts. Carved at the center notch were the conjoined planetary faces. The bow's edges curved out and were capped with sharp metal tips. Adrian gently tapped the taut string with the pad of his thumb. It vibrated with a hum.

The Bull God then handed Adrian an arrow quiver with a leather strap so it could hang across his back. The quiver was fully stocked with golden arrows with the white tail feathers of an eagle attached to their ends. Mixed in among the others were three arrows larger than the rest, made from the same lightweight metal as the javelin and tipped with black feathers. Adrian withdrew one and balanced it in his hands. There were two red bands painted on it, one below the tail feathers and the other above the triangular tip.

"Those were forged in the fires of Hephaestus." The Minotaur spoke. "They are tipped with the black feathers of the Erinyes, and charged with their vengeance."

The last thing the Minotaur gave to each man was a small dagger and a shield. The knife was a foot in length and the blade looked sharp. Adrian, like Zack, put the dagger into the sheath and strapped it around his waist. The men strung the shields over their shoulders and onto their backs.

"These weapons are older than the memories of mountains," the Minotaur said. "They are from the original Titanochomy. These are the sacred weapons of the gods. Use them wisely and they will serve you well."

Adrian attached the javelin onto the quiver with a clasp and strung it over his shoulder. The quiver was so light he barely noticed the weight on his back. The bow he held in his left hand, ready for use when needed.

The Minotaur waited until Adrian met his eyes. The demigod's muscled arm reached out and he slowly opened his hand. Sitting in the center of his palm was a silver oval pendant. The design was a swan swimming under a crescent moon; the curve of the bird's neck mirrored that of the moon reflected in the water. The Minotaur nodded, indicating that Adrian should take it.

Adrian took the silver charm. He ran his thumb over the raised design and felt warmth radiating from it.

"This is not for me." Adrian knew this immediately. He looked up and met the Minotaur's gaze. "Who is this for?"

The Bull God held his stare for several long moments.

"When the moon shines where no moon shines," the Minotaur solemnly answered, "plant it at her feet."

"What does that mean?" Adrian asked.

The demigod put his fist out. He turned his hand over and opened his palm to reveal six gold coins.

"Three for each," the Minotaur explained. "To pay the fee of the ferryman."

Zack and Adrian took the coins. The tokens were the size of a half dollar, with the image of a weeping willow engraved on both sides. The men carefully put the coins into the pocket of their leather vests.

The Minotaur took a step forward until he was centered between the two pillars. He stood with his legs evenly spread and his bull's tail sweeping out from underneath the kilt. His took the Trident in both hands and raised it over his head, pointing the silver tip at the floor. With one sweeping motion, he lifted the weapon; a purple light created a glowing arch between the pillars. The crescent hung in the air and the Minotaur rapped the base of the Trident three times on the floor.

The space between the two columns shimmered. A thick, rolling smoke stretched between them from floor to ceiling. The vapor became thicker, and more solid, forming a cloth tapestry hanging between the columns.

A rocky path wound its way through mountainous terrain with high jagged peaks on either side. The path disappeared around a bend.

The Minotaur stepped back. He offered the Trident held tightly in his fist to Zack. Zack hesitantly reached out, his hand trembling, and took the Trident with a respectful nod. The Bull God pointed to the path leading between the pillars and into the tapestry.

"I'm guessing there's no going back?" Adrian whispered.

"Nope," Zack confirmed. "And no way else to go."

Zack held out his arm, offering a hand to Adrian. Adrian accepted the gesture with a slight nod. They took their first steps onto the Road of the Underworld.

CHAPTER TWENTY-SEVEN

E chidna was thrown to the floor of the temple.
      She landed hard, reawakening the pain from the wounds
received from the Olympian's attack. She rolled onto her side, pain
shooting through her body. Bile burned in her stomach. She pressed
herself to the cool tiled floor of the dark sanctuary, waiting for the
nausea to settle. As she lifted her head, the Temple of Hecate swam
into focus.

The three torches were already placed in their proper holders: one
in each corner, burning their dark amethyst flames. In the center of
the room the enormous statue of the three-headed goddess stood on
its pedestal. The three veils hung lifelessly over the lower half of each
stony face. The torch in each of the goddess's hands was extinguished.
Each head faced out into a different corner of the temple. The empty
eyes stared down, coldly disapproving.

Echidna prostrated herself before the statue. Her arms extended
out to her sides and she pressed her palms into the tiles.

"Dark Goddess," she prayed. "I come to you once again, begging
your help and seeking your guidance."

The temple remained still. The acrid scent lingered around her.

"I went forth in haste and underestimated my enemy," Echidna
pleaded. "I seek your help once more."

The statue's pedestal rose from the floor, leaving flame in its
wake. The torches in the goddess's stone hands burst alive with fire.
Dark plum-colored flames cast monstrous shadows on the walls. Gray
marbled color receded from the three faces as flesh emerged. All six
eyes blinked with life. The single neck turned, allowing the heads to

glare at the creature prone before them. The veils fluttered, and the lips moved with speech.

"You throw yourself on holy ground," the Dark Mother's voice rumbled, "when thunder rings all around. Prayers in vain I have heard; you broke your vow and broke your word."

"Ancient One. Great Mother," Echidna said. "The world is not as I remembered. It has changed too much. I went forth too fast with not enough strength."

"The words you speak all sound like lies—you have been a disappointment in my eyes."

"I beg for mercy, my Black Mistress." Echidna's voice wavered in fear. "I can still do what I have promised. I have not yet failed."

"Listen to the words that I have said before you race on your path ahead."

The flames burned low. The temple was cast into an eerie pale purple light. The goddess's eyes burned. Her voice thundered throughout the chamber, echoing off the walls.

"When the ground starts to shake, then the earth shall split and volcanoes give up their fire; for revenge is found when prisoners are freed and their captors feel their ire. Beware the meshing of sun and moon when thunder shakes the skies, for if Heaven shall journey into the World of Night, even the mightiest can die."

"I have imprisoned the spirit of one," Echidna said. "If her body dies, she will be locked here forever. The others will be trapped and I shall kill them here."

"A moon shut in darkness still shines bright," Hecate's statue said. "And lightning still flashes in the sun's light. Open eyes are often blind, and what you see is not what you find."

"I have lured them here," Echidna insisted. "To the Underworld. They are not familiar and will easily be killed. They will go to the Dark Palace and I will attack them there."

Echidna pushed her human torso up by her hands. She lifted her head proudly and looked directly into the stone goddess's eyes. The air was siphoned from the room, leaving dust to settle in Echidna's mouth. Her hands reached for her throat as it closed, choking the breath from her lungs. She rolled onto her back, the dragon's body convulsing on the ground.

"I will grant you one last time, but should you fail, your soul is mine." The three voices of Hecate echoed. "Your imprisonment was torture, that is true. But it is a dream compared to how I shall punish you."

Air rushed into Echidna's lungs. She gasped with a sharp breath.

"I pledge my life to you." She swore her oath. "I shall destroy the Olympian or I shall be destroyed. I bind myself with my vow to you."

"And if your words ring true, a final chance I'll give to you." Hecate's ferocious voice rolled through the temple. "If you do not do as you say, a final curse will come into play."

A chill spread throughout Echidna's body. Her skin itched as if insects were gnawing out from within her veins. She tried to move and found she was bound immobile to the floor.

"My last prophecy I give to you: I shall invoke the ancient rule. This is how you shall repay your debt. This is how the curse is set. Only one or the other shall leave this land, and Death will be given from a godly hand."

"I will kill them," Echidna pledged. "I promise you, I shall kill them all."

The goddess lifted her neck. The three heads returned to staring in their corners. From one of the torches a purple light shot out, igniting the tapestry. The rich plum flames quickly burned the woven rug hanging between the two pillars. The ashes fell into a neat pile. As if stirred by a wind, the ashes flew back up, weaving a new rug with a different design.

The picture of a tower appeared, woven intricately with finely colored thread. A dark-colored road led through marshes up to the gate of a tall, black-bricked tower. The single turret loomed upward into heavy clouds. A storm raged, lightning flashing around the donjon. The path emerged from the tapestry, creating a short ramp from the temple floor.

"Go!" the three sets of lips commanded. "I can help you next and then no more. For you I will open this portal door. And to the Kingdom of the Dead, you shall travel the path ahead."

The three living heads went mute and returned to stone. The veils fluttered briefly before settling. The pedestal slid back into place, extinguishing the circle of flames burning around it. The Temple returned to silence.

Echidna lifted herself from the floor. She slithered over to the two columns and examined the magical doorway. Without hesitation, she took a step into the tapestry. Her foot touched solid stone and she crept farther until her entire body entered inside the tapestry. The ramp retreated behind her. She looked back and saw the Temple of Hecate blurring, as if she were looking through water. The torch flames shimmered, a light flashed, and the Temple went dark and disappeared.

Echidna began down the blackened road, the Dark Palace far in the distance.

Chapter Twenty-eight

The door of the Minotaur's portal disappeared. The path before them stretched far through the rocky terrain. Perpetual twilight illuminated the path, casting great shadows on the mountainous shapes around them.

"Have you been here before?" Adrian asked.

"No," Zack answered. "I have read of this place and have had visions of being here. I've never visited. Nor did I want to, until my time comes up."

"Then this entire adventure is the blind leading the blind, so to speak?"

"Not exactly," Zack said. "We know where we have to go."

He pointed to the dark peaks of the castle looming ahead of them. "Is it a good sign that lightning is flashing around the top?" he asked. "I mean, you're supposedly descended from the God of Thunder, right?"

"That's not mine," Zack answered. "I had nothing to do with that."

"But you can combat it?"

Zack didn't answer.

They followed the road as it twisted until it ended at the side of a mountain.

"That was a quick end," Adrian said. "Now what do we do?"

"Nothing is as it appears," Zack said. He studied the side of the rock. "If the path goes this way, there must be a way to follow it."

"You know an awful lot for someone that hasn't been here," Adrian replied.

"There are rules for everything," Zack answered. "Even in magic.

The problem is they are never written down, and they are neither clear nor easy to follow."

"So glad I came along on this trip."

"You were warned."

Zack handed the Trident to Adrian and put his hands flat against the solid mass. He closed his eyes and slid his palms along the stone.

"We're just going to have to trust there's some sort of hidden latch or something," Zack commented. "The Minotaur wouldn't have put us on this path if there wasn't a way to get around each obstacle."

"Zack," Adrian said quietly.

"Wait a minute," Zack said. His fingers explored a small crag. "I think I may have something here."

"Zack," Adrian said, slightly louder.

"Damn it!" Zack pounded his fist against the stone.

He stomped his foot, scattering small dirt clouds and loose gravel. He threw himself against the rock, trying to see if it would give way and slide to the side. It didn't.

"We must have missed something back there," Zack said.

"Or we could try to slide underneath." Adrian pointed down to the foot of the rock. "It's an illusion. The path goes under."

Zack looked at the base of the stone. Adrian kicked at the gravel, the pebbles disappearing through a passageway. The two men bent down and looked through. A small rectangular breezeway was cut through the stone. It was a little over a foot high and maybe two feet wide at most. The path was colored in the same tones as the rock hanging above, creating the illusion of the path ending in stone.

"I'm going to slide through," Zack said. "Then, as long as everything is okay, you can follow me. Don't argue with me. I'm going first."

Adrian opened his mouth to protest, but simply nodded. Zack dropped to all fours and rolled over on his back. He stretched his hands out under the stone. Slowly, he slid through, pulling himself from the other side. His legs disappeared and Adrian waited.

"Adrian." Zack's voice came from under the stone. "You need to see this. It's amazing."

Adrian slid through and found himself in a carved grotto. He stood up and looked out the opening. Adrian stepped to the cavern's edge, to Zack's side. Neither man said a word as they gazed out in awe.

The path continued. It gently sloped down before meandering through the terrain. Gravel gave way to dirt and soil. Spreading out beyond was an open field of ripening grain. The stalks were tall and healthy, with long pale green leaves growing low on the thick shafts. Long, wiry hairs grew around tightly knit golden kernels toward the top. The stalks swayed in a breezeless wave, rippling in a golden sea. The path continued through the center.

"It's beautiful," Zack whispered. "Breathtaking."

Adrian gazed out over the field, agreeing. "It seems so out of place. I thought there'd be nothing but darkness and destruction. I've never seen a field as beautiful as this one."

"And that's exactly why we should be wary."

A howling sound echoed across the field. The wailing entered the cave, thundering as it reverberated between the stalactites hanging from the ceiling. Small avalanches barreled down the walls. Zack fell to the ground, motioning for Adrian to do the same.

The stalks bent away from the sound as if pushed by a powerful wind. A shimmering of colors washed across the budding wheat and grains. The harvest season passed in an instant and the stalks slowly shed the bright pink and lavender colors of spring for the burnt gold of fall. The kernels ripened, falling alongside the dried, twisted leaves.

Adrian was covered in gooseflesh.

The mournful sound rang out. A new path blazed through the decaying wheat field. A short distance behind ambled the frightful figure of an ancient crone, dressed in a flowing black robe. A translucent green shroud covered her head and hung past her bony shoulders. She held her gnarled hands in front of her ancient frame, wringing them over and over. Her frail body drifted across the field, the stalks of grain changing and bending before her.

The ancient crone stopped where the two paths intersected. She paused and lifted her veil from her face. The oval face was wrinkled with time and memory. Empty black eyes stared out and her twisted mouth hung open with her haunting mournful cries. One of the gnarled hands clutched the shawl beneath the creases of her neck. She took a deep breath, briefly pulling the fallen stalks toward her.

"Kore!"

The single word was the cause of so much sorrow. It filled the field with pain and bereavement. The stalks bent away from the crone, shedding their kernel seeds, marking their loss.

"Kore!" She twisted her body to search every direction. She continued across the field, leaving the decaying harvest in her wake.

Adrian and Zack remained still, pressed onto the cliff's ledge. Silently, they watched the crone disappear farther into the field. The heartbreaking wailing slowly faded until only the burnt path through the wheat was left behind.

"What was that?" Adrian asked, once he was certain the hag was gone.

"The Grain Mother," Zack answered.

"Should we help her find whatever Kore is?" Adrian asked. "Maybe she could help us find Annelise."

"No," Zack answered. He watched over the long, brown path of grain. "We shouldn't initiate contact with anything we find here. There's no telling how it will respond to the living."

Zack started down the path toward the field, Adrian a step behind. They paused at the entrance to the wheat. The harvest path of the Grain Mother crossed ahead of them, a scorched brown road flattened across the field. They entered, cautiously making their way through the stalks. The moment Adrian stepped in, the tall shafts shifted in the breeze and closed in on him from all sides.

Adrian spun around and took a single step backward. He grabbed hold of the shafts, trying to pull them apart.

"Adrian." Zack took a firm hold of Adrian's shoulder. "We can't go back."

"It's trying to push us forward, isn't it?" Adrian asked.

"I don't know," Zack answered. "I only know there's no going back the way we came."

The wheat stalks towered above their heads, confining them on three sides. The path continued to unfold before them as they made their way through the field. The broomlike hairs scraped against their legs.

"How do we get back?" Adrian asked.

"I don't know that either," Zack said. "I can only trust there will be a way."

Adrian's hand snapped forward, stopping Zack in his tracks. "What was that?"

"What was what?" Zack looked around.

"There." Adrian pointed to a brief spark of light. "There. And there."

The tinkling of bells sounded through the field.

"Did you hear that?" Adrian asked. He leaned closer to Zack. "There's another firefly."

Adrian pointed over Zack's shoulder. A colorless light briefly twinkled on the path ahead. It blazed for an instant before fading and going dark. The high-pitched sounds of ringing bells echoed as it flashed.

Zack positioned the Trident in his hand. His body tightened and he gazed around cautiously.

"We need to hurry up and get through this field," Zack muttered.

"There's another." Adrian pointed to it. Amused delight crept into his voice. "That's really cool. What are they?"

The number of blinking lights quickly increased. The delicate sounds of wind chimes echoed from within the stalks. Three lights pulsed on the path ahead. They delicately floated toward them and started circling around their heads. The bells tinkled like cracking ice.

Adrian reached up and captured one of the lights. He could feel the warmth emanating from the light blinking between his palms. The pulsing continued for a moment before flashing bright and going dark. His palms started to itch. The sensation intensified until it started to burn. The pain grew until he couldn't handle it and Adrian opened his hands.

A small winged creature sat huddled in Adrian's palm. It flashed in his hand and quickly floated away, shrill ringing laughter echoing after. Red jagged lines crossed both of Adrian's hands, swelling into welts.

Adrian swung his arm toward a small light cluster. They fluttered back, weaving among the wheat stalks. The high-pitched sound rang out around him. His palms burned and itched, causing his rage to build. Two fireflies twinkled in front of him and Adrian darted forward.

He stepped off the path and immediately disappeared into the stalks of wheat.

Another light blinked, leading him a farther step away. Adrian clapped his hands together, trapping the light and crushing it between his palms. The blisters on his hands broke, painfully leaking a burning discharge across his palms.

He wiped his hands on the leather tunic and turned back to the path. Thick stalks of wheat surrounded him. Adrian reached out and pulled the stalks apart, taking another step. The path was nowhere to be seen.

"Zack?" Adrian called.

"Zack." The shrill sounds surrounded him.

Adrian spun around and saw nothing but wheat. The fireflies continued blinking deeper within the field.

"Zack." Adrian tried again.

"Zack." The taunting ringing echoed.

"Stop it," Adrian commanded.

"Stop it," echoed the laughter.

Adrian's rage came to a boil. The itching in his palms inflamed until it felt like his skin was burning. His head rang with the tormenting laughter. A light sparked next to him and Adrian swung at it, losing his balance and falling to the ground. The stalks of wheat towered above, growing taller by the moment and blotting out all traces of light. The rotten air settled into his lungs, causing them to constrict on the emptiness.

Roots popped out of the ground, wrapping around his wrists and ankles. They shot over his chest and legs, locking them in place. A thick braid snapped across his throat, constricting the last breath from his lungs. His eyelids fluttered, the darkness descending heavily. His fingers slowed their desperate flailing. Adrian felt the life being drained from his body.

A deafening snap cracked through the air. Light exploded from over the tops of the wheat chaffs. The mocking sounds of laughter stopped and the air went silent and cold. Adrian forced his eyes open as another thunderous clap echoed over the field.

The roots relaxed their hold. Adrian snapped the binding at his wrist, pulling his arm free. He tore at the root around his neck, desperately trying to dig his fingers under the braided growth. They slid between the root and his skin, and he pried it from his throat.

Adrian inhaled the air greedily. Light flashed behind his eyelids and the darkness seemed to clear overhead. The roots fell away from his body, withdrawing back into the ground. Adrian pushed his way up to a sitting position, still panting, the pounding in his head slowly receding.

The wheat stalks around him parted to form a path. The trail led only a few feet away from where Zack stood. Handfuls of grain were tightly clutched in each of Zack's hands, and he ripped them apart, creating a new path ending at Adrian's feet. Adrian stood up, his head still spinning. Slowly, he crept back to where Zack stood on the main trail. Zack waited until Adrian was out of the field before letting go of the stalks. The wheat fell back into place like a dropped curtain.

"And that is why we don't stray from the path," Zack said. "Are you all right?"

"Yeah," Adrian said, his voice still husky from the strangulation. "My hands feel like they are on fire."

"Will-o'-the-wisps are full of venom," Zack explained. "They appear harmless to lure you with their lights and chimes. They are coated with magical poison. If you get bitten or scratched by one, the venom seeps in and makes you very susceptible to their call. It will slowly drive you mad."

"How do I get their poison off me?"

"Heal your hands," Zack suggested simply. "The same way you healed Annelise after she was attacked."

Adrian nodded and closed his eyes. He put his hands together and immediately felt the itching and burning intensifying.

"Ow," Adrian gasped. He pulled his hands apart.

"Work through it," Zack advised. "Keep going."

Adrian put his hands back together. The heat and pain flared up. A moment later it began to ebb away. When it completely stopped, Adrian opened his palms. Red lines still ran over his skin; the pain and itching were gone.

"Good," Zack said. He took hold of Adrian's fingers and briefly studied the skin. "You're getting better at that."

"It seemed to flow naturally," Adrian said. "I felt it moving through me like…breathing."

"The more familiar you become with your abilities, the better off you'll be."

They followed the path through the rest of the field. The will-o'-the-wisps kept their distance, not bothering them as the men continued walking. Ahead, a river cut through the sea of golden wheat. The strong current flowed rapidly, dividing the end of the field from several large trees growing on the far bank. Round steppingstones led across the water and to the bank in front of a weeping willow tree. The whip-like branches hung downward, swaying gently in front of another cave opening.

"I'm guessing that's where we go," Adrian said. "It's the most uninviting thing I can see."

Zack led the way down to the riverbank and started across the stones. Adrian followed until they were across the river and standing in front of the willow tree. The trunk had grown so thick it almost blotted out the cavern opening. A thin way past remained on either side, and the men held their breath as they squeezed beyond the bark.

The cave was dark and sloped down to a narrow path leading into the earth. It smelled dank. Two steady drips sounded like a heartbeat and echoed from deep within the cavern's bowels.

"Stay close," Zack said. He looked down into the sloped darkness. "There's not going to be much light there."

Adrian tapped him on the shoulder and held up a single finger, signaling for patience. He closed his eyes with a deep breath. His lips puckered and he slowly exhaled a line of light that curled into the size of a baseball. When the breath was extinguished, the light floated before him.

"That's pretty good," Zack said. "You learn fast."

"My intuition is getting stronger," Adrian replied. "I can feel it."

The glowing sphere led down the path and hovered, waiting for the men to follow. Adrian started first with Zack quickly behind. They continued the steep slope until the path became level. It continued through a narrow crag, forcing the men to slide through one at a time. Adrian reached back, taking hold of Zack's hand.

The path widened and eventually opened on the side of a steep cliff, continuing downward. The sound of dripping water echoed, keeping rhythm as they walked. Adrian listened to the wind that swept through the steep pathway between the mountains. It whispered like a long-drawn breath.

"Do you hear it?" Zack asked. "That's the breath of the Earth."

"I thought Mother Earth was killed when they drilled too deep in the ocean," Adrian said. "Isn't that what started all of this in the first place?"

"The Earth always finds a way to rebuild itself," Zack replied. "This is a good sign."

"How do you know all of this?" Adrian asked.

"I've spent the last forty-five years studying mythologies from all over the world," Zack answered. "I've traveled all over, learning how to work with my abilities."

"When did you first know what you were?" Adrian asked.

"In my early twenties," Zack answered, "I met a woman who showed me what I was capable of."

"Are you bisexual?"

"I never thought so until then. Misha was exotic and had a sexual energy about her that could break down any barrier," Zack answered. He smiled. "She was a descendant of Venus and was very skilled in her magic."

"And the two of you had a relationship?" Adrian asked. He wasn't sure if he wanted to know the rest.

"Briefly," Zack answered. "Once she showed me who I was, the relationship ended. I came by her apartment one day, and it was empty. She moved and I've never heard from her again."

The sound of running water gently rolled toward them. The path exited the jagged mountains and came to a rocky shoreline. Black sand formed the beach, stretching down to a dock jutting out over another fiercely flowing river. The water was black as night.

"That must be the River Styx," Adrian said. "The only thing more sacred than the gods themselves."

Zack turned his head.

Adrian smiled smugly. "The gods swear their oaths by the River Styx and it is considered holy. I do know something about Greek mythology."

"Let's hope it's enough," Zack said.

The glowing ball continued to lead them down to the black sand beach.

CHAPTER TWENTY-NINE

The dark, murky river stretched far before disappearing into the horizon. Glimpses of iridescent lights glinted on the beach, shining ghoulishly against the black sand. As the pathway leveled off, Adrian saw they were translucent human figures hovering with open mouths and hollow, pleading eyes and aimlessly gliding over the sand like specters.

"Extinguish the light," Zack whispered into Adrian's ear. He nodded at the guiding glowing sphere. "We don't want to draw attention to ourselves."

Adrian followed his instincts and took a deep breath. He blew out a single cone and the sphere shimmered briefly before finally fading away. They stood on level ground, peering out from behind a large dune leading from the path to the beach.

"Who are they?"

"The dead," Zack answered. "Those buried without payment for the ferryman, or those who couldn't afford it."

"What happens to them?"

"They are condemned to wander aimlessly on the beach, never to move on."

"That's not fair."

The spectral parade stopped. The wandering wraiths turned as one, spotting the two living souls emerging from the mountain path. They charged, running toward them across the sand.

The swarm circled around Adrian and Zack, trapping them against the sand dune. Adrian pulled the bow into action, notching an arrow and holding it taut. Zack bent his knees, nervously shifting his weight and spinning the handle of the Trident in his hands.

The ghostly horde closed in, coming to an abrupt halt only feet away. The hollow eyes stared ahead and their open mouths formed a sea of blackened ovals. The swarm hovered in place, drawn to the rarity of something alive and radiating with light. Suddenly, the wraiths parted down the center creating a path to the dock.

The men lowered their weapons. Adrian started down the clearing with Zack behind him. The iridescent phantom forms bowed respectfully as they passed. The path closed behind them as the specters followed with great reverence.

"What's going on?" Adrian asked.

"They're drawn to our life," Zack answered. "They can see our wyre-lights."

The two men walked to the end of the dock. The ebony planks did not creak as the men crossed. The wraiths followed.

"This is dismal," Adrian muttered. He shivered at the cold, looking down at the rapidly flowing, murky water. "Does anything actually live down there?"

"Things you don't want to think about," Zack answered.

"Something's moving out there," Adrian said. He pointed across the vast river.

Four brightly glowing green lights cut through the thick blackness. They blinked in the dark. A large form careened out of the thick veil, forming a ship's outline. The sail billowed out at full mast, the silver embroidered willow tree winking from the darkness. The canine masthead stared straight ahead from both sets of red burning eyes. The dogs' teeth were bared, ready to snap at anything in their way. The vessel raced toward them, noiselessly gliding up to the docking station.

From the rear of the boat stepped the giant Kharian.

"Good Lord," Adrian gasped in a whisper.

The wraiths shifted their attention from the two living men to the giant ferryman approaching. The silent ogre stopped in front of them, extending a muscled arm and holding out a meaty palm, ready for the coin.

Adrian reached into the pocket of his tunic and removed the three coins the Minotaur gave him. He held one out and dropped it into the waiting hand. The palm closed around the coin and held it up before the giant's cold stoic face. The ferryman's eyes glowed with dark emerald fire. He stepped aside, permitting Adrian to pass.

Adrian held up a second coin between his finger and thumb. The burning green eyes focused sharply on the gold. Adrian's fingers moved and the third coin appeared.

"These are for them," Adrian bargained. "Let me pay for two more passages."

"What are you doing?" Zack asked. He was surprised by Adrian's action.

"Somehow I just know this is right," Adrian said. "I don't know how, but it is."

"Let us pay for four more passages," Zack added. He stepped behind Adrian and proudly put an arm around his shoulders. "And I have one more for myself."

The coins clanged against each other as they fell into Kharian's palm. The giant hand closed around the payment and ushered four wraiths past them. The specters rushed by and climbed onto the boat. The ferryman motioned for Adrian and Zack to take their seats. Once they were seated, he climbed back into the stern and pushed off.

The sail snapped in the windless breeze and the boat darted away from the dock. The shore disappeared as the vessel flew across the water, the sail fully engaged and the unmanned oars silently rowing on either side. The dorsal fin of a great beast broke the surface with a sweeping arch, its spiked tail flailing above before smacking down on the water.

"Is that rain?" Adrian pointed to the glimmering sheet of sparkling mist ahead.

"No. That's the Lethe Gate," Zack explained. "It's more beautiful than I ever imagined."

"Why does it look like rain?"

"It's a kind of cleansing," Zack said. "The gates are really enchanted mist. When they bathe over you, they wash away your memories. That way you can start clean on the Shores of Rebirth."

"How do we find Annelise if our memories are wiped clean?" Adrian asked Zack with confusion. "How do we get around that?"

"We don't," Zack answered. "We're going to jump overboard and go underneath."

Adrian looked over the boat's side and saw huge shadowy creatures swimming beneath the murky waters.

"You're crazy," Adrian declared.

"There's no choice," Zack insisted. "We're going to jump when I count to three. Hold on to me and don't let go. The Trident will protect us for a short time. We're going to have to get the rest of the way across the river on our own."

"Do you have *any* idea of what I saw swimming in that water?" Adrian's voice leapt up an octave. "And you think I'm going to jump into it? That's suicide. There's no way."

"There's no choice," Zack declared. "And no time to argue about it."

He went to the side of the boat and looked over. He kept watch on the rapidly approaching Gates of Lethe. Zack climbed onto the boat's edge and motioned for Adrian to do the same. He held tight to the Trident and held Adrian's hand even tighter.

"Get ready," Zack warned. "When I count to three, jump. And remember, don't let go! One. Two. Three."

The two men sliced into the murky water without a splash. The river swallowed them as the ferry shot away.

Adrian struggled with only one free hand, kicking wildly for balance. He wasn't sure if his eyes were open or not. The Trident burst into light, a sphere glowing around the three points and spreading outward, creating a sustaining bubble around them. Adrian stopped flailing as his feet touched the solid boundary. The force field provided oxygen, an internal dim light, and safety. His heart pounded in his chest.

"It's the Trident," Zack explained, with a nod toward the glowing instrument in both their hands. "It possess strong magic, I can feel it racing through me. The Minotaur said it is the Trident of Poseidon. I didn't think he meant the original."

The globe continued to sink until finding its balance and remained still, floating in the water. They carefully took a step within the boundary and the giant sphere rolled forward, catching the fast-paced current of the Styx. Sea creatures never seen by the living swam by the giant globe, curious yet repelled by the dim light. Some menacingly bared their teeth or tried to attack, only to find the sphere's magical charge repelling them.

"What's that?" Adrian asked.

Something moved in the darkness in front of them. The shadow shimmied through the river, causing dark ripples to cut through the current. Schools of fish increased their speed, darting past and away from the approaching shadow.

"There's something glowing up ahead," Adrian said. "Wait. There are two of them."

"Those aren't lights," Zack warned.

A huge black form wriggled toward them in the water. The set of glowing eyes focused on the bubble and the two men inside. The creature's thick body was tubular and roughly the size of a football field. The sleek body was covered with sickly gray-colored scales. A gaping mouth opened, revealing tusk-like fangs. Rows of sharp, ragged teeth lined the insides. Long strands like the feet of a centipede hung down from its body, twitching in the water, creating tidal pools with every stroke. The Leviathan came toward them. It propelled swiftly through the murky waters against the powerfully sweeping current of the Styx. Adrian watched as the giant creature came toward them. The cold, lidless eyes remained locked on its prey.

The Leviathan's jaws opened wide. The sea serpent's fangs snapped down on the glowing sphere. A spark ignited and the beast was brushed aside. The massive creature rolled back from the repelling force. It recovered, turning back to the bubble. The beast made slow circles predatorily around the glowing globe.

Leviathan circled its body around the vessel. The magical force field kept its scales from touching it. It swam around, examining the object from all sides. It stopped swimming and remained still, floating loosely around the protected globe. The giant head turned and looked at something approaching in the darkness.

Four decaying bodies swam close to the sea creature. A dorsal fin rose from the swimmers' backs and their calves. Webbing connected their fingers and the inner part of their elbows. The faces were round with lidless dark eyes staring out, watching every move. Gills flexed from under their jawlines, allowing them to breath in the abysmal river. The two male Merfolk carried tridents in their hands, while the two mermaids brandished spears.

Leviathan opened its mouth and snapped several times. A merman raised his spear and hurled it like a torpedo, striking the monstrous creature. Leviathan unfurled itself from around the bubble, revealing its massive size to its enemy. It snapped at the merman in front of it, smacking its tail and sending another one rolling away. The great sea creature doubled back and opened its mouth to attack.

A dull roar echoed through the water. The sonar force pushed back against the glowing sphere, knocking Adrian and Zack from their feet. The globe floated backward until they could once again find their footing.

The giant Leviathan remained perfectly still. It looked out into the darkness before coiling back onto itself and darting away. Two of the Merfolk quickly followed the beast.

Another roar rippled through the River Styx. The two remaining Merfolk quickly moved to either side of the protected bubble. A mermaid's grisly hand raised a conch to her lips and she blew three solid notes into the water.

Without warning, the ocean was alive with schools of fish racing by. The colors flew past the bubble as the fish tried desperately to avoid hitting the force field. The mermaid was knocked back and caught in the sudden rush, being flushed away with the fish.

The bubble floated in darkness.

A set of eight tentacles sprang out from the dark. They reached forward, wrapping themselves around the sphere. Huge oval suction cups lined the underside of each of the monstrous arms; a circular row of teeth lined the inside of the suckers. The moment they touched the sphere, a blinding light flashed and powerful voltage repelled them. The beast waved its appendages in the water before trying again. A dimmer flash exploded. The tentacles pulled back.

The monstrous body of a huge squid appeared out of the darkness. Its slithered through the water until a set of glowing eyes appeared, focused on the two men in the protective sphere.

The Kraken's bulbous head held a large, lidless eye on either side. Two slits were cut above a cavernous mouth lined with sharp teeth angling back. The jaw looked powerful enough to snap through a ship. A set of curved spikes ran back over its skull and down the spine to where eight powerful arms protruded. All eight limbs retreated into a tight ball then shot forward, attempting to attach themselves to the glowing sphere. Electricity crackled and the suckers writhed as they absorbed the attack. The monster turned, opening its jaws to take them into its mouth. The sharp teeth glinted in the murky water.

The fangs snapped down. Sparks shot off into the dark. The tips of the pointed teeth broke. The Kraken opened its jaws and released the sphere. It let out a howl of rage, sending the giant bubble rolling backward. The Kraken balled up its body, preparing for another attack. Motion swirled around the globe surrounding them with a Merfolk army armed with weapons. The decaying Merfolk regiment charged the Kraken with attacks from tridents and spears.

The monster unfurled its limbs, striking out at the attacking army. The tentacles trapped individuals onto its gaping suckers, crushing them within its folds. A long thin tongue shot out of its mouth, pulling the closest army members into its rotating teeth.

The rotting recruits continued to appear, all brandishing weapons. They formed a line between the Kraken and the glowing sphere, holding their sharp instruments outward, facing the beast. The tentacles smacked against the defensive wall, causing disruption but not breaking their ranks.

An incredibly large seahorse swam behind the Merfolk army. Holding the reins was a venerable warrior. He wore a breastplate of black pearls over his chest. On his head he wore a seven-tiered crown, each one capped with a black pearl. An ancient beard of kelp swayed from his chin, and in his strong hands was a Trident exactly like Zack's. The king swept his arm in an arch and the tips of his Trident began to glow.

Zack felt his hand begin to tingle. His hand felt melded onto the Trident and an electrical charge ran through his body. The fire burned through his veins, running down his arm and into the Trident's handle. The three points started to glow bright. Three beams of light shot out the end and connected with the one in the Merfolk king's hand.

The king reared back on the white seahorse. He held the Trident with both hands, circling the points above his head. The power from both weapons created an intensely charged light that formed around the Merfolk king. He thrust the Trident forward, pointing the tips at the Kraken.

Three powerful charges of light flew out from the Trident tips. They shot over the defensive wall created by the Merfolk army, and attacked the Kraken directly. The electrical charge sent the great squid rolling backward.

The Kraken recollected itself and pushed back. All of its legs smacked into the light beams and its attack was instantly repelled. The three beams increased their power and pushed back against the monster. The force collided with the bulbous head. The Kraken howled with fury and swam away from the attack, with half the regiment in quick pursuit.

The remaining Merfolk army turned to face the glowing sphere and the two men within. They lowered their weapons, holding them at ease by their sides. The king swung his arms forward, propelling the protective vessel by the connecting lights of the Trident. The great sphere rolled across the bottom of the river until it slowly crept up on shore.

Once on the bank of the river, Adrian and Zack pushed the great sphere onto the black sand beach. Zack motioned to Adrian and they let go of each other's hands. The giant sphere shimmered around them and melted into the ground. The men fell to their knees, panting heavily on the sand. They looked up as the webbed feet of the king approached.

The mighty lord opened his mouth, letting a series of clicking screeches emerge from decaying lips. He finished speaking and stood over the two men. He pointed his Trident at Zack's, letting the tips touch. Zack took hold of the Trident's shaft without breaking the connection between the two.

"Mighty Oceanus," Zack said, bowing his head with reverence. "How can we thank you for your help against the Kraken?"

The clicks and screeches continued for several moments. When they stopped, Zack reached down and took his Trident in both hands. Keeping his head bowed, he held the Trident out as offering.

"I offer you this as payment for your help."

The dead Sea King reached out and grabbed the Trident from Zack's hands. He slowly raised a Trident on either side of his head, looking from one to the other with great awe. He nodded at Zack, screeching and clicking before turning around and remounting his seahorse. The animal dove beneath the waters. The small troupe lingered behind for just a moment before diving after their lord and disappearing under the surface.

"You could understand him?" Adrian asked.

"You couldn't?" Zack asked with the same surprised tone.

"Why did you give him the Trident?" Adrian asked. "That's our most powerful weapon."

"It wasn't mine to keep," Zack answered. "Oceanus never wanted a part of the Titanochomy; the Titan Triton took over his kingdom and killed his brother. Oceanus has no domain except for the Dead Waters, and he should have complete rule there."

"So what do we do now?" Adrian asked.

Zack looked over at the twisted road winding away from them. He nodded with his chin, motioning the way. Adrian turned and saw the obsidian road leading away from the dock. The Dark Palace loomed in the distance. Lightning flashed through the hovering black clouds that hid the tower tops from sight.

"That's the place I saw in the vision," Adrian confessed.

"That's the Dark Palace."

CHAPTER THIRTY

The road from Hecate's Temple was long and treacherous. Echidna moved through secret pathways and ancient mazes of cavern tunnels. She emerged from a stone doorway and out onto the banks of the Acheron River. The calming waters of healing held no interest for her and she followed the shores back to its source, where it became a tributary of the Styx. Once she found the ancient river with its dark, acrid waters, she followed it back to the ferry dock and on to the road to the Dark Palace.

A silted waterway linked an interlocking system of marshes and bogs, all of them leading back to the swiftly flowing River Styx. The stagnant waters of the obsidian highway led to the Black Gates. The noxious smells increased the closer Echidna came to the castle. Sulfurous scents burned from the pits, and the bog's noxious vapors filled the air with a heavy scent of decay. Foul gasses emitted from the marshes, and the saffron-colored smoke created an ethereal railing for the silver-gray road.

Echidna approached the Black Gates as if she were returning home. The obsidian road ended at the massive onyx doors. She stood still, staring up at the ancient symbols etched into their surfaces, and trembling with excitement. Echidna brought her wrist to her lips, her fangs tearing at the flesh. When the black blood bubbled to the skin, she turned her arm and let three drops fall in offering.

Rumbling shook the palace doors. The gates grated inward. Stale air rushed from the halls, bringing with it the lingering foul stench of the rotting earth. Echidna let it wash over her, bathing in its putrescence.

Some Underworld insect flew past Echidna's ear. A sharp stinging pain burned at the base of her neck. She reached up to find blood flowing across her shoulder. She turned at her waist, looking behind, and saw her enemy approaching.

The two male Olympians stood facing her. The younger was notching an arrow to his bow. The Thunderer stood with his arms at his sides, raising the power to throw a second lightning bolt. The red wyrelights radiated powerfully around them.

Echidna started wringing her hands and muttering a spell. Her hands summoned a fireball and she raised it over her head. She hurled it at the Olympians, aiming for the space between the two men. The missile grew and split in half as it hurtled toward them.

The Usurper shot two bolts of lightning, one at each fireball. They collided in an explosion of spark and flame. Smoke and debris filled the air. When it thinned, the younger Shining One was on the ground, while the Thunderer still stood, undisturbed.

A buzzing spear of electricity flew toward Echidna. She darted to the side, letting it fly by her. She raised her spiked tail and slammed it on the ground, cracking the obsidian road. Her clawed hand grabbed hold of a large rock. She threw it in the air, letting it grow to the size of a boulder, and smacked it with her tail. The two men dove for ground. The stone crashed on the pavement in front of them.

Echidna scurried through the doors of the Dark Palace. Once inside, she knew where she could hide and plan her attack. Two arrows flew past, barely missing her head. A bolt of lightning crashed into the onyx doors, silver scorch marks appearing on the black stone. She spun around, readying for defense.

Two more arrows flew toward her. Echidna twisted at the waist, avoiding being hit. The Olympians were taking small steps forward, forcing her to back up inside the palace. The boy was notching another arrow and the Usurper held a flaming bolt in his hand. He let it fly, and she was ready. Her tail hovered and she easily hit it back toward them.

They were not as fast as before and the reversed missile exploded in the air. The burning shrapnel flew out in all directions. She summoned another and lobbed it after the first. It erupted with flowing lava and burning tar. As the smoke cleared, both men lay on the black pavement.

The boy lifted his head, coughing to clear his lungs. Burnt debris darkened his face. His arms shook as he pushed himself up to his knees. Blackened scorch marks spotted his skin and tunic. The Usurper slowly moved by his side. Blood ran down his arm and a large gash opened his thigh. Fire burned on the pavement in front of them.

Echidna's cankered lips curled in a cruel smile. She took a deep breath and reached her gnarled fingers into her mouth, took hold of her upper right fang, and ripped it from her jaw. She spat dark blood onto the ground and held up her prize. Her forked tongue licked at the blood running down her chin.

"One shall bring two and two shall bring four," Echidna muttered. She spat out more blood. "With each one cut, it grows two more."

A bolt of lightning flew toward her. She tried to dodge it but was not fast enough. The arrow struck the scales below her human flesh. Her soft pink skin tore and burned, blood running down from the wound. She clamped her hand over it, immediately starting to heal herself. Her scales were only discolored. Another arrow was launched at her head. She raised her hand to deflect it, but the pointed tip ripped through her palm.

The bloodied fang flew from her clutches. It bounced on the broken road, spinning in a circle on the edge before toppling over into the bog. A black bubble formed, rising above the surface until it burst. Several more began to brew as the silted water came to a boil. Auburn smoke curled from the swamps, filling the air with the scent of burning sulfur. The thick fog spread across the road, hiding everything from sight. A firebolt cut blindly through the smoke, missing her.

Echidna darted into the main hall of the Dark Palace. She scuttled through the grand open room, letting the memories of its branching hallways come back to her. There would be no hiding in plain sight. She needed to heal and regain her power.

Echidna darted down a hallway. She tried a door and found it open. Entering an empty room, the Mother of Monsters created a temporary nest for herself in the dark. From here, she would be able to detect any living thing entering the castle. She would wait from her lair, watching, if the Olympians could get past her guardians. If somehow they managed to succeed and rescue the Greek bitch, then the Mother of Monsters, the last of the Titans, would be ready for the final attack.

CHAPTER THIRTY-ONE

The thick orange smoke gathered on the edge of the obsidian road. It hovered over the lip, growing denser, blotting everything behind it from sight. Adrian stood on his knees, breathing heavily, bow still in his hand. Zack stood a few paces away. A large slash went from his shoulder down his arm to the elbow. Blood ran freely from the wound.

"Can you move your arm?" Adrian called out. He kept an eye focused on the dense cloud of smoke.

"Not easily." Zack grimaced in pain as he walked toward Adrian. "It got cut pretty badly. Where's Echidna?"

"She's gone, disappeared into the castle," Adrian said. "But I don't like the looks of that."

Adrian gestured with his head toward the burnt umber–colored smoke. It continued to grow until it was about the size of a compact car. The vapor swirled, becoming opaque and forming a monstrous shadow inside.

"That's not good," Zack muttered.

Adrian took hold of Zack's arm, ignoring his cry of pain. He wrapped his hands around the open gash, letting his palms channel healing energy into the wound. The heat intensified between his palms until the wound was closed. When he removed his hands, only a three-inch scar remained.

A screech rang through the air. Both men looked up to see a serpent's head emerging from the thick smoke. The head rose from an elongated neck, uncoiling from a python's body. The serpent was covered with indigo scales, and the head swayed, studying each man in turn. Its forked tongue slid out.

The serpent opened its mouth, hissing. A set of fangs curled from the mouth. The neck pulled backward and two clicks sounded like the striking of a flint. Its mouth opened wide and a thin line of fire shot out. The serpent hovered in the air, its body coiled underneath it.

"Fuck me." Adrian's hand flew to the quiver on his back and withdrew an arrow. In an instant, he had it notched. He pulled back the string and and let it fly.

"No! Don't!" Zack cried too late.

The arrow flew, clearing away the remaining wisps of smoke. The point hit the hydra's mouth, slicing through its neck and decapitating the creature. The head spun as it flew away from the body, rolling when it hit the ground. The serpent's empty neck thrashed wildly until it thumped on the ground and after a few final twitches, became still.

Adrian lowered the bow to his side. A satisfied smile spread across his face and he turned to Zack.

"What were you saying?"

Zack's shoulders fell. "I was going to say"—spoken through clenched teeth—"not to aim for its head. It's a hydra; you cut off its head, more grow back."

Adrian's head slowly turned back to the snake's carcass. The decapitated neck pulsed on the ground. It lay still for a brief moment before twitching again. Suddenly, a thick neck sprang up from the wound, splitting down the middle. Two fully developed heads blossomed at their ends. The necks stretched out so that each serpent's head could focus on its prey.

Adrian notched another arrow. He aimed for the center base where the body connected to the two necks. The arrow flew and struck the target, bouncing off the scales without any damage. Both heads opened their mouths, releasing streams of fire.

Adrian swung the shield from his back, lacing his arm through its handle. He held it before him as the flames hit and spread out over the shield's edges. When the fire ceased, the snake heads lunged forward, alternatively snapping at his arms.

"I'll distract it," Adrian called over his shoulder. "You attack the damn thing!"

Adrian swung his arm. The face of his shield knocked one of the heads to the side.

Three lightning bolts flew past Adrian in quick succession. They bombarded the hydra, forcing it to take a step back. Another bolt flew by, striking the mountain behind. A small avalanche rumbled down the side and crashed into the bog below.

The hydra rolled on the ground, avoiding the lightning onslaught. It extended a head toward Zack, the fanged mouth snapping at his arms. Zack swung his shield before him. The serpent's mouth clamped onto the edge, trying to wrestle it from his hands. Zack pulled the shield, slicing across the serpent's mouth. The cut severed the head and the neck flailed on the ground before the body sprouted two more necks and heads.

One of the new necks lunged forward and swept Zack's legs from under him. The head spun around and snapped at his feet. He desperately crawled backward, avoiding its clutches and kicking the open mouth when he could. The neck swung low and wrapped itself around Zack's left leg. It hauled him into the air, hissing triumphantly. Zack swung helplessly, trying to avoid the two other snapping mouths.

Adrian reached for his javelin and rushed forward as fast as he could. He leapt into the air and landed on the hydra's tail. Hugging its body, he rode the thrashing tail. Locking his legs at the ankles around it, he raised the javelin with both arms. Using all his strength, he thrust the javelin into the wormlike body, pinning it to the ground. The creature rose in pain, dropping Zack on the pavement.

High-pitched screeches pierced the air. Stones tumbled down the side of the mountains, splashing the fetid waters as they crashed into the marshes. The serpent body thrashed, sending Adrian rolling across the obsidian road, the bow knocked from his hand. The three heads spun in unison, baring fangs and screeching in anger.

Adrian barely had time to pull himself to his knees. He saw the hydra heads flying toward him and knew there was no way to defend himself. He thrust his hands out before him, clasping one hand tightly to the other. A powerful glow ignited around his hands. As the serpent's fangs crashed into the barrier he'd created, they were instantly repelled by the light.

Seeing the giant snake held at bay gave Adrian the moment he needed. He took a deep breath, fighting to take a step forward. The light barrier advanced and the hydra was pushed back several paces. He positioned himself to keep the hydra between him and the mountains.

"Zack," Adrian called out. "Do you see that pointed ledge hanging off the cliff? Can you hit that with a lightning bolt?"

"Yeah," Zack answered from behind. "I can do that."

The repelling beam was sapping Adrian's energy and strength. "When I say 'now,' I want you to hit right below that and cause an avalanche."

"Got it!" Zack answered.

Adrian took another deep breath and summoned his might. He felt the energy rising inside him, rushing through his body and radiating out his palms. The glowing force field pushed back until the three heads extended over the marsh and toward the mountain.

"Now!"

Zack released three firebolts. The lightning flew, striking the mountain directly under the extended lip. Fragments of rock and smoke exploded, causing the mountain to shiver. Boulders became dislodged and rolled down the sides, pelting the hydra's heads and necks. Zack fired another and the jutting ledge began to shake. The lip cracked at the base and the pointed edge flew down the side of the mountain. Shards of rock flew out in all directions, barely missing Adrian.

Adrian summoned his last bit of strength. He forced the hydra back until the boulders pounded down onto all three of its heads, crushing them. The pointed ledge came down like a missile, piercing the hydra in the chest.

The body twitched, the sharp rocks tearing into the flesh. The heavy rocks pummeled down, crushing the hydra beneath their fall. The necks twitched, thrashing before finally remaining still.

Adrian appoached cautiously, until he was sure the beast was dead. He strode over to the body, removing the javelin from the serpent's tail.

Adrian spoke with a heavy breath. "That did it."

Zack didn't answer. Adrian looked over his shoulder and saw Zack lying on the side of the road. He was on his back with his head facing away, his right leg sprawled out from his body, while the left was bent at the knee. His right arm was draped across his stomach, and his left arm lay at his side, twisted at an odd angle. A boulder thrown from the mountain lay a foot away.

"Zack." Adrian ran to the body. "You can't be dead!"

Adrian carefully touched two fingers to the side of Zack's neck, hoping to find a pulse. He clenched his eyes tightly shut. The pulse was there, but weak. Adrian sat behind Zack's head, one hand cradling Zack's neck and the other resting on his chest.

Adrian closed his eyes and took a deep breath. He let it out, feeling his breathing slow, becoming steady and drawn. His palms felt warm, and he felt the pulse leaping from his fingers into the back of Zack's skull. The steady rhythm continued until Adrian could feel the pulsing answer in Zack's chest. The energy cycle flowed several times through Zack, entering through his skull and flowing out through his chest. Adrian felt their pulses synchronize and become one.

Adrian's eyes opened and he looked down into Zack's face. The bleeding at his lip stopped, already starting to heal. His body twitched with shock and the broken arm returned to its natural positon with an audible snap. The rising of his chest became smooth and Zack's breath became regulated. His eyelids fluttered and opened slowly.

"You're alive," Adrian said, with ecstatic relief.

The electrical pulses in Adrian's hands slowed and stopped. Carefully, he lowered Zack's head onto his lap. Adrian's hand remained on Zack's chest, feeling the strong heartbeat through the leather tunic.

"You healed me," Zack said weakly.

"Yeah." Adrian smiled. "I guess I did."

Adrian glanced around for any signs of movement. Nothing stirred, other than the dissipating smoke and vapors.

"I think everything's clear," Adrian said. He looked down into Zack's blue eyes and smiled. "At least for the moment."

"Thank you," Zack said.

Zack's hand shook with weakness as he reached up to Adrian's neck. He massaged it for a moment, then pulled Adrian close. Their lips touched. Adrian resisted at first before returning the kiss.

CHAPTER THIRTY-TWO

The halls of the Dark Palace were wide and cold. The walls extended into high vaulted ceilings where dim green lights glowed, illuminating each room. The main hallway stretched far back into the palace, with numerous hallways branching off.

Oil paintings hung on the walls featuring either scenes of the Titanochomy or terrible scenes from the Land of the Dead. Tapestries with dancing skeletons of the Danse Macabre hung between the paintings. The Olympian Lord of the Underworld was depicted frequently, often sitting on his throne brooding next to Kore, the bride he'd abducted in the flower of her youth, or running on the black shores with the three-headed Cerberus at his feet.

"That thing could be anywhere," Adrian said. "There are so many halls and closed doors."

Cautiously, they walked through the Main Hall, stopping in the center. Their sandaled padding on the stone floor was the only sound, and it echoed in the cold air. The room seemed to swallow them, towering above on every side. Adrian closed his eyes and listened to the silence. When he opened his eyes again, he pointed to a hall branching off the back left corner of the room.

"That's where we need to go," Adrian said. "I don't know how, but I know that's the way." He strode to the back of the room.

They stood gazing down the long, empty hallway.

"Are you scared at all?" Zack asked.

Adrian shook his head. "No," he answered casually. "I'm really not."

They started down the hallway.

"It's odd," Adrian continued. "I'm feeling more in tune, not only with what's happening around me, but with myself as well. I'm feeling...empowered."

"You're following your instincts more, instead of asking me what to do," Zack commented.

Ahead, on either side of the hall, were two platforms with large sphinxes resting on top of them.

Their upper bodies were human, with the heads of beautiful women. Both faces were framed by long black hair hanging down past sets of human breasts. Slim waists disappeared into sleek lioness bodies that sat relaxed on their haunches. Their eyes were cold and blank.

A shimmering curtain stretched across the hallway, connecting the backs of the two platforms. A single beam of light shining from the ceiling lighted the other side of the curtain. Its translucence allowed a lone figure to be seen on the other side: a woman dressed in a Greek peplos. She moved slowly, uncertain.

"Annelise!" Adrian called.

Annelise stopped abruptly, cringing in pain. Her hands flew to head, covering her ears and trying to block out sounds only she heard. Adrian stopped calling and Annelise hesitantly removed her hands. She studied the air around her, seeing nothing, and continued to walk aimlessly.

Adrian took a step forward. Zack grabbed him by the arm.

"What are you doing? Can't you see her?"

"I see her," Zack assured him. "I also see them."

Zack signaled for Adrian to look up at the statues. Both sets of the sphinxes' eyes were now lit. They glowed yellow, with black lightning. The eyes moved, following every movement Adrian and Zack made.

"I don't care," Adrian stubbornly said. "That's Annelise."

Adrian pulled free from Zack's grip. He took off running, calling his sister's name. The moment he called, she cringed. He charged forward into the shimmering curtain but was thrown backward several feet in the air. He landed hard on the stone floor, the wind knocked out of his body. Zack ran to his side as Adrian rose to his elbows and shook his head slowly, trying to clear the ringing from his ears.

The huge feline bodies of the sphinxes began to glow. They came alive, stretching out their front legs and raising their hindquarters in unison. Their tails swayed and twitched behind them. Both creatures leapt from their perches, passing each other in midair, and landed softly on the ground. The sphinxes studied the men, reaching their human heads out and sniffing the air. They pulled back with smiles on their faces and then sat back on their haunches, waiting.

Adrian drew an arrow from the quill. He notched it and pulled the string back, holding it taut with warning. The feline smiles broadened; neither sphinx moved. Adrian let the arrow sail between the two creatures. It bounced off the invisible curtain and burst into flames.

"In order to pass by our curse, you must answer our simple riddle first." The sphinxes spoke in rhyming unison.

The two cats began pacing in front of Zack and Adrian. They moved with feline grace. They walked in an infinity pattern, crisscrossing in the middle.

"Is this the only way we can pass?" Adrian asked.

The sphinxes nodded and purred.

"What happens if we turn around?" Adrian asked.

"You are free to turn and go," one of the sphinxes answered.

"But the reward beyond you'll never know," the other completed.

As the two cats met at their crossing, they hesitated. The female faces leaned out, touching noses before rubbing their cheeks against each other. They continued to follow their pattern.

"Is there any other way to rescue my sister?" Adrian asked.

"There are many secrets in the castle deep," a sphinx responded.

"And these are secrets we must keep," the other added.

"To get to your prize and save the day?"

"We do not know another way."

The sphinxes let out loud purrs. The low rumbling echoed down the hall. Their whiskers twitched as they wrinkled their human noses.

"What the hell do we do now?" Adrian asked.

"We either go back," Zack answered, "and hope we don't wander around these hallways forever, or worse, run into something else that kills us. Or we try and answer their riddle."

Adrian watched as the sphinxes prowled in front of them. Beyond the two cats, Annelise wandered farther away.

"I don't think there's a choice." Adrian succumbed.

The two sphinxes turned to face Zack and Adrian. They sat back. Their human heads faced out and their breasts hung above the carefully groomed fur-line. They spoke as one.

"Once we play our game with you, there is no other path to choose. It's us or you, and no other way. Answer our riddle or you will pay."

"Agreed," Adrian said solemnly.

The sphinxes looked at each other, purring loudly. The room rumbled. Zack and Adrian were thrown to the floor. A wall emerged from the side, sealing off the hallway behind them.

"There's no winning," Adrian said. "We're dead if we do and dead if we don't."

"Ask your riddle," Zack said.

The sphinxes spoke their riddle: "I can bring tears to your eyes. I can resurrect the dead. I can make you smile, and reverse time, it is said. I can last a lifetime but form in the twinkle of an eye. I can bring both fear and happiness; shared or private, what am I?"

The words echoed in the chamber.

"Can we hear it again?" Adrian asked.

They repeated the riddle, speaking alternating lines. The sphinxes stood and stretched forward. Sharp claws extended from the ends of their large paws. They returned to their pacing, the nails clicking on the stone with every step, sounding like a ticking clock.

"Any ideas?" Zack asked in a whisper.

"Not really," Adrian said. "Give me a minute. How many guesses do we get, three?"

"I doubt it," Zack answered. "Whatever our answer is, we need to make it a good one."

"Let's take it one line at a time," Adrian suggested. "The first one was bringing tears. That doesn't really help. It could be anything bad."

"Not necessarily bad," Zack suggested. "People shed tears over good things, too. We may need to think out of the box. I remember the second line. It struck a chord. 'I can resurrect the dead.' "

One of the sphinxes spiritedly attacked the other. They rolled across the stone in a feline ball, splitting apart with a playful growling.

"What's the rest of it?" Adrian asked.

"Ah," Zack sighed. "I can't remember. Will you repeat the riddle again?"

The sphinxes regained their composure in a flash. They took three steps away from each other before sitting back and repeating the riddle. When they were finished, they returned to playfully stalking each other.

"Okay. We have something that makes you cry and brings back

the dead," Adrian puzzled out. "It makes you smile, and time is not a restraint. It sounds like some sort of fantasy."

"No one fantasizes about bringing back the dead. Maybe in a dream." Zack snapped his fingers. "A dream. That's it! Think about it."

"How does a dream resurrect the dead?" Adrian asked.

"Haven't you ever dreamed about someone that died?"

"I don't know," Adrian said. "There's something not right about that answer."

"No. This is it," Zack said. "Dreams bring tears. The dead visit in dreams. Dreams can make you smile. They happen in an instant."

"What about reversing time?" Adrian cautiously asked.

"How many dreams have you told me about being in ancient Greece?" Zack countered. "Or any other time period, for that matter? Think about the rest of the riddle."

Adrian took a moment to replay the rhyme.

"Dreams happen in an instant and last a lifetime," he rationalized. "You can have nightmares, too. That's fear and happiness. It sounds right."

"Then why the hesitation?" Zack demanded.

"It doesn't *feel* right," Adrian argued.

"Look," Zack said. He reached out and took Adrian's hands in his own. "I'm not giving any answer if you're not comfortable with it. This isn't just me anymore; it's you, too. I need to remember that. If you have a better answer, I'm willing to hear it."

Adrian racked his brain trying to think of something. He played the riddle over in his mind, yet something nagged at him each time. Adrian looked into Zack's eyes, knowing that Zack would never press forward without his consent. He looked at the pacing lionesses and the hallway beyond, leading into darkness. He turned back to Zack.

The two felines broke away from their playing. They retreated to either side of the hallway. They reached up, stretching at the base of their podiums, sharpening their claws on their scratching posts. The nails scraped down the metallic base, sending sparks shooting in the air and ice running down both men's spines.

"Okay," Adrian said. He let out a heavy sigh and dropped his shoulders. "Go with dreams."

"Are you sure?" Zack asked. Their hands were still joined.

"No," Adrian answered honestly. "But I have no other answers."

"I need you to be sure," Zack insisted.

Adrian opened his mouth and found he could not speak. Tears welled up in his eyes, and he snapped his jaw closed. Both lips disappeared as he pressed them tightly together. He could only nod his answer.

Zack gave both of Adrian's hands a reassuring squeeze.

"Okay then," he said. "Here it goes."

Zack leaned forward, kissing Adrian on the lips. Adrian wrapped his arms around Zack's chest and hugged him tightly. They held each other for several long moments. Zack patted Adrian's back and gently pushed him away. He swallowed hard and walked away without speaking a word.

Adrian watched the sphinxes relax from their scratching posts and stretch their feline bodies. He marveled at how majestically they moved. There was a reason lions were called kings of the jungle. His mind flashed on a memory of when their parents had taken Annelise and him to the zoo.

It was their seventh birthday. The family spent the day watching the different animals and making their way through the special petting zoo section. It wasn't until the end of the day that they came upon the lions' den. In a giant outdoor facsimile of the natural habitat, several lions were being fed. The zookeeper was throwing pieces of meat to the great cats. The audience applauded in delight as the animals caught their meals. Adrian stayed back, hugging to his mother's skirts. Annelise was unafraid. She dropped her father's hand and pushed her way to the front to watch the lions literally tear into their lunch. For years she teased Adrian about being afraid.

Adrian yelled, "Don't say a word!"

The sphinxes had taken their sitting positions and were waiting for Zack to answer. Their heads turned to face him, the same patient, knowing smile.

"What's wrong?" Zack asked. He spun around, startled.

"It's not the right answer." Adrian reached out and firmly took Zack by the shoulders. "It's not dreams."

"Then what is it?"

"Memory," Adrian insisted. "Think about it. Memories can

make you cry. They bring the dead to you. They make you smile and remember the past, a different time period. Memories form in an instant and last a lifetime."

"They both work." Zack agreed. "How do we know which one it is?"

"It's memory," Adrian insisted. "Watching the two sphinxes playing like cats reminded me of something that happened when Annelise and I were kids. It involves us at the zoo, and a lion's cage, and blah blah blah...the point is, she remembers it differently than I do."

"Okay," Zack said. "People remember things differently."

"Yes," Adrian insisted. "But not dreams. 'I can bring both fear and happiness; *shared or private*, what am I?' Memories can be shared. Dreams cannot."

"You and I shared a dream," Zack said. "After...you know, we had sex. You said I was in your dream."

"You were," Adrian said. "But we were awake, so that would be a vision. Besides, you didn't see it also, so it wasn't shared between us. I told you about it, but that's not the same thing."

"Are you sure about this?" Zack stared.

Adrian nodded. "Definitely. Now ask yourself the same question."

Zack stood quiet for a long minute. Slowly, he nodded. A smile crept across his lips. "Yeah," he said. His confidence came back quickly. "You're right, this *feels* correct."

Adrian smiled. He took a few steps toward the sphinxes. They returned to their sitting positions.

"Please repeat the riddle," Adrian asked.

"I can bring tears to your eyes. I can resurrect the dead..." they rattled off in their soothing voices. "I can make you smile, and reverse time, it is said. I can last a lifetime but form in the twinkle of an eye. I can bring both fear and happiness; shared or private, what am I?"

Adrian glanced back at Zack for reassurance. Zack nodded with a grin on his face. He stood next to Adrian and took his hand.

"Ready?"

"Ready," Adrian confirmed.

They walked toward the line of the force field. Zack gave Adrian's hand a reassuring squeeze and nodded.

"I have the answer to your riddle," Adrian announced.

The sphinxes smiled as they approached.

"The answer is memory."

Everything in the hallway remained perfectly still. The last echoes of Adrian's answer faded. Zack's hand held Adrian's tightly. Adrian returned the squeeze with equal strength.

The sphinxes returned to all fours and crouched low. They let out a menacing growl, baring animal teeth in their human mouths. The claws were exposed, freshly sharpened, ready to cut and slice. The sphinxes leapt at one another, no longer playing. The two animals rolled across the floor, howling and biting with deadly menace.

Two strong paws swung in the air. The razor-sharp claws met with the human throats, slicing them open from ear to ear. Blood fanned out and bathed them in crimson red. The two sphinxes collapsed on the floor, one atop the other.

The translucent curtain shimmered and shimmied, cascading down like a waterfall. It fell, covering the dead sphinxes and flooding the immediate area between the broken statues. The water drained into the base of the pedestals, carrying away the lionesses' bodies.

All traces of the bloodbath disappeared.

In the distance a figure slowly walked toward them. It was human and dressed in a Greek peplos. The woman crept forward. The single beam shined down on her, illuminating her face.

"Annelise?" Adrian called.

"Adrian," Annelise called back.

Adrian ran toward her with open arms, ready to embrace her. As the two siblings were about to touch, Adrian's hands passed into Annelise, and he moved directly through her. Both of them turned around with an equally surprised expression.

"What's happening?" Adrian asked.

"I don't know," Annelise answered.

"Are you...dead?" Adrian choked out the words.

"No," Annelise confirmed. "I don't feel like I am dead. I feel kind of numb and just...present."

"You're a wraith," Zack said as he approached. "Your body isn't dead, so your soul isn't ready to come here yet."

"Then why am I here?" Annelise asked. "In fact, where am I? How did I get here? And why are you both here?"

"We're here to rescue you," Adrian said.

"It's been, literally, an odyssey," Zack said. "Right now, we need to get out of here. We'll get you caught up on the way."

Adrian stepped into the circle of light and gave Annelise a hug. He felt something burning at his side. His fingers dug into the pocket of his tunic and he withdrew the silver pendant with the swan.

"Oh," Adrian exclaimed. "I almost forgot. The Minotaur gave me this."

"The what?" Annelise asked, incredulous.

"I'll get to that," Adrian said with a smile. "I'm supposed to plant this at your feet."

Adrian fell to his knees in front of Annelise.

"What are you doing?" Zack asked.

"The Minotaur told me that when a moon was shining where none should, I should plant this." Adrian pointed at the beam shining from the round opal light in the ceiling.

"That looks like a moon to me," he said. "And this thing is burning in my hand. There's a crack in the floor, and I'm planting it here."

Adrian wedged the pendant into the crack. The necklace was swallowed. He stood up and the three of them looked down at the floor, staring in silence, waiting for something to happen.

A brilliant pale blue light erupted from the crack in the floor. The slice widened until it became a square tile. The newly cut stone danced in its frame, the blue light shaking it from underneath. It stopped as suddenly as it started, and the light disappeared.

Adrian nodded for Annelise to retrieve whatever was underneath the tile. She hesitantly bent down and pulled at the loose piece of flooring. Inside the hole was a silver woven coronet with a crescent moon on the front. She reached in and picked it up, holding it out for all to see. The piece was three-quarters round and simply designed. Two tiny swans were woven on the side with combs underneath to hold the small crown in place. The crescent moon was prominently displayed in front. The sides of the moon curled upward, four inches between the points, glinting in the dim light.

"You guys obviously get cool shit," Annelise nodded to the weapons and shields both men carried, "and I get a tiara. Somehow that doesn't seem fair. What is it for?"

"I have no idea," Adrian said. He looked to Zack, who shrugged.

"If I've learned anything on this journey, it is that whatever it's for will present itself when the time is right."

"It is beautiful," Annelise said with a sigh.

She took the coronet in both hands and gingerly placed it atop her head. Her wraithlike appearance became more solid. Annelise reached for Adrian's arm, her fingers still pressing through the flesh.

"I can feel that," Adrian said. "It feels like you have a tight grip on my arm."

"And you got this from a minotaur?" Annelise asked.

"Let's get out of here," Adrian said, "and we'll get you caught up."

"Sounds good," Zack asked. "But where do we go from here? The halls are sealed off."

"Ow. Ow!" Annelise cried.

She put her hands to the sides of her head. The swan on the coronet's left side fluttered off the silver tiara. It swam in the air around the startled mortals. It slowly led the way down the hall, hovering and waiting for the three humans to follow.

"And now we know the reason for the tiara," Annelise said.

The other two nodded. The three of them began walking, following the ethereal silvery white swan.

"Why do the two of you have red halos burning around your heads?" Annelise asked.

Adrian and Zack looked at each other. They both burst out laughing.

CHAPTER THIRTY-THREE

I felt like I would never get out of the endless halls," Annelise concluded. "I heard my name but it sounded like it was piercing my ears. The path would only go forward, repeating itself over and over. I tried to count the times I went through, but eventually I lost track of everything except wanting to go on."

They followed the swan as Adrian and Zack recounted the long story of Echidna's escape from Tartarus. Zack explained their shared history and heritage, eventually leading up to Echidna's attack on Annelise and how all of them ended up at the Dark Palace. When they had finished, Annelise told them her story.

"You've been here since the attack at the gallery opening," Zack said. "That's when you went into a coma back in our world."

"Echidna imprisoned your soul here since technically you haven't died," Adrian said, intuiting the truth. "That's why you're a wraith. Your body isn't dead."

"I'm glad to hear that," Annelise said. "How long ago did all this happen? It seems ages ago."

Zack and Adrian stopped. They looked at each other, puzzled.

"I have no idea," Adrian said.

"It's a different world," Zack said. "Time is altered from how we measure it."

The three stopped at the open main gates of the Dark Palace. The ghostly swan swam around the human trio in the air. It gently floated to the side of Annelise's head, hovering momentarily before reattaching itself to the side of the silver crown.

"Ow!" Annelise said. She straightened the tiara on her head. "I will be glad to put this place behind me."

"I hear you," Adrian added with a shudder. "I'll accept my death when it's time, but not now. I'm not ready yet."

Zack led them out the door. Annelise went next, having no weapon and still not fully corporeal. Adrian followed behind, scanning the black road and the swampy marshes on either side.

An explosion erupted from behind them. The force propelled Adrian forward, and he pushed into Annelise. Her body only being partially corporeal, he tumbled through her, feeling cold, before pushing into Zack. They tumbled to the ground, debris flying through the air. Adrian rolled onto his stomach and grabbed an arrow from the quiver. He held the bow on its side and quickly notched it, waiting and watching.

From out of the smoke emerged Echidna. She emitted an ear-piercing shriek that rang across the obsidian highway. Her tail flailed up and smacked on the ground, causing tremors to rip a crevasse through the black stone road. The vibrations caused Adrian to drop his arrow.

"Is that what Camille turned into?" Annelise said.

"Stay here," Adrian commanded. "You're still vulnerable. Don't go near her or let her get to you."

"He's right," Zack confirmed. He crawled up beside them. "You're already trapped here, she won't bother with you. She's after us, at least for now."

Adrian notched the arrow and let it fly at Echidna. He followed it with two more. She dodged out of their way, taking a step toward the mortals.

"Follow this road down to the crossroads," Zack said to Annelise. "You'll be safe and we'll catch up to you there."

"I'm not letting you risk your lives for me again," Annelise argued.

"You don't have a weapon," Zack yelled. "And you can't hold one, being a wraith. There's no time to debate this."

Zack pushed himself to his knees. He put his hands in front and immediately they started to glow. Standing up, he hurled three lightning bolts as Echidna approached.

Adrian stood and let another arrow fly, to gain cover for Annelise.

"Go!" Adrian yelled. "Now, while she's distracted."

"Adrian," Zack yelled. "Watch out!"

Adrian turned around too late. He pulled his shield into place as the fireball collided with him. A great explosion knocked him backward. He landed on his back, completely winded. Lights flickered before his eyes, everything blurred. There was a low-grade ringing in his ears. He shook his head to clear it. Fresh waves of pain throbbed through him. His bloodied hand clutched the broken shield. He threw the useless metal aside.

Zack hurled a barrage of lightning bolts at the monster. Echidna deflected each one, batting them away with ease. Her powers growing, she raised her tail and slammed it to the ground. Another tremor rippled forth, causing Zack to lose his balance. He fell to the pavement.

Adrian shot two more arrows. The first bounced off the scales harmlessly. The next flew directly at her head. Echidna used her hand for balance as she ducked. The arrow sliced off three fingers. She let out a scream of pain.

Echidna looked at her bleeding hand for only a moment. She lifted her head, her eyes glowing with hatred. She raised her hand, letting the blood run freely down her arm. With a snap of her wrist, droplets of blood flew into the air, transforming into a swarm of flies. The dark cloud buzzed with anger and flew directly at them.

Adrian and Zack swung their arms wildly, trying to ward off the attacking vampire insects. Each bite drew droplets of blood, while their stings injected miniscule amounts of venom, causing the men's skin to itch and burn. Adrian's neck and arms radiated with pain and raw, red welts.

Zack pulled the shield from his back and slid it onto his arm. Stepping in front, he pushed Adrian down to the ground and swung the shield in a wide circle. The attacking bugs collided with the metal. He raised the shield so the emblem of the eagle pointed to the sky.

"Evohe!" Zack yelled.

A clap of thunder echoed from the sky above them. A flash of lightning shot from the dark clouds hiding the turrets of the Dark Palace. The bolt struck the center of the shield and a blinding flash radiated outward. A golden dome covered both him and Adrian, protecting them from the onslaught attack of the flies. Drops of raining fire fell from the skies. The falling beads pelted the swarm until they lay dead.

The globe of light swelled into a blinding flash. It disappeared, taking the shield with it.

Echidna stood watching, clutching her torn hand. She raised her arm and again flicked her wrist, fanning the foul blood before her. The droplets flew and landed on the black road, burning into the stone. The rising smoke took form, becoming an army of skeletons. They formed two rows of ten, each soldier holding a sword in its bony grasp.

Adrian slowly stood and stared out at the skeletal army.

Zack threw a lightning bolt at the skeletons. It struck the four end soldiers, sending bones flying in every direction. Two of them re-formed from the dismantled pieces, rejoining their comrades. The regiment closed ranks and continued marching forward.

Adrian rapidly fired arrows at the approaching skeleton crew. A few struck their mark, knocking loose an arm or becoming lodged in a leg, but most flew through the bones without any damage.

A series of bombs came flying toward Zack, releasing a hailstorm of stone and fire. Zack was knocked back to the pavement and sent rolling to the edge. His legs fell into the bog and he desperately clawed at the polished obsidian before sliding into the swamp.

The skeletons turned to face Adrian. They took a step forward in perfect unison, raising their swords above their heads, readying for attack. The ranks spread out until they confined Adrian on three sides, forcing him back toward the brink of the marshes.

Adrian stood on the edge. He threw his arms out in front of him, pressing one hand over the other and locking his elbows. A powerful light shot out from his palms, becoming a powerful funnel opening. The tornado shot from his hands.

The skeleton army stopped. They started to vibrate and shake from the force of the tornado. One by one, their swords and hands were ripped from their bodies and pulled into the funnel's open mouth. The more skeletons it engulfed, the larger the tornado grew. It ripped through the army, knocking into them like a wild top and scattering the bones.

Zack struggled to pull himself from the bog. His hands slipped as he tried to grasp to the sides of the road, and the fetid water weighed him down. Finally, he crawled out of the marshes, panting, hunched over on hands and knees.

Echidna slammed her tail onto the ground, sending another tremor. It knocked Adrian off balance, the arrow falling from his hand. She clapped her hands together, summoning a flaming ball of tar. Echidna hurled it at Zack. The bomb exploded, sending burning tar into the air. Zack was thrown to his back, bouncing on the stone road. The tar continued to burn as it landed on his tunic, melting the leather and scorching his skin. He extinguished the burning tar on his body and collapsed to the ground.

Adrian pushed himself to his knees. He reached back and felt for another arrow. His supply was dwindling and there were only another dozen arrows left. He felt through them and grabbed one of the Smith God's arrows with the black tail feathers of the Erinyes.

If not now, his mind debated, *when?*

Adrian notched the ridges to the string and held the arrow still. He closed one eye and focused as Echidna released the flaming tar. The edge of the arrow's tip glinted and blurred as Echidna's chest came into view. Adrian drew a quick breath and the bowstring, holding both tightly.

"Let's end this once and for all."

The arrow flew from Adrian's bow. It pierced the fleshy human skin on the left side of Echidna's abdomen and passed through. The dragon's body stopped moving, and the tail twitched rapidly in the air. Echidna's upper body swayed, and she looked down at the blood running from her stomach. Her hands covered the wound. She wavered as one of her arms reached out for balance, finding no support to hold. She teetered on the edge of the road. Echidna looked up with a stunned expression and fell backward into the bog. The water bubbled ferociously.

Adrian limped cautiously to the road's edge. His skin burned, but he would not let it stop him. He peered over the side to where Echidna's body had fallen. The bubbling was slowly returning to silted stillness. Hesitantly, he raised his bow and fired an arrow. He shot two more arrows into the water before he felt satisfied. Adrian limped his way to where Zack lay.

Zack was on his back, completely still. Small puddles of tar burned around him, smoldering with thick smoke. Adrian fell to his knees, ignoring the pain shooting through his body, and spread his palms over Zack's chest. The heat raged in his hands, spreading up into his arms, soothing the welts and burning fly bites. Adrian felt the healing energy flow into Zack until their heartbeats became one. Zack's eyes snapped open and he gasped. Adrian withdrew his hands, watching the welts retreat from both their bodies.

"Where is she?" Zack asked. He choked on the words. "Where's Echidna?"

Adrian helped him to a sitting position. "Gone."

"Gone?" Zack looked at him disbelieving. "Or dead?"

"I shot her with the Smith God's arrow," Adrian explained. "She fell into the swamp."

"You think that's the end of her?" Zack asked.

Adrian leaned down and gently kissed Zack's forehead.

"I hope so," he answered.

CHAPTER THIRTY-FOUR

Adrian helped Zack up from the broken ground. He moaned from the movement of his sore, bruised muscles. Adrian healed them both and they walked back to the crossroads, where Annelise was waiting for them.

"Is that thing dead?" Annelise asked. Her tiara was glowing in the dim lighting.

"The arrow went through her belly," Adrian confirmed. "Then I shot several others into the bog after her. If she's not dead now, she will be shortly."

"The water is toxic," Zack said. "I could feel it burning my skin when I was knocked into the marsh. And if she isn't dead now, she'll be pulled into the Styx eventually. All of these bogs and marshes may be silted, but they still connect to the main rivers of the Underworld."

The three of them stood at the crossroads. The Dark Palace loomed silently behind them. The obsidian road continued to the far ends of the Underworld.

"Where do we go from here?" Annelise asked. "How do we get home?"

Zack put a single hand on his hip and looked down the black stone roads. "That way leads into the heart of the Underworld," he said. "That way is the Black Palace."

"I don't want to go back there," Annelise said. "Wait a minute. What's that?"

She paused and listened. A smile crept to her lips, gently tugging at the sides of her mouth. "It's beautiful."

"What is?" Adrian asked. "I don't hear anything. Do you?"

"No," Zack asked. He was concerned. "What do you hear?"

"Music," Annelise said in a dreamlike state. "I can hear faint music. Singing."

Annelise looked in every direction for the source and saw nothing. She pointed opposite the castle and took a step in that direction.

"It's coming from down there," she said. "It sounds like a choir. Adrian, you'd love it; it's so beautiful."

Zack reached out and took hold of Annelise's shoulder. "It's the Elysian," he explained. "It's the home of paradise."

"It sounds like it." Annelise tugged at her arm, trying to continue on her way. Zack stopped her.

"You can't go," he argued. "You're not dead."

"I don't care," Annelise said, hypnotized by the music. "It's so beautiful."

"How come we can't hear it?" Adrian asked.

"We're not dead," Zack explained.

"Neither is she."

"No," Zack continued. "But she's a wraith and was imprisoned here. If we don't get her back soon, her spirit will be locked here forever."

"That's not good," Adrian muttered. He looked at his sister, who was totally lost in the music. "Annelise." He tugged at her peplos. "Ignore the music. We need to go."

"Go where?" she argued. "I'm not going back to that castle. That way goes into the heart of hell, and this way is paradise. Can't we go? Even if it's only for a few moments?"

"There is no 'only a few moments' when it comes to the Elysian," Zack said. "Once the Elysian is entered, there's only one way to go, and that's on to rebirth."

"And what's so bad about that?" Annelise replied. "After all we've been through, I could use a little bit of paradise. Couldn't you?"

She tugged at his grip, trying to pull free. She took several steps, leading them to the edge of the road.

"Then where do we go?" Adrian asked.

"The ferry," Zack answered. He walked over to Annelise, making sure she didn't go any farther. "There's no other way back."

"Can't we find another portal or something?" Adrian said, joining them.

The swamps on either side bubbled, releasing foul stenches and rancid smells.

"I told you," Zack explained. "Those are rare, hard to find, and usually only one-way. The ferry is the only way out."

"We don't have any coins left for passage," Adrian said. "How are we going to pay?"

"I don't know," Zack answered. "Considering the circumstances, we can only hope we won't need to."

Annelise stopped still. Her shoulders fell and her face saddened.

"It stopped," Annelise said. She looked around, desperate to hear more. "I don't hear it anymore."

"Good," Zack said. "Hopefully you won't be tempted any more either." He leaned over and looked at the marsh. The simmering sulfur bubbles broke on the surface, releasing their rancid smell. The current moved quickly, flushing out the marshes and emptying the deposits into the River Styx.

Zack turned from the foul, stinking water. "We need to go to the ferry if we are getting out of here."

He took a step away. A thick tail sprang out of the water and wrapped around his ankle. Echidna leapt out of the bog, landing on the edge of the black road. Her body was covered in slime and debris from the rancid waters. The wound at her side was still raw but no longer open and bleeding. Her amber eyes flashed pure, unadulterated hatred.

Her tail held Zack upside down over the marsh. She clapped her hands together and threw a firebomb at Adrian and Annelise. Annelise tumbled to the ground, avoiding the explosion of sparks and flames. Adrian was knocked over, landing on his back, not moving.

Echidna dangled her prize in front of her. Zack struggled helplessly, his arms and leg flailing in the air. He tried to summon a lightning bolt in his hands, but Echidna thrashed her tail, disrupting his spell. The fire fell into the marsh, where it settled with a serpentine hissing. She swung her tail high until she looked directly into his upside-down face.

"Did you think you would conquer me again?" the Mother of Monsters whispered. Her breath was foul.

Echidna's tail slammed Zack onto the ground, which cracked under the pounding. She lifted him into the air before hurling him a short distance. He crashed onto the ground and rolled to the edge. He lay there panting, conserving his strength and pushing himself upright.

She wrapped her tail around his chest, pinning his arms to his sides. She lifted him in the air, squeezing like a python.

"Did you think I would let you leave?" Echidna hissed. "I don't *think* so. The prophecy is clear. Now that the Heavens have entered the World of Night, your reign is over."

Echidna took Zack's arm in her hand. She snapped the bone. "You are no match for the true children of the Universe."

She threw him onto the ground, watching him roll across the pavement. Echidna slammed her tail onto the ground. The body jumped but otherwise remained still. She tossed her head back, cackling triumphantly to the dark wasteland.

"The Olympian rule has ended!" Echidna screeched. "Dark Mother, I avenge you!"

Echidna's sounds stuck in her throat. Her words stopped. Her eyes were locked, opened wide. A fire ignited and ran through her body. It burned in her stomach, sending out horrible waves of pain. Her breath caught, allowing only a high-pitched whistling sound as her lungs clawed for air.

With short, shaky gestures Echidna lowered her head and looked down at her body. The silver javelin cut through her back, leaving the pointed blade sticking out below her breasts. The razor-sharp tip was covered with her blood, and the viscera torn from her body. Her hands shook as she wrapped them around the weapon's shaft, the enchanted metal burning her palms. Summoning her strength, she pulled the javelin from her chest. She held the weapon before her, staring at the blade with disbelief and despair. She looked over her shoulder to see Adrian falling to his knees, panting heavily.

The mercurial silver glistened in the dim light. As the blood ran off the metallic point, she saw the etching on the flat part of the blade: the conjoined profiles of the sun and crescent moon.

Hecate's words came taunting back. She whispered them, finally understanding.

"For if Heaven shall journey into the World of Night, even the mightiest can die."

The godly blade clanged on the stone pavement. Echidna swayed as her life drained from her body. She coughed black blood from her mouth, droplets dribbling down her chin.

Zack moaned from where he lay on the pavement. The fingers on his good arm twitched. His legs moved slowly and stopped. He groaned with pain and tried to push himself up. His arm gave way and Zack fell back down with a sharp breath of agony.

Echidna turned her body with great effort. She saw him twitch and knew he was alive. Summoning her strength, she stumbled to his side, looking down at the broken man. Her spiked tail rose, aiming down at the flying eagle on his breastplate. She coughed up blood, spitting it onto Zack's leather tunic.

She would complete her mission with her last, dying effort.

"Hey, bitch!"

Annelise's voice took Echidna by surprise. The great monster froze in place. Slowly, she turned, keeping her tail poised over Zack's chest, until she was facing Annelise directly.

"Forgot about me, didn't you."

Annelise reached up and took the crescent moon from her tiara. She held it in her fingers and with one motion, snapped her wrist. The silver blade flew, leaving a blue-white trail behind.

The ends of the crescent struck Echidna in both eyes. The monster screamed. Black blood flowed from the sockets, leaving large trails down her face. Her hands shook with shock, slowly reaching up and dislodging the silver moon from her eyes.

The Mother of Monsters stumbled a few short steps. Her dragon's body collapsed on its side, falling on the road's edge. The human torso blindly swayed, her bloodied head rocking on the neck. Her hands hovered before her body, the clawed fingers clutching at nothing. As her upper half wavered, she pressed her hands to her chest and pushed herself into the marsh.

The water bubbled ferociously as Echidna's body sank below the surface. The undertow quickly took hold, allowing the tip of her spiked tail to resurface before finally dragging the body under. The current carried the carcass to the River Styx.

No one lamented the death of Echidna, the Mother of Monsters.

CHAPTER THIRTY-FIVE

Annelise ran over to where Adrian lay on the pavement. She bent down, reaching for his hand. Her wraith palm hovered over his flesh.

"I will never mock you playing Frisbee golf again," Adrian said, panting heavily.

"Thank God you're all right!" Annelise said. She bent down to kiss his cheek. Her cold wraith lips made him flinch.

"All things considered," Adrian said, pushing himself up to his elbows, "you'll have to be more specific. Think she's dead this time?"

"I think so," Annelise said with a smile.

"Where's Zack?" Adrian asked.

They saw Zack lying unconscious on the pavement. The two of them scrambled to his side. Adrian checked for a pulse.

"He's alive," he said, relieved.

Adrian kneeled next to Zack. He pressed his fingers together, tucking his thumbs underneath, and laid his hands over Zack's breastplate. His hands burned immediately and he felt the energy flowing through him and into Zack's body. Annelise watched in awe.

Zack's broken arm wiggled on the ground and unbent, fixing itself. The breastplate glowed bright silver and Zack opened his mouth, gasping for breath. The cuts and bruises began healing, leaving only red welts and dried blood that started to flake off. His body jerked as if an electrical shock ran through it. His eyelids opened, and his breathing slowed to normal.

"Holy shit," Annelise said. "I thought he was dead."

"Nope," Zack mumbled. He let out a soft moan and attempted to sit up. "I just feel like I'm dead."

"Give me a hand," Adrian said.

Annelise and Adrian hoisted Zack to his feet. Wincing only a little from pain, Zack threw his arms over their shoulders, and together, they slowly made their way down to the ferry deck. By the time they stepped onto the ebony planks jutting out over the Styx, Zack was walking on his own with only a slight limp.

"How's your arm?" Adrian asked.

They reached the end of the dock. Zack reached up and pulled the silent bell, ringing for the ferry.

"It's still a little swollen," he answered. "Hurts a bit, but considering it was broken and almost ripped from my body not too long ago, I can't complain."

He smiled softly at Adrian.

"What is that?" Annelise asked, pointing to the dark that spread over the rapidly flowing waters. Shining green lights appeared. The silver outline of the willow tree on the black sail twinkled in the dark. Within moments, the crescent-shaped barge docked silently at the ferry station.

The giant Kharian stepped from the boat and sauntered down the ebony planks toward them. Trotting behind him was the black dog, Cerberus. The size of a Shetland pony, the pitch-colored canine walked behind the giant; three sets of burning red eyes stared out of three separate heads, and three sets of bared teeth were accompanied by low growls. When Kharian stopped in front of them, Cerberus sat on its haunches, panting; drool glistened from its mouths like a spider's web at twilight.

"You two may leave." Kharian nodded at the men. "You may not."

"No," Adrian argued. "We came here to rescue her. We're not going back without her."

"She is still part of our world," Zack added.

"And she is part of mine." Kharian's baritone voice rolled over the sounds of the river.

"We are not leaving her," Adrian argued. "We've been tested enough."

Kharian studied Adrian. His ruby eyes burned with ancient secrets and knowledge.

"She may go with you," Kharian answered. "But never look back."
The giant ferryman spun around on his heel like a military guard.
He slapped his leg as he strode back to the boat's boarding ramp.
Cerberus leapt to its feet and bounded after the giant. They climbed
into the boat, waiting for the three left standing on the pier.

Kharian directed Adrian and Zack to the front of the boat. They
moved quickly and stood under the dual-canine masthead. Annelise
stepped onto the ramp and Kharian extended his muscled arm, directing
her to the rear. She opened her mouth to protest. The burning coals in
Kharian's eyes blazed darker. He took a step forward to prevent her
from going to the ferry's front. When she took a seat toward the rear,
Kharian reclaimed his position at the rudder. Cerberus stood next to
him. The boat pushed away from the dock and bounded across the
water.

The Lethe Gates quickly came into view. The translucent curtain
misted down, spreading across the river. Kharian shifted the rudder as
the ferry approached the gates. Half of the manless oars backpedaled,
shifting the direction of the boat. The barge turned away from the opal
mist and was led through the locks to the side gate. The ferry slowed,
letting the magical current carry it through the enchanted gates. The
curtain drew back over their part of the gate, and the barge drifted
through without being rained upon.

The ferry docked at the Shores of the Living. Kharian left the
rudder and set up the exit plank. He motioned for Adrian and Zack to
exit. Zack stepped onto the platform while Adrian hesitated.

"Where's my sister?" Adrian confronted Kharian. He looked up
into the giant's eyes. The top of Adrian's head only came up to the
ferryman's nipple.

"She will be behind you," Kharian said. The muscled arm slowly
lifted and he pointed for Adrian to exit the boat. "Do not look back."

Adrian looked at the shores. The wraiths hovered over the black
sand, crowding the dock to pay the passage.

"Where?"

Kharian pointed to the mountains beyond the black sand dunes.
He turned his hand over and opened his palm. A tiny finch appeared
made of golden yellow light. It flew off his hand, flitting about their
heads before darting off toward the mountain. It left a burning trail in
its wake.

Adrian exited the ramp and stood next to Zack.

"You should go first," Zack suggested. "This way, I can hopefully stop you before you turn around."

Adrian looked at him, confused.

"That wasn't literal, was it?" he asked. "I thought it meant we couldn't return until it was our time, and that's perfectly fine with me."

"No," Zack answered. "You did hear what Kharian said, right? There's no looking back. It's like the Greek myth of Orpheus and Eurydice. Annelise is allowed to leave, but we can't look behind us until the journey is over."

"How do we know he'll keep his end of the bargain?" Adrian asked.

The three heads of Cerberus growled and barked. Kharian folded his arms across his massive chest, his shoulders rocking with silent laughter.

"You have no choice, little godling," Kharian answered. His fingers curled and he pointed to the fading glowing trail. "Go."

"Go," Zack whispered to Adrian. He forcefully spun Adrian around and pushed him between the shoulder blades. "Don't look back."

Annelise watched the two men start off toward the mountain. She took a step to follow but Kharian blocked her way. She looked up into the burning red eyes. The giant raised his hand and clamped it over her mouth. Annelise struggled in the strong grip. Her lips burned and she yelled muffled protests into the giant's palm. When he removed his hand, Annelise found she could not speak.

Kharian smiled, an oval opening with yellowed, crooked teeth. He extended his arm and pointed after the men. Annelise hastily disembarked the ferry to the triple barking sounds of Cerberus.

Annelise caught up to Zack and Adrian as they started through the sand dunes. The golden finch circled overhead and flew directly into a large pile of black sand. The yellow light spread out until a doorway was created, and a portal opened.

"That does not look inviting at all," Adrian said.

"No other choice," Zack said. Both hands rested on Adrian's shoulders and he gave them a quick squeeze. "After you."

They walked into the darkness. The inside of the dune opened into a large antechamber. There was nothing except a narrow set of stairs carved into the rocks and curling upward. Adrian looked up at the steps, seeing them spiral above them, and felt overwhelmed by vertigo.

"Oh God," he muttered. "I think I'm going to be sick."

"Don't get sick," commanded Zack. "Just go. There aren't any options."

They began climbing the slow-twisting circular steps. Their leg muscles soon started cramping.

"Adrian." Annelise's voice called out from behind the other two.

The sound made Annelise pause on the steps. Her hands flew to her muted mouth as she realized the phantom voice came from elsewhere.

"Adrian." The voice sounded casual and normal. "Do you remember when we were kids, and we went to Greece to visit the relatives?"

"Yeah," Adrian answered. Fatigue was evident in his voice. "What about it?"

"What about what?" Zack asked from behind him.

"This climb reminds me of when we went to the Parthenon." The voice continued, "Remember how we raced each other up the stairs?"

"Yeah, I do." Adrian's voice softened at the fond memory. "That was a fun trip."

"Your idea of fun is a twisted concept," Zack said.

"What are you talking about, Zack?" Adrian said over his shoulder. "I'm talking to Annelise."

"I remember I beat you to the top."

"That's because you pushed me and I fell," Adrian said. "Don't you remember my knee was bleeding, and Aunt Sophia yelled at you all week until we went home?"

Annelise felt her heartbeat quicken. Cold panic flushed through her veins. She reached up to tap Zack on his shoulder when her hand stopped in midair. She couldn't speak and he couldn't turn around; there was nothing to do but to endure the torment. Annelise silently prayed they wouldn't rise to the bait and turn around.

"Is Annelise talking to you now?" Zack asked.

"Can't you hear her?" Adrian answered.

"You always make excuses when I beat you at something," the voice said.

"I wouldn't have to," Adrian teased, "if you didn't cheat to win."

"No," Zack said with concern. "I can't."

"You can't what?" Adrian snapped at him from over his shoulder. Frustration added to his fatigue.

"You always were a little baby when it came to competition." The torment continued.

"I can't hear anything Annelise is saying," Zack answered.

"Fuck you, Annelise," Adrian said.

"You and Uncle Nico. The babies of the family."

"What does Uncle Nico have to do with anything?" Adrian asked.

"Adrian." Zack tried to interrupt, to no avail.

"Dad always said you and Uncle Nico were very much alike. He always said you both were the wimps of the family."

"What the hell are you talking about, Annelise?"

Adrian stopped short. He started to turn when Zack grabbed him firmly by the sides of his head.

"Don't look back," Zack commanded. "It's not Annelise."

"Get the hell off me." Adrian struggled in Zack's grip.

"Both of you are big crybabies, Dad used to say; always complaining about something."

"It's not Annelise. Don't turn around," Zack insisted. "Whatever she says, do not listen."

Adrian stopped struggling, nodding to show he understood. He took a breath and continued climbing the stairs.

"Wah wah wah," the malicious voice teased. "Always crying, always afraid of something. Remember when we went to the zoo?"

"Shut up," Adrian growled over his shoulder.

"Who was a little pussy boy, afraid of the big bad lions?"

"Shut up." Adrian's tone deepened. His body tightened.

"Sure as hell wasn't me. Dad and I laughed about that for so many years."

"You're not real," Adrian insisted.

"I remember one night, Dad and I were laughing about it...again. And I'll never forget what he said."

"Adrian," Zack warned, "fight it. You're better than that. It isn't real."

"It was so funny." The phantom voice giggled. "I can still hear him, clear as day."

"Fuck you." Adrian quickened his pace, trying to get away from the voice behind him.

Zack increased his pace to keep him in sight, and Annelise followed helplessly.

"Don't listen, Adrian."

"It was hysterical. Dad turned to me and said, 'Too bad my *other* daughter isn't as brave as you.'"

Annelise felt her body run cold and her heart break. She watched Adrian tense, tucking his elbows tightly against his sides. He raised his hands to cover his ears.

"His other daughter." The voice laughed mockingly. "We even nicknamed you Lady Pathesia, High Priestess of Whiners."

"Fuck you!" Adrian erupted. "Fuck you, Annelise!"

"Adrian!" Zack said. "It's not her! I don't hear a thing. Whatever it is saying, it's trying to get you pissed so you'll turn around. Ignore it. You need to fight it."

A high-pitched ghostly laughter echoed eerily throughout the cavern.

"La la la laaaaaa…" Adrian started loudly humming Beethoven's Fifth Symphony. "La la la laaaaaa…"

The sounds of giggling echoed off the walls. The travelers continued to climb with only Adrian's singing of Beethoven to encourage their steps. It was a while before Adrian stopped, and the trio continued in silence.

"I do like your artwork, Adrian." The phantom voice saccharinely tried again. "You definitely have great potential…for a grade school student."

Adrian didn't answer. He snorted and stomped forward.

"Do you think you have any real talent, Adrian? Those little sketches you do are so cute. You're so protective of all those doodles in your book. It's totes adore!"

Adrian's body grew tight. He opened and closed his fists.

"To the average eye, you might even pass for having basic talent. From a professional, let me save you some time," the voice went on. "You're better off getting a matchbook and learning how to draw Winkie the Turtle."

"Shut up," Adrian commanded.

"What?" Zack asked. It took him a moment to follow. "It's happening again?"

"Yes," Adrian snapped.

"You may want to start with a kit," the tormenting continued. "There's a novel idea. You could be the Picasso of Painting by Numbers."

"Shut up!"

"Fight it, Adrian," Zack said. "You can do it."

"Unoriginal to cut off your ear," said the voice. "With your dating record, why not cut off your dick? Really, who would miss it? You're just a big girl anyway; we were Daddy's two princesses. Rival siblings, like Mary Tudor and Elizabeth the First, and we both know who the Mary here is!"

A fire geyser erupted in front of them. The flames leapt high, burning dark red. The travelers raised their arms to shield their faces from the inferno, which burned out as quickly as it started. The Minotaur appeared with the fading smoke curling around his muscled body. He held a labrys in both hands, the light glinting off the blades of the double-headed axe.

"Return to your master," the Minotaur commanded.

Adrian paused, unsure if he should turn around and go back. Three dogs barking sharply sounded from behind. Cerberus's low growls were followed by the soft padding of the large dog walking away.

"My brothers," the Minotaur addressed Zack and Adrian, "your journey is almost ended. Follow the path and you will find your way."

The Bull God stepped aside. Zack nudged Adrian from behind, and the two men scurried past. They continued climbing the stairs. The Minotaur turned his attention to Annelise. He raised his hand and placed it over her mouth. She did not resist. The smell of leather and musk filled her nostrils. His palm rose, hovering in front of her eyes.

The cavern in front of Annelise blurred with swirling colors. Her head felt light and dizzy. She closed her eyes, feeling the room spin around her. She reached out to grab something to keep her balance. A hand held hers and she squeezed it, tightly.

"It's a miracle!" Yvonne screamed. "Nurse!"

Annelise opened her eyes. The first thing she saw was Yvonne's face lighting up with excitement, smiling broadly. The hospital room around them slowly came into focus. Monitors were beeping loudly and a rush of activity was happening in her room.

"I can't believe it, you're back," Yvonne cried. "You're back."

Two nurses ran into the room. One turned the alarm off and the other began to check Annelise's vital responses.

"Where's Adrian?" Annelise gasped.

A doctor stepped in front of Yvonne, blocking her out. A flashlight beam briefly shined in each of Annelise's eyes.

"We don't know," Yvonne said from behind the doctor. "No one's heard from him in over a week."

A doctor and another nurse charged into the room. Yvonne stepped aside. She wiped her eyes, clamping a hand to her mouth.

"How long have I been here?" Annelise choked out.

"Ms. Petrakis, can you hear me?" the doctor asked.

"I hear you just fine." Annelise lay back on the hospital bed.

"You've been here eight days," the doctor said slowly. "Can you show me, on your fingers, how many that would be?"

Annelise looked at him as if he were an idiot. She raised her hands and held up eight fingers. "Call Adrian!" she said. "I need to know he's all right."

"I call him three times a day!" Yvonne said. A doctor was telling Yvonne she needed to step out of the room. "No one's heard from him."

"Try again," Annelise begged.

"Miss Petrakis," the doctor said. "I'm going to need you to calm down so I can check your vital signs. It's 3:40 in the morning. Do you know what day it is?"

Annelise thought for a moment and shook her head. As she sank back in the hospital bed, she realized she felt exhausted. Her body ached, and her head was heavy. There was so much going on in the room around her that she couldn't focus on any one thing. She looked toward the hospital room's door.

Yvonne stood in the door frame, her shoulders gently rocking with silent sobs.

CHAPTER THIRTY-SIX

Adrian's body ached as the stone stairs finally leveled off to a flat plateau. The bruises on his skin's surface were practically healed, but the muscles underneath still ached from the journey. His body longed for sleep.

The path led to a wall of solid stone. As they approached, the surface shimmered into a translucent curtain. Zack's guest bathroom came into focus on the other side.

"We must be behind the black mirror," Zack said. "We step through there and we're home."

Zack offered his hand. Adrian took it firmly in his palm, lacing their fingers together. He smiled at Zack. They walked through the curtain together.

The tile floor felt cool against Adrian's bare feet. He was bare-chested and only wore the pair of boxers he'd originally brought to Zack's home. Zack was only dressed in his gray cotton shorts. Adrian looked at the mirror behind them.

"Did you know that was a portal this entire time?" Adrian let go of Zack's hand. His face was drawn and his shoulders slumped forward. Both arms hung listlessly at his sides.

"There are all sorts of things hidden behind mirrors." Zack shrugged. "That's why we only see what they reflect."

Silence hung heavily between them. Adrian felt awkward. After everything that happened, there seemed little to say.

"Hey," Adrian said. "Do you mind if I shower?"

"No," Zack answered. "No, of course not. I'll do the same in my shower. There's plenty of hot water. Take as long as you want. I'll get out of your way."

The two men shifted clumsily around one another. Zack paused in the open doorway, the gallery of photos hanging in the hall behind him. He looked into Adrian's tired and drawn face.

"Okay then," Zack said awkwardly. He left Adrian alone.

Adrian waited until he heard Zack farther down the hall before closing the door. The silence weighed heavily in the small bathroom. He reached into the shower and turned on the hot water. He slowly slid the boxers off his hips and climbed into the tub, shutting the sliding doors and letting the small enclosure fill with steam.

Adrian rested his palms flat against the wall and let the water pelt his skin. The thought of what day it was briefly entered his mind, and he realized he had no idea. Visions of the Underworld danced behind his closed eyelids. He did his best to push them away. Slowly, his muscles relaxed under the water pressure. He finally succumbed with a heavy, audible sigh. Turning his back to the water, Adrian inspected his naked body for signs of damage. Miscellaneous red scrapes ran over his body. Bruises dotted the skin's surface, many already starting to fade.

Adrian turned the water off and reached for a towel. He stood in the tub, naked and dripping, his energy completely sapped. After forcing himself to complete the arduous task of drying off, Adrian wrapped the towel around his waist and trudged down the hall. He stood in the guest room's doorway, silently looking at the pristine made bed, feeling detached from everything. His backpack still sat in the corner. The hard rectangular shape of the sketchpad was visible inside. The black clothes from the gallery opening lay crumpled on the floor, undisturbed, next to his shoes. Adrian's cell phone lay on the nightstand next to the bed, exactly where he'd left it, fully charged. The screen was lit up with messages.

The solitude and silence became oppressive. Adrian turned around and walked back down the hallway. Dawn was trying to slither between the curtains of the back sliding glass doors, and Adrian ignored it, reaching for the doorknob to Zack's bedroom. The door was slightly ajar and Adrian gently pushed it open.

The dim glow from the alarm clock was the only light in the room. It was enough for Adrian to make out the bed's shape, and the man curled beneath the blanket. He crept around, letting the towel drop at the bedside before pulling back the covers and sliding between the sheets.

Zack was curled on his side when Adrian spooned behind him. Adrian gently laid his arm around Zack's body, his fingers trailing through chest hair before settling on Zack's flat stomach. He realized Zack was wearing a pair of briefs and, for a moment, felt awkward about his own nakedness. Exhaustion took over, and he gently pressed against Zack's back, enjoying the warmth of his body.

Zack acknowledged Adrian's presence with a soft, subconscious moan. He reached back and sleepily patted Adrian's leg. His fingers slid off and curled around Adrian's arm wrapped across his chest.

Adrian nuzzled his nose against the nape of Zack's neck. The skin smelled fresh, of natural musk and lightly scented soap. He brushed his lips against the tender flesh. His lips puckered. He kissed the sensitive skin. Zack softly moaned. Adrian moved his hips, pressing his body against the back of Zack's briefs. Adrian's hand lightly slipped over Zack's side, tracing the muscles of his abdomen. His fingers crept lower until reaching the stretched pouch of the cotton briefs. They traced the length of Zack's penis and gently cupped his scrotum. Zack softly growled at the touch. Adrian pushed himself up on his elbow and leaned over Zack's chest.

Their lips brushed together. Adrian covered Zack's mouth with his, gently probing the welcoming lips apart. He felt Zack's tongue gently darting forward, sensing pleasure and exploring further in his mouth. He pushed himself into Zack's body.

Adrian's hand crept between them, down over Zack's erection, pressing the hard shaft as his fingers closed around it. His other palm searched over the tight muscles of Zack's chest until he felt the erect nipple between his thumb and forefinger. He pinched the taut tissue, making Zack gasp and thrust his hips upward in Adrian's lap.

Zack's strong hands slid down the sides of Adrian's torso, and he pulled Adrian on top of him. His right hand gently palmed the curve and firm roundness of Adrian's naked buttocks. The fingers of Zack's left hand massaged Adrian's tailbone. Zack's arms wrapped tightly around Adrian's lower back.

In one quick motion Zack rolled them over until he was pressing down onto Adrian. They continued to kiss deeply. Zack tickled up the sides of Adrian's torso, gently lifting his arms and pinning them down to the pillow over his head. Zack pressed his mouth hard against Adrian's, letting his tongue explore Adrian's mouth and grinding their hips together. Zack let go of Adrian's arms. He moved his mouth lower on Adrian's chest, his lips brushing over the taut nipple and his teeth nipping at the sensitive tissue.

Adrian gasped. His hands slid down Zack's muscular back, feeling Zack's spine ripple under his touch. His fingers spread over the stretched cotton briefs, and he anxiously worked his way underneath the waistband. He shimmied the briefs down to mid-thigh, where Zack maneuvered them off his legs. Their bodies pressed together, Zack's hard cock rubbing alongside his. Adrian rubbed the firm curves of Zack's ass, feeling the thin brushing of hair across the muscled mounds and the more wiry ones between them.

Zack pushed up onto his palms and toes. Adrian slid underneath until Zack's hard-on hovered above his face. He opened his lips, raised his head, and took Zack's cock into his mouth. He opened his throat as Zack slowly pushed in. Adrian choked. He pressed his palm against Zack's pubic hair, gently guiding the speed and depth of his cock's exploration. Adrian's throat slowly opened, letting Zack comfortably find his rhythm.

Zack pushed himself off Adrian and lay next to him. Their arms wrapped around each other's backs, bodies pressed together, and they kissed deeply. Zack's fingertips traced down Adrian's body, brushing through the curls of pubic hair below Adrian's waist. He let his finger traipse across the underside of Adrian's hard erection, sending gasps and shivers through his body. His hand crept lower until Zack cupped Adrian's balls. He ignored the light stubble, letting his middle finger sneak lower, subtly moving between the curves of Adrian's ass. His finger slid down, brushing over the sensitive opening of Adrian's anus. He tapped the warm opening, feeling the muscles clench and blossom open, Adrian sharply gasping at each touch.

Zack hovered over Adrian's face, studying his beautiful features. The brown eyes stared up hungrily, his mouth hanging open, catching short breaths.

"You are fucking hot," Adrian panted.

He lifted his head, pushing their mouths together. He reached down between their bodies, wrapping his fingers around Zack's hard dick. Slowly, he stroked the shaft, teasingly pulling back the foreskin. Adrian ran his thumb over the slit at the end, spreading the emerging droplets of pre-cum.

"Fuck me," Adrian whispered into Zack's ear. He bit into the lobe. "I want you to fuck me."

Zack stretched across Adrian, reaching for the nightstand and withdrawing a condom and a small bottle of lubricant. He shifted until he was kneeling between Adrian's legs. He hovered over Adrian's thick cock and covered it with his mouth. As his lips expertly slid along the length of Adrian's slightly smaller shaft, his fingers deftly applied the lubricant to Adrian's body.

Adrian let out a slow breath as Zack's finger eased inside him. The muscles tightened before relaxing enough to allow Zack a second entry. Zack's mouth worked Adrian's cock. His fingers continued liberally lubricating Adrian's hole until they easily slid in and out. Zack braced Adrian's legs against his shoulders. He squeezed a handful of lubricant onto his hand and generously applied it to his throbbing, condom-covered cock. Zack leaned down, positioning the thick head at the well-lubricated opening, and entered.

Adrian gasped as Zack slowly pushed inside him. He initially resisted the penetration until his muscles started to relax. The instant assault immediately transformed from pain to pleasure, letting an electrical charge loose in Adrian's veins. His body welcomed Zack's cock, and Adrian felt the shaft sliding farther into his ass. Adrian took another breath, completely succumbing to Zack's advances, feeling him fully enter his body.

Zack held the position, grinding slowly until his pubic hairs scraped and tickled the sensitive skin under Adrian's ball sac. He felt Adrian's body become accustomed to his cock's length and girth, allowing him further entrance. He leaned over Adrian, bending the younger man in half, pressing his mouth to his and kissing deeply. Zack moved his hips slowly with rhythmic precision. Adrian's eyes fluttered closed.

"Look at me," Zack commanded. "I want you here with me."

Adrian's brown eyes opened to see Zack's face hovering inches over his. Lightning flashed across the blue fields and Adrian felt himself being drawn into Zack's eyes. The blood red wyre-lights began to pulse with each thrust of Zack's hips. Adrian's hand tightened around his cock, matching his strokes with Zack's rhythmic tempo. His moans became short whimpers. His chest tightened and he gasped for breath. Adrian felt the slow, agonizing, ecstatic building of orgasm constrict his muscles.

Zack pushed himself to rest on his palms and toes. His breathing increased and his chest and stomach rippled with each thrust. His hips moved faster, sending electrical shocks into Adrian's body. Adrian's mouth opened with an inaudible squeak. His eyelids fluttered and Zack's image blurred, exploding in bright lights.

He felt the wind rushing past him at an exhilarating speed. A woven wreath of laurel leaves kept his curly black hair pushed away from his face. The wind roared in his ears and he opened his eyes to see a field of crystal blue. Four white horses in harness galloped in front; the reins were in his hands. The great steeds were larger than the average equine and pulled his chariot with haste, knowing by instinct the route they traveled. They barely needed guidance from the reins, and he kept the cords loosely wrapped in his hands.

He wore a lightweight blue shirt that blended perfectly with the open field of sky around him. A leather kilt was around his waist, the straps of leather hanging above his knees. Through the sandals on his feet he felt the gentle vibrations from the great wheels of the chariot. He looked over the edge without fear or hesitation.

The earth stretched far below. Patches of green and brown appeared, looking like parts of a quilt, laid out to cover the earth entirely. Forests of trees came into sight, their green crowns swaying reverently as the Sun Lord's chariot crossed the sky far overhead. As the chariot ascended, clouds appeared more frequently, revealing only occasional glimpses of the patchwork below them.

A mountain range came into view. The peaks rose high into the vast blueness, and he pulled the reins of the horses to lead their climb upward. The chariot raced toward the peak of Mount Olympus, rising majestically out of the clouds. He snapped the reins and the horses lurched forward, increasing their pace, anxious to return to their home stables.

A starburst of light exploded behind Adrian's closed eyelids. His cock erupted in his hand. The ejaculation flew with such force, the first few shots splattered on the lower part of his chin and neck. Adrian's body shook violently with each orgasmic wave. Every muscle clenched and released, pulsing with short electric shocks. He gasped for breath, trying hard to suck air into his constricted lungs. Pleasure rippled through every nerve in his body.

Zack's thrusting increased. He slammed his hips forward, feeling Adrian's muscles clench in the throes of orgasm. Zack fell to his knees, convulsing, with his cock shooting deep in Adrian's body. He collapsed onto Adrian's chest. He covered Adrian's mouth with his, moaning his orgasm through a deep kiss. Their bodies rubbed together as passion slowly ebbed away.

Zack rolled onto his back next to Adrian. Both their breathing came in short pants, slowly settling down and blending silently together. Zack smiled at Adrian's face beaded with perspiration.

"You really are a pretty boy," Zack said.

"And you're such an asshole," Adrian answered.

Adrian pressed to Zack's side, snuggling into his open arms and warmth.

CHAPTER THIRTY-SEVEN

I don't mean to interrupt you boys," Annelise said. "I'd like you to join me in the main gallery when you get a moment. That is, if you don't mind."

Zack and Adrian cut striking figures in their tuxedos. Annelise smiled affectionately, her fingers absently going to the silver crescent moon pendant she wore about her neck. The forest green dress was simple. It hung off her shoulders, leaving her upper bosom exposed, and allowed the necklace to catch the light.

"Be there in a moment," Zack answered for them. "Your brother is still feeling a little nervous."

"There's no reason," Annelise said. She walked across the foyer to where her brother nervously paced. She took Adrian's hand in hers. "You'll be fine."

"Easy for you to say," Adrian said.

"Adrian," Annelise said. She gave his hand a reassuring squeeze. "I'm a capitalist bitch. Brother or not, if I didn't think I could make a buck off your work, I'd never waste the time displaying it in my gallery." She gave his hand a condescending pat and smiled.

"That's true," Lily said. She came from the main room into the foyer of the Petrakis Gallery. "I think we can all testify to that; she can be a bitch."

"Hey." Annelise laughed playfully. "No comments from the minions."

Lily pantomimed a sarcastic bow. "Everything's all ready, your Majesty," she reported.

"Guys," Annelise said, "come on in when you're ready. Adrian, you'll be fine."

"He is fine," Lily said. Her straight black hair shined in the foyer lighting. "All the handsome ones are always gay."

"Yes," Zack said. He beamed proudly, throwing a reassuring arm about Adrian's shoulders. "The handsome ones always are."

"Ah," Lily said. She pushed between them, snaking an arm around each of their waists. Her full-length red dress stood out between the two tuxedo-clad men. "You two would make such beautiful babies."

"We do try," Adrian said. "But I think I'm barren."

"I meant with me," she replied.

"Lily," Annelise called back over her shoulder. "Leave the boys alone so they can finish…whatever it is they're doing."

"My master's voice." Lily waited until Annelise was out of the room. "'Minion,' my ass. After running the gallery and making excuses for her while she was in the hospital, believe me, she's lucky I settled for manager and not partner."

"You have no desire to be partner, we all know that. Annelise would never make you partner; we know that, too." Adrian teased her. "My sister knows you're good at your job. And you can't bitch with the salary she gave you."

"You're not supposed to know what my salary is." She playfully batted his arm. Lily kissed Adrian's cheek. She rose on her tiptoes to do the same to Zack. "Congratulations. To you both."

Zack's eyes followed Lily out of the room. The moment she disappeared into the main gallery, he snapped around and wrapped his arms around Adrian's waist, gently pulling him closer by the hips.

"Honestly. Before this night starts," he asked, "are you doing okay?"

Adrian felt nervous and anxious. He looked into Zack's blue eyes, finding reassuring comfort, and started to calm down.

"It's not natural that you're not nervous," he said.

"I am nervous; I've just learned how to hide it better." Zack leaned down and gently kissed Adrian. "You'll be fine. I promise."

Adrian looked away at the framed advertisement of the exhibit.

"'Men, Myth, and Magic,'" he read aloud. He wriggled out of Zack's embrace and picked up the ad. "I told Annelise to use one of your sculptures on the brochure. You're the more experienced of the two of us."

"It's your debut," Zack said. "If it makes you feel better, she and I talked about it, and I insisted she use the Bellerophon. It's a beautiful piece, well drawn, and even slightly erotic. Perfect for the cover advertisement."

"We have equal numbers of work represented." Adrian spoke in a low growl. "It isn't right and makes me feel weird."

"Don't," Zack insisted. "Several of those pieces were in storage for a while and haven't been on display. My work is part of this simply to fill it out. Nothing more. This really is more about you than me."

Adrian was about to protest when Yvonne stuck her head around the corner.

"Hey, guys," she called with a patronizing edge. "You may want to get in here. Annelise is already getting that nervous-bitchy tone in her voice."

"We know," both men answered in unison.

"I don't know how I let her talk me into being a server tonight." Yvonne sighed. "As far as I'm concerned, both you and your sister owe me a huge favor."

"Annelise is the one that suggested an all-female staff for an all-male exhibit, and she asked you for the favor. I don't owe you anything," Adrian replied. "Count yourself lucky. I tried to convince Annelise to get you to wear heels."

"Gloves are one thing." Yvonne scoffed. "But not even your sister would have gotten away with putting me in heels." She spun around and went back into the main room.

Adrian called after the disappearing figure, "Have you never met my sister?"

Zack waited until Yvonne was well out of the room. "The gloves were your idea, weren't they?"

"Yup," Adrian confirmed.

"She's still giving you attitude, I see." Zack smiled. He ran his knuckles up and down Adrian's arm.

"Yeah, but I can suck it up."

"It's been almost three months," Zack insisted. "You think she'd stop by now."

"Yvonne? Stop giving me grief because I wasn't there for the eight days my sister was in a coma?" Adrian asked incredulously. He wrinkled his nose and shook his head. "I'll hear about it until the day I die. And we both know there's a good possibility I'll hear about it after that, too."

"Okay," Zack said with a heavy sigh. "We've stalled long enough. You ready to go?"

Adrian held the vaporizer up, clicking the On button. He took a long draw and held it in his lungs. Adrian offered the pen to Zack, who turned it down with a headshake.

"I'm telling you it's not natural not to be nervous." Adrian blew out the vapor and smiled. "The edge is off, now I'm ready."

The two men entered the main gallery to the smattering of the small group's applause. Marcus and Teddy were both giving wolf whistles. Teddy was dressed in a dark Henley shirt, a pair of blue jeans, and black shoes. He was shoving his phone into his pants pocket. Marcus stood next to him wearing a teal button-down shirt that hung outside his khaki pants. He held a silver-tipped cane under his left arm, applauding. Lily stood on the other side of Marcus. Her face was beaming brightly and she blew kisses as both men approached.

Yvonne stood toward the rear of the gallery and next to the small dais. She pulled her second glove up to her wrist, offering belated golf claps. Standing next to her, applauding without attitude, were two more female servers wearing dresses that matched Yvonne's—and gloves.

Scattered about the room on various-sized pedestals and boxes were six of Zack's wood sculptures. Different figures of mythology were decoratively displayed with shaded hues of lighting to amplify different emotional stirrings. Each figure faced an accompanied drawing hung on the wall.

Adrian's work lined three walls of the gallery with Bellerophon's battle with the Chimera prominently displayed. The drawing was surrounded by olive-green matting and mounted in an ornamental classic frame. Bright lighting caused the smaller details to emerge, letting the taut muscles and conjoined moon and sun sigil be more readily observed by the onlooker.

The Eagle carrying Ganymede was displayed only a few feet away. The drawing of the giant python, named *The Revenge of Leto*, hung on the other side. Smaller sketches of related images surrounded the larger pieces. Four new drawings, including an erotically charged minotaur holding a trident in its hands, were framed and mounted in a group in one corner. Every drawing, sketch, painting, or sculpture on display celebrated the male mythological hero, god, and beast.

Adrian left Zack standing with the boys and joined his sister standing in front of the platform. His eyes sparkled. He held his arms in front of him, lacing his fingers together, waiting for the applause to settle.

"I asked Annelise if I could say something before the evening starts," Adrian said to the group of friends and family. He opened his mouth to continue and found no words came to mind. He coughed an embarrassed laugh, trying desperately to search for the speech he prepared.

"Thank you," he finally said. He blinked back tears. "That's all I can think of to say, is thank you."

"Any time my brother is that succinct," Annelise said, "it calls for a celebration."

She glanced up at the clock in the corner to synchronize the time with her wristwatch. "We still have time before we open," she announced. "What do you say we all have some champagne and toast the exhibit?"

The two female servers hurried out the back door to open the champagne and pour the glasses.

"Adrian," Lily said, approaching. She curled up next to him, playfully running a finger under his chin. "I know you have your vape with you, right?"

"Forget him, Lily," Marcus said. He patted his left pant pocket. "I have some with me."

Lily spun around, throwing an arm around Marcus's waist.

"You can lean on me, sweetie," Lily purred. She glanced back over her shoulder. "See you outside."

"Slow down, bitch," Marcus said with a laugh. "I have a limp."

"A limp wrist," Teddy added. He followed them to the gallery's rear.

"Zack." Lily stopped in the doorway. She called back over her shoulder. "You coming, or are you all nerves of steel?"

"I'm good. Thanks."

"Really?" Lily baited. She put her hand on her hip and stared him down. "Not a bit of nerves? I call bullshit!"

Zack held her piercing stare for as long as he could. He cracked with a chuckle. He started for the back door.

"Hey," Adrian called after him. "How come when I asked, you said no?"

"Never argue with a woman, pretty boy." Zack turned in the door frame. He smiled and shrugged helplessly. "It'll make life a lot easier."

Annelise and Adrian watched the small group disappear out the back.

"He's been off the cane for a month now," Annelise commented. She accepted a glass of champagne and handed one to her brother. "How often does Marcus play up the limp?"

"Whenever he thinks he might have to do manual labor," Adrian said. "Or if he thinks it might get him a little sympathy action. He's taking it slow with his clients and working hard at getting better. He misses being a gym rat."

"What does he remember from the wreck?" Annelise asked.

"The storm," was the nonchalant answer. "A large tree branch crashed down and he lost control of the truck."

"That's as good an explanation as any, I guess."

They touched glasses and took a sip.

"It's better than your excuse to Yvonne," Adrian teased. "Did you have to make me look like an asshole?"

"I just woke up from being in a coma." Annelise defended herself. "I grabbed at the first plausible excuse that came to my mind. Sorry, but there was no time to agree on an alibi."

Adrian raised an exasperated single eyebrow. "Really? Telling her that it was all too much for me, and that I snapped and ran away to Orcas Island for a week? Making me look like a big baby was *really* the first thing that came to mind?"

"It explained why you had no cell service," Annelise argued. "And why no one could reach you. Anyone that's met you knows you're high-strung. You'd snap from the truck wreck alone, never mind Marcus's accident, or me getting attacked."

"I swear." Adrian folded his arms across his chest. "I save your ass from eternal damnation, and you make me look like a wimpy basket case."

"Yeah, well," Annelise replied, "I told her that it doesn't bother me, so it shouldn't bother her. She'll get over it."

"Is Lily any better?" Adrian lowered his voice. He stretched his neck to make sure he wasn't overheard. "Is she still freaked out that some lunatic in a mask tried to attack you?"

"She's better now that we have motion sense lighting surrounding the building," Annelise said. "And now we've launched a good Neighborhood Watch here on the island, so something good has come out of all this."

"I guess so."

"How are things going with you and Zack?" Annelise asked. "Any better?"

Adrian sighed heavily and took another large sip of champagne. "For the moment."

"What's the issue?" Annelise said. "He's a good guy, and he definitely cares for you."

"Zack *is* a good guy," Adrian agreed. "And I like him, too. But…"

"It's the age difference, isn't it?" Annelise interjected.

Adrian thought a moment and shook his head. "Not really. I think we're too alike and too different at the same time. We're both comfortable with our independence. We don't *need* each other. Do you know what I mean?"

Annelise smiled. She nodded with a soft chuckle. "I do, little brother. I do. It must be that twin thing I've heard so much about."

"Zack and I have talked about it," Adrian continued. "I think we're both aware of our differences."

"That's very civilized," Annelise said. She weaved her arm through Adrian's and slowly led him across the gallery.

"For now we're both enjoying ourselves," Adrian said. "We're letting things run their course and trying not to have too many expectations. We'll see what happens."

"That's a new attitude," Annelise commented.

"Maybe," Adrian said. "With everything that's happened, I feel it's time for one. I feel the need for some change."

"Why?" Annelise asked with a smile. "Nothing ever happens on Bainbridge Island."

About the Author

Eric Andrews-Katz (EricAndrewsKatz.com) lives in Seattle. His first story, "Mr. Grimm's Faery Tale"—a 2008 Spectrum Short Fiction Award nominee—was published in *So Fey: Queer Fairy Fiction*. Other works are included in: *The Best Date Ever, Charmed Lives, Gay City Vols. 2, 3 & 4* (co-editor of *Vol 4*), *Best Gay Romance 2015, The Advocate, Chelsea Station*, and the *Seattle Gay News*, where he was a contributing writer. His first novel, *The Jesus Injection*, and its sequel, *Balls & Chain* (Agent Buck 98 Adventures) are from Bold Strokes Books.

Books Available From Bold Strokes Books

Tartarus by Eric Andrews-Katz. When Echidna, Mother of all Monsters, escapes from Tartarus and into the modern world, only an Olympian has the power to oppose her. (978-1-62639-746-0)

Rank by Richard Compson Sater. Rank means nothing to the heart, but the Air Force isn't as impartial. Every airman learns that rank has its privileges. What about love? (978-1-62639-845-0)

The Grim Reaper's Calling Card by Donald Webb. When Katsuro Tanaka begins investigating the disappearance of a young nurse, he discovers more missing persons, and they all have one thing in common: The Grim Reaper Tarot Card. (978-1-62639-748-4)

Smoldering Desires by C.E. Knipes. Evan McGarrity has found the man of his dreams in Sebastian Tantalos. When an old boyfriend from Sebastian's past enters the picture, Evan must fight for the man he loves. (978-1-62639-714-9)

Tallulah Bankhead Slept Here by Sam Lollar. A coming of age/coming out story, set in El Paso of 1967, that tells of Aaron's adventures with movie stars, cool cars, and topless bars. (978-1-62639-710-1)

Death Came Calling by Donald Webb. When private investigator Katsuro Tanaka is hired to look into the death of a high-profile lawyer, he becomes embroiled in a case of murder and mayhem. (978-1-60282-979-4)

The City of Seven Gods by Andrew J. Peters. In an ancient city of aerie temples, a young priest and a barbarian mercenary struggle to refashion their lives after their worlds are torn apart by betrayal. (978-1-62639-775-0)

Lysistrata Cove by Dena Hankins. Jack and Eve navigate the maelstrom of their darkest desires and find love by transgressing gender, dominance, submission, and the law on the crystal blue Caribbean Sea. (978-1-62639-821-4)

Garden District Gothic by Greg Herren. Scotty Bradley has to solve a notorious thirty-year-old unsolved murder that has terrible repercussions in the present. (978-1-62639-667-8)

The Man on Top of the World by Vanessa Clark. Jonathan Maxwell falling in love with Izzy Rich, the world's hottest glam rock superstar, is not only unpredictable but complicated when a bold teenage fan-girl changes everything. (978-1-62639-699-9)

The Orchard of Flesh by Christian Baines. With two hotheaded men under his roof including his werewolf lover, a vampire tries to solve an increasingly lethal mystery while keeping Sydney's supernatural factions from the brink of war. (978-1-62639-649-4)

Funny Bone by Daniel W. Kelly. Sometimes sex feels so good you just gotta giggle! (978-1-62639-683-8)

The Thassos Confabulation by Sam Sommer. With the inheritance of a great deal of money, David and Chris also inherit a nondescript brown paper parcel and a strange and perplexing letter that sends David on a quest to understand its meaning. (978-1-62639-665-4)

The Photographer's Truth by Ralph Josiah Bardsley. Silicon Valley tech geek Ian Baines gets more than he bargained for on an unexpected journey of self-discovery through the lustrous nightlife of Paris. (978-1-62639-637-1)

Crimson Souls by William Holden. A scorned shadow demon brings a centuries-old vendetta to a bloody end as he assembles the last of the descendants of Harvard's Secret Court. (978-1-62639-628-9)

The Long Season by Michael Vance Gurley. When Brett Bennett enters the professional hockey world of 1926 Chicago, will he meet his match in either handsome goalie Jean-Paul or in the man who may destroy everything? (978-1-62639-655-5)

Triad Blood by 'Nathan Burgoine. Cheating tradition, Luc, Anders, and Curtis—vampire, demon, and wizard—form a bond to gain their freedom, but will surviving those they cheated be beyond their combined power? (978-1-62639-587-9)